# how
# i got
# to be
# this
# hip

The Collected Works of One of America's
Preeminent Journalists

## Barry Farrell

Edited by Steve Hawk
Introduction by John Gregory Dunne

**WSP**

New York · London · Toronto · Sydney · Tokyo · Singapore

A WASHINGTON SQUARE PRESS *Original* Publication

A Washington Square Press Publication of
POCKET BOOKS, a division of Simon & Schuster Inc.
1230 Avenue of the Americas, New York, NY 10020

Copyright © 1999 by Marcia Farrell

ISBN: 0-671-02810-3

First Washington Square Press trade paperback printing February 1999

10  9  8  7  6  5  4  3  2  1

WASHINGTON SQUARE PRESS and colophon are
registered trademarks of Simon & Schuster Inc.

Cover design by Brigid Pearson
Cover photo by Mary Ellen Mark

Printed in the U.S.A.

# Acknowledgments

Putting together this collection on Barry Farrell's behalf barely dents a debt I'll never be able to repay. Like most of the writing students who took Barry's class at the University of California at Santa Barbara in the mid-1970s, I quickly became—to steal John Dunne's fitting description—a Farrell disciple: a true believer in the man and his work. I can't imagine what mundane turns my life and career would have taken had Barry and I never become friends. So although there are many people who deserve credit for helping to get this book published, the one who must top any list of acknowledgments is Barry Farrell himself. He did all the work; my role was merely clerical. I simply hope he would have selected many of the same pieces had he lived long enough to compile his own anthology.

Second on the list comes Bill Dwyer, one of Barry's oldest and closest friends. Without Bill's wise suggestions and limitless support, this book would still be a stack of photocopies in my closet.

John Dunne also played a big part—bigger than he may realize. He lent his name to the project early and without hesitation; his generous effort speaks for itself.

Steve Hawk
July 1998

# Contents

# Introduction

I t was 1960, or maybe 1961, the winter, when I first became
aware of Barry Farrell. I was a floater at *Time* magazine. A floater
is a writer, usually a new young writer, who floats from section to
section each issue, sitting in for the regular who is sick or on vacation.
I was writing sports that week, and the lead piece in the section was
going to be on a West Coast college basketball team, UC Berkeley, if
memory serves. Now: I happen to detest basketball—bounce ball, Red
Smith called it, an attitude that sums up my own—and I was looking
forward to the assignment with low dread. The reporter on the piece
was not even a staff correspondent but a stringer attached to *Time*'s
San Francisco bureau, another cause for alarm. I waited all day
Wednesday—filing day for the back of the book—for the file; nothing
came in. Thursday A.M., still nothing. Thursday afternoon, nothing. I
was in a rage. Then at dinnertime, the first take. More TK. I read; the
fury abated. The file was—there is no other word for it—stylish. Not
facts—six foot eleven, 19.7 ppg., 2.3 steals, 6.1 assists, that sort of
thing—but an appreciation, a love of the game of basketball, a sense

of its subtext and the fluid interplay of its personalities so lucidly explained that it almost made me rethink my own antipathy to the game. There was nothing I had to do, except trim to fit. The cable went into that week's magazine, virtually as filed—and what a rarity that was at *Time*. I did not even know the name of the stringer until I hit the tag at the end of the file: "Regards, Farrell."

Regards, Farrell. Rarely have two words so perfectly summed up a single human being. Barry Farrell passed through life bestowing his regard as if it was a benediction, a kind of sanctifying grace. Of course he was hired by *Time* as a regular correspondent, and in due course he moved to New York as a staff writer for the magazine. It was there that we became friends, and we remained so until he died nearly twenty-five years later. Writers do not make easy friends of one another; they are professional carpers, too competitive, mean-spirited, and envious for the demands of lasting friendship. With only occasional lapses from grace, Barry and I were an exception to this rule.

How do you describe a friendship of a quarter of a century? You can't really. There is only a blur of images, shards of memory, and with each memory an angle of distortion, my psychic light meter adjusting differently than someone else's. Physical impressions first. He was tall, and somewhat stooped, as if to compensate for his height, bearded, strawberry blond with jug ears, and the most extraordinary eyes, the eyes of someone who had seen too much, too many violations of the human contract. The first story he ever covered, as a young police reporter for the *Seattle Post-Intelligencer,* was a homosexual suicide, and then not so much a hanging as an accident, a homosexual who had strung himself up to increase the pleasure of onanism, and then had slipped during climax. Orgasm and strangulation, the ultimate death trip, and an exposed limp dick mocking the authorities who had cut the body down. A few stories like that and the capacity for surprise is soon lost. I once told him he had the look of a Graham Greene priest; he had heard too much in confession, his pitch for

evasion and deceit was too perfect. And yet always he was ready to
absolve; it was not for him to cast the first stone.

Women loved him. He was that rare writer who looked the way
a writer should look. I remember once seeing him standing at the
elevator at *Time,* wearing a trenchcoat and smoking a Gauloise (another wonderful affect, as was the occasional joint he would sometimes puff while in conference with the managing editor, confident in
that innocent time that the editor would think it only some particularly
noisome foreign tobacco he had picked up on his travels). He was on
his way to France to romance a movie star. Forget that the movie star
in question had romanced half the Western world; he was the first
person I had ever known, the first person of my generation, who had
been in the feathers with an eminence of the silver screen. I envied
his panache, and I wanted to cheer.

He was stylish, but there was so much substance beneath the style.
Those eyes, the voice—Barry was that rare person who talked in complete
sentences, every sentence perfectly parsed, plural predicates for plural
subjects, no dangling participles, every clause modifying what it was supposed to modify, *that* never confused with *which*—people trusted him,
they told him things they would never tell another reporter. He liked
cops and coroners and city hall bureaucrats, and to him they would
confide the most appalling tales of municipal mendacity. Barry was a
great chronicler of the city, any city; he understood the internal rhyming
scheme of city hall meetings and committee reports, finding in the impen-
etrable diction of officialdom the broken meters that concealed collusion
and fraud. The hostility between the homicide squads of the two police
agencies in Los Angeles—the sheriff's office and the LAPD—was a situation made for him. He would intimate to the LAPD homicide cops that
the sheriffs thought they were no good, nothing more than traffic cops
in polyester double knits, and then give the reverse rap to the sheriffs,
with the result that both squads could not wait to tell him about the
boneheaded screwups in the other's murder investigations.

Vietnam, the Middle East, Latin America—wherever Barry went, first for *Time,* then for *Life,* then on his own—his method was the same: never trust the official version, hang around, persevere, work the telephone, anticipate (and of course appreciate) what V. S. Naipaul once called "the chain of accidental encounters." The spook he caught in a lie was a source of rare value—someone he then did not have to believe. He was a tenacious questioner, never deflected, following a kind of quiet Jesuitical logic, a holdover from the Catholicism he had long since abandoned, one that allowed him to illuminate dark corners. "Was he well hung?" he suddenly asked a jailhouse snitch about the stoolie's former cellmate, Gary Gilmore; it was a startling question, posed without judgment, perfectly evoking a prison world without women where any member, any orifice might offer opportunity for sexual release. "A bum bandit," he would call a cellblock sexual imperialist. Above all, Barry had that gift in which Henry James placed so much importance, ". . . the power to guess the unseen from the seen, to trace the implication of things, to judge the whole piece by the pattern." Henry James again: "Try to be one of the people on whom nothing is lost." Nothing was ever lost on Barry.

The cruelties of life did not pass him by. His two-year-old son was killed, electrocuted in a freak household accident, and his first marriage fell apart. His daughter Anny, adored and too rarely seen, lived with her mother. Then marriage again to Marcia, and after a time they adopted Joan, named after my wife. He left the warm embrace of the Time-Life Building and moved to California, and the freelancer's life. In retrospect, it was probably a mistake. Barry always had difficulty making deadlines—remember the first file he sent me; he needed some kind of corporate whiphand, and the possibility of a paycheck withheld. In the freelance world, his passion for perfection—the perfect world, the perfect image, the perfect example—led to pieces being a week late, then a month, two months, a year. He needed one more fact, there was someone in Reno, a whore in Salt Lake, a narc hiding out in Miami, this will nail it down, another trip was scheduled, another deadline postponed. Happiness was a motel on the Utah sand flats, interviewing Gary Gilmore on death row through a filter of law-yers; it was the obstacle that obsessed him, and the adrenaline and the ingenuity needed to overcome it, and if his interviews only pro-vided the subsoil out of which grew Norman Mailer's *The Executioner's Song*, what the hell, he would get back to his own work later; this was a moment in history not to be missed. He "was at a point of frustration," Mailer wrote in *The Executioner's Song*, "where his best pleasure was taking notes." Mailer had him pegged:

> Someone was always dying in his stories. Oscar Bonavena getting killed, Bobby Hall, young blond girls getting offed on highways in California. One cult slaying or another. He even had the reputation of being good at it. His telephone number leaped to the mind of various editors. . . . Led his life out of his emotional exigencies, took the jobs his bills and his battered psyche required him to take, but somehow his assignments always took him into some great new moral complexity. Got into his writing like a haze.

Pure Norman, true Barry. I could give Barry the Philistine's argu-ment: finished is better than good. He did not listen, could not heed.

And yet, it was in this period that his best work was done. He and Marcia and Joan lived in a small house in Hollywood, and God, it was fun to go there for dinner. There were actors and NBA basket-ball players and writers and defendants and vice cops and lawyers and every kind of oddball—I remember one sweet old woman with a wooden leg who designed turn-on clothes for the hookers who worked the legal Nevada whorehouses, outfits with little heart-shaped openings framing the pubic symphysis—a little dope and a lot of booze. He was also teaching now, nonfiction writing, first at UC Santa Barbara, and then at colleges around Los Angeles, both to earn a little money and because he genuinely enjoyed it. He did not have students so much as disciples, acolytes who hung on his every word; he was E.T. as whiskey priest, bringing them communiqués from a world they could not believe existed.

Every morning, precisely at 9:15, he and I would talk on the telephone; a natter, he would call it. He had usually been up all night; he was always trying to find the best time to work, some schedule that would allow him to crack his writing block. In the background, I could hear the noises from the mean streets outside his Hollywood office, the wailing sirens and the voices of the dispossessed floating up through the open window. The New York and Los Angeles newspapers would be read by then, and with ribald shrewdness he would give me a close textual exegesis of the morning's news. I would often tell him I wished a tape-recording device could be implanted under his skin to record his conversation, those beautiful sentences, throwing out its tape at the end of the day. That, I said, would solve his writing block. His private life was becoming more untidy: he could not write and drank; he drank and could not write. He looked terrible. And then one day it happened—a minor automobile accident, a stroke, and a massive heart attack; none of the medical attendants on the scene knew which had occurred first. For six months, he lay semicomatose in a Veterans Administration hospital not five minutes from my house in Los Angeles. Finally he died. I cannot hear the telephone ring at 9:15 anymore without a frisson. It will not be Barry.

I read these pieces and I can see him, hear him. "He has an enthusiasm for tragedy," he once said about a noxious self-dramatizer who had done him harm; I had never heard anyone so effortlessly eviscerated; a simple declarative sentence in six perfectly chosen words; if only writing came so easy. So many times in the years since his death something has happened and he is the only person I wanted to call, the only one who would intuitively understand what was on my mind, what stuck in my throat. Perhaps that is how to define friendship. "Regards, Farrell." Regards, Barry. Regards, regards, and love.

John Gregory Dunne
October 1988

# innocence
# and
# guilt

# On a Sailboat of Sinking Water

I didn't really resent the way the poets laughed and talked and
ran around the room. If that was their way of writing so well,
only a fool would call for silence and order. It was just that watching
them from my seat at the back of the big sunny room made me feel
delicate and dry, a burnt-out case compared to them. The fact that
the oldest of the poets was eleven was no consolation at all.

I had encountered these poets a few weeks before when an anthology of their writings arrived in the mail from Chelsea House, a
book called *Wishes, Lies and Dreams.* It began with a long essay by the
poet Kenneth Koch on new methods of teaching children to write
poetry, but I skipped on to the poems themselves and soon found
myself lost in wonder at the secret places they revealed.

A few of the poems were cute enough to let you off with a safe
adult chuckle:

> Goodbye crawling hello walking.
> Goodbye diapers hello panties
> Goodbye hairy hello baldy.

3

And there were others that were exceedingly gentle as they drew you into the universe of imagination:

I was born nowhere
And I live in a tree
I never leave my tree
It is very crowded
I am stacked right up against a bird . . .

But then came feats of the child's unharnessed vision, the ability to imagine anything, to *be* anything at all. A first-grader named Andrea Dockery wrote

I used to be a fish
But now I am a nurse . . .

and I began to perceive that my parental pleasure in these verses was tinged with professional envy. Then, in a poem by Eliza Bailey, a fifth-grader, I came upon the sailboat of sinking water.

I have a dog of dreams . . .
I have a sailboat of sinking water . . .

A sailboat of sinking water. An image as calm and mysterious as anything of the deep. What could she have meant by it? What did she see in her mind's free eye? It was beyond my imaginative reach, and as a fellow writer I couldn't help but experience further pangs and stirrings. Something in these poems reminded me very acutely of my own childhood and of sensibilities I'd forgotten I ever possessed. Remembering, I felt sabotaged by my education, crippled for life by all the rules and manners I'd learned. In such a mood, it did my confidence no good to come upon lines such as Eduardo Diaz's "The big bad pants lay faded on the chair." Or Iris Torres' "A breeze is like the sky is coming to you." Or Argentina Wilkerson's incredible "I wish planes had motors that went rum bang zingo and would be streaming green as the sea." Thinking it might serve me as a tonic, I made arrangements to visit the poets at their school, P.S. 61, on the Lower East Side of Manhattan.

Koch's method was in fact no more than an attitude that began with the assumption that children are natural poets. Teaching them meant only encouraging them with enthusiasm, respect, ideas, and a general amnesty on all the obstacles to free expression such as spelling, meter, and rhyme. Koch had spent a year working at P.S. 61 and by experiment had discovered a variety of ways to elicit the best responses. He would tell children to be mean or crazy if they wished and give them plans for poems that left them completely free. The children differed greatly by age, he said, with the first- and second-graders "buoyant and bouncy, the third-graders wildly and crazily imaginative, and fourth-graders warmly sensuous and lyrical, the fifth-graders quietly sensuous and intellectual, and the sixth-graders bitter, secretive, and emotional." We chose a fifth-grade class to visit, and Miss Pitts, the teacher, took a seat to the side and let Koch take over the class. The children cheered and pounded their desks at the sight of him, and he responded excitedly, looking as he waved, like Chico Marx, all hair and friendly smile.

Once he had got them started by suggesting they write about the months of the year, Koch came back to warn me not to count on today's session producing anything inspired. Like all writers, the young poets had their days. There was a birthday party going on in the hallway outside, and the students were also disturbed by an article about Koch in *Newsweek* which referred to them as "slum children." They had answered with poems to the editor drawing the distinction between a poor district and a slum, and they seemed happily avenged.

"I know it looks like they're just raising hell," Koch said, "but that's part of the approach. Children make a lot of noise when they're excited, so it's a good sign if poetry does that to them."

Koch agreed that the catch in his method lay in finding teachers who could tolerate the anarchy of creation and could also face up to the fact that children are better poets than their teachers. To criticize or correct or single out the best were all out of the question if the children were to be free of inhibition. Koch spent the hour spelling out words when asked and offering advice to those few who were stuck. Ten minutes from the end of the hour, he told the poets to stop writing. "Who wants to read?" he asked. A dozen hands shot up.

One after the other, the children came up to the front of the class and read their work, with no trace of embarrassment or self-consciousness.

> . . . I was to be a lion but the skin tore . . .
> March, in France, the gray tower falling . . .
> I think of going ice skating in the sewers . . .

I could have sat in that room forever without thinking of ice skating in the sewers. Writing, for me, has always been in the service of some demanding standard. I inch along, dreading inelegance and error, finding my words on a tightrope stretched over canyons of falsehood and inhibition. There is no doubt a very good argument that even the most permissive and encouraging education might not be able to protect these poets' access to their imaginations from all the other disciplines and conventions designed to brick them up. Perhaps you have to be ten to think of sailboats of sinking water; at eleven, your science teacher informs you that water doesn't sink and from then on it is inevitable that the boundaries of reason and fact will draw in on you, ensnarling your free inner life forever.

But there was a moment in the classroom, with the lovely chaos all around, when it seemed to me I could almost picture a sailboat of sinking water. It was one mind, one imagination, free and riding on the sky that comes to you with the breeze.

1970

# Second Reading: Bad
# Vibrations from
# Woodstock

I've been having trouble with my mental compass since coming home from Woodstock, and I'm afraid that nothing I've heard or read about it has been much help in setting me straight on what I saw there. The press and even the police seem content to write it off as a victory for peace and love, which, in a way, it was. But I would have thought that the significance of a half-million young Americans spontaneously creating a society based on drugs would have caused some slight concern. I half expected Senator McClellan, at least, to demand an investigation.

Not that I would have made a helpful witness—I went to Woodstock, after all, in pursuit of the promised Aquarian pleasures that lured the stoned multitudes. Beyond that, the experience turned out to involve so many incongruities and surprises and so much that seemed to belong to the future that my memory of it resembles a flying-saucer story, where you get caught in a three-day time warp and witness a universe of wonders from some forgotten swamp.

I knew I was in for more than a mere festival from the mood of the approach. The road was like a Day-Glo Ganges cutting through the safe billiard green of Archie and Jughead's America. Townsmen stood at the roadside for miles around, observing the exotic pilgrimage with smiling faces and ambiguous eyes, conveying just the shade of nervous welcome they prayed would keep the peace. White-haired ladies waved V from their porches, as did squads of Jewish Boy Scouts in short pants and yarmulkes.

But the sights along the road left me unprepared for the jolt of laying eyes on the ceremonial pasture itself—a good thirty acres, filled to the horizons with a stew of cushioning bodies, nestled together, it seemed, as nicely as puppies in a pet store window. It was as if the population explosion had occurred then and there in the burst of a stupendous life-bomb.

The impact on the eye brought strong emotions welling up in everyone—I felt brotherly and joyous, awed and a little alarmed. I even felt a surge of patriotism for the country that had created, however accidentally, such a vast, benign generation. Everywhere I looked, people stood gaping at the spectacle. No one could pretend to have any experience to compare with what lay before him, and feelings of nationhood were quick to grow from being caught, one and all, in the same historical pinch. No one seemed to doubt that we were crossing a cultural Rubicon.

Until that moment, I would have stopped short of calling rock-dope an American religion. Now I am struggling to think of another religion that could summon such a mass of believers whose lifestyle and social ethic has so much in common. Many minds seized upon the metaphor of religion that day: the people were seekers, the rock stars their prophets, drugs pretty nearly their staff of life. As one might expect of such an electrochemical church, the prophets had little to say by way of guidance. Richie Havens, the first to perform, set the standard for philosophical speculation when he took the mike and said, "Wow! Phhhew! I mean like wow! Phhhew!"

The scene by night was more dramatic still, disclosing an image of the future worthy of Orwell or Huxley. From the fringes of the crowd, the stage looked like a pearl at the bottom of a pond, a circle of acid-tinted light fired down from towers as big as missile gantries. Just beyond it, helicopters fluttered in and out of a landing zone ringed with Christmas lights, bringing in the rock groups, evacuating casualties and stars. Much music was lost under the beat of their blades—an annoyance, until it was perceived as a higher music than rock alone: rock-helicopter music, space music to accompany the sound-and-light vision of the American seventies.

The speaker's expert voice purred across the breadth of the vast crowd, reading off lists of the injured and ill, urging respect for the fences. In the newspeak of our age, he praised the crowd for being groovy, cautioning them not to blow the cool thing they had going by breaking any house rules. Then he would give way to another rock group, and the prophets would appear, tiny forms bathed in lurid light, moving a half-beat ahead of the thunderous sound of their music.

By the festival's last night, the field had turned to slime, and abandoned sleeping bags lay sprawled underfoot like corpses. But the crowd was scarcely diminished. Many had wrapped themselves in plastic covers, like figures in a painting by Hieronymus Bosch. The rest stood shivering under soaked coats and blankets. Their bonfires, fed with newspapers and milk cartons, cast up a stench that hung above the meadow in a yellow haze. Ambulance beacons swirled through the trees. On the dark roads, the pilgrims had become refugees. Unseen faces whispered the names of drugs to passing strangers. "I got hash, speed, acid, downers, snappers, and glue." At the central crossroads, anxious voices shouted the names of lost friends into the bewildering night. *Gloria! Donald!*

The great stoned rock show had worked a countermiracle, trading on the freedom to get stoned, transforming it into a force that tamed and numbed and kept tens of thousands content to sit in the mud and feed on a merchandised version of the culture they created. In the cold acid light, the spoiled field took on the aspect of a concentration camp, a camp of the future, stocked with free drugs and music, staffed with charming guards. The speaker's coaxing voice only encouraged the nightmare, which became complete when I asked a shuddering blue-faced boy standing next to me if he was sure he felt all right. "Groovy," he said, adding a frozen smile.

Only the rare crank came away from Woodstock with complaints. Most took it as a thrilling confirmation rite, some kind of triumph for the youth rebellion. But as one who has believed that the justification for using drugs lay somewhere in the zone of psychic freedom, I was disturbed by the bovine passivity they induced in this mass of free minds. For almost everyone present, the freedom to get stoned together was more than freedom enough.

The Rubicon we felt ourselves crossing was the line of restraint between the old drug culture of the underground and some new authorized form, dangerously adaptable to the interests of packages, promoters, the controllers of crowds. It was a groovy show, all right, but I fear it will grow groovier in memory, when this market in our madness leads on to shows we'd rather not see.

1969

# Celebrity Market

I hope it won't sound like bragging if I say that I happen to be a person of exceedingly strong brand loyalties. I can look back over the years and see a bright thread of coherence in the way that my addictions have endured. I don't go larking around with competing coffees. I have no interest in the other fellow's cigarette. Yet I have never given a thought to doing a celebrity endorsement. Neither has Newman or Brando.

So far obscurity of name and face has spared me the nuisance of being greatly importuned. Sponsors who cater to mass tastes want to see a readout, and mine is weak on viewer recognition, aura spillover, and the glamour-sex-excitement curve. I'll admit that if someone came along who really believed in me, who thought I could deliver for the product, who offered me the kind of package that kisses your worries goodbye, I might be tempted to go on TV and tell how this wonderful crutch or elixir keeps on improving my morale. They could show me and a bunch of young women horsing around outdoors, my hair sort of bouncing, my shirt unbuttoned to the waist. You would sit there thinking, What's he got that I haven't got? Then it would dawn on you.

For the moment I can only say that inviting the world to copy my secret tastes and hungers hasn't been consistent with the type of image I've been trying to project; Newman and Brando won't do endorsements for exactly the same reason. We see nothing but compromise in tying our personae to a bottle or box of something you can buy. We don't need the exposure. We don't need the money, either, I guess.

The touching thing is that so many celebrities do appear to need the money. No matter how great the income of one's heroes, one must never be surprised to see them on TV, assuming the humble stance of the paid enthusiast. Nobody here is a show-business innocent. I used to be, but I grew up around the time that Willie Mays quit baseball to become a full-time armpit. Now I am beyond embarrassment or shame. I won't deny that Dorothy Provine lost a hint of mystery for me when I first observed her boasting coast to coast of a hospital-fresh vagina. But much of her allure has returned with the thought that she might have been paid to lie.

Perhaps I seem naive in my belief that celebrities are lying when they claim to be the satisfied consumers of products that everyone can buy. In real life, I know, celebrities give much of their time and attention to the search for costly alternatives. A single Vegas booking can make it almost impossible to find shirts and pajamas that fit. When in Rome one shops for shoes, as in Paris for neckties. Eventually, one learns the name of a little man in Zurich who can make a decent wristwatch. Lying on TV is an excellent way to support indulgences of this kind, and I would like to encourage all celebrities who have done so in the past to continue lying now in the face of the recent FTC ruling that "endorsements must reflect the honest views of the endorser."

I need hardly point out that this silly ruling discriminates against celebrities who refuse to traffic in ready-made goods, not to mention products that may be lacking in celebrity appeal. When a celebrity admits to a special weakness for a certain brand of wart-removing paste, he is addressing his admirers on the airiest levels of mass consciousness, and neither side profits from a spurious insistence that his claim be true. The competent television watcher does not ask if Joe Namath is in fact a reliable authority on popcorn popping—he only dreams of resembling him vaguely through the purchase of the popper of Joe's choice. It is an open-and-shut case of caveat emptor, and the FTC ought to stay out of it.

Endorsements give the most pleasure when taken only as frank and occasionally charming confessions of personal greed, of a willingness to barter what one is or used to be for a fistful of dollars more. The public would be better assured that every endorsement is a useful little fiction that does not reflect the tastes or mental imbalance of anyone involved. For while the false enthusiast is merely turning a well-paid trick, the person who actually believes that his status as the leading actor in the English-speaking world or the top rebounder in basketball makes his personal choice of flea collar a matter of public concern is suffering from serious delusions and is someone the law should punish, not reward.

A distressing case in point is the ubiquitous commercial in which Patricia Neal comes on to say that her husband, a writer, is terribly fussy about his coffee and won't drink anything but Maxim. Unhappily, this is all too true, as I can attest from having spent the summer of 1965 hanging around the kitchen of Miss Neal's house in Great Missenden, a small town an hour north of London. Maxim was a novelty in England at the time. It had to be flown in. We would drink it in front of the English and remark to them on the freeze-dried character of the crystals in our cups. Every so often the writer would bound in and be terribly fussy about his coffee. It was a fabulous summer, and when I saw it played back on TV I was alarmed that such a privacy had been so thoroughly invaded—one's kitchen, one's cups, one's husband's tempers, all traded up for a mess of freeze-dried pottage.

This sense of alarm, of Faustian danger, became all the more acute a short time later, when I happened to witness Peter Ustinov appear on behalf of Gallo wines. The soul of urbanity was saying that when last in California he had paid a visit to the winery of "my friends Ernest and Julio Gallo," whose "passion is to create fine wines." For those who have never seen it, the Gallo Winery in Modesto needs only a seagull dying in the goo to complete the image of a vast petrochemical plant, and I found it delightful to picture Peter there, sipping a chilled glass of Ripple with his friends Ernest and Julio.

Although the wines Peter was praising were the company's new line of varietals (and not Ripple, Boone's Farm, or Thunderbird, of which the Gallos create about ninety million gallons a year), I was at first amused by his pretension in claiming a fondness for these naive domestic *ordinaires*, assuming, of course, that he was being paid to lie. Why else would the owner of a fifty-eight-foot ketch; an apartment in Paris and a country house in Switzerland; a large collection of original drawings by Daumier, Tiepolo, Forain, and Toulouse-Lautrec; six thousand classical phonograph records; and, I believe, an English sheepdog—why else would such a marvelous spendthrift and sybarite confess to practicing the small and comparatively painful economy of drinking Gallo wine?

I did feel, however, that Peter had gone a step far in revealing his friendship with the Gallos. It was precisely the sort of intimate detail I have always believed celebrities should never put up for sale, especially since in this case it had the charm of such beguiling incongruity. Ustinov and the Gallos were as unlikely a group of merrymakers as one might expect to find in a year of table-hopping. Where had they met? Gstaad? Fresno?

I called Peter with the intention of disguising my voice and passing myself off as another old friend from the valley—"Ernest said to be sure and call." But Peter was off cruising the Mediterranean on his fifty-eight-foot ketch. So I called Modesto instead and spoke to a Gallo executive who said he had been present at the meeting where Ustinov's name first came up. Someone had suggested Johnny Carson, but Carson had been blackballed as lacking the transatlantic sophistication the Gallos had in mind. Then someone else thought of Ustinov—"who it was shall remain ever nameless, unless you want to say it was Ernest Gallo"—and within a few months Peter had been brought up to Modesto to taste the wines and shoot the ads.

. Naturally, I was relieved to learn that Peter was only lying when he claimed to be the Gallos' friend. He hadn't given away anything he ever really owned. It was just another small act of prostitution—feigning affection for money—a victimless crime, as it were. Still, it struck me as a lapse of taste on Peter's part. There are rules to every game, including this one. And everyone knows you're not supposed to kiss the customers on the mouth.

1975

# For the Only Freak
# in Ohio

Even if reading the dirty papers had endangered me or my loved ones by arousing my prurient interest in some unmanageable way, I never would have thought of complaining to the city about it. I was calling the license commissioner simply to ask by what miracle of tolerance the city had allowed the sidewalk trade in pornographic tabloids to become such a conspicuous success, with a take of more than $400,000 a week from the newsstands of Manhattan alone. "I'd call it a case of bad smut driving out good," the commissioner answered suavely.

The bad smut arrived in the streets last winter—first *Screw*, then *Pleasure*, then *Kiss*, a new genre of shock-value digest defiantly free of any word or thought that might convey a hint of redeeming social value. The district attorney filed charges, of course, and the police went on mercurial antismut campaigns that brought repeated arrests to the editors, publishers, distributors and to some fifty sidewalk newsdealers, at least two of whom could claim blindness as a defense. But the question of obscenity has come to acquire such murky status in

17

the law that it has been easy for the papers to keep publishing while their cases proceed through the courts—so easy, in fact, that a choice of sixteen straight sex papers now greets the browser's eye at news-stands all over the city.

The good smut—meaning *Playboy* and the like—having profited so richly from what used to excite, was now made to suffer for its relative tameness, and in this there was surely an avenging justice: He who lives by the center spread shall die by the center spread. But the underground press, with its free use of language and radical vision of new lifestyles, contained good smut, too—the kind meant to dissolve fear, not exploit it. I hated to see it caught in the irony of being stomped out from below. Having created the atmosphere that made the bad smut even thinkable, such worthy old repression-fighters as *The East Village Other, Rat,* and *Other Scenes* were being shuffled into the shadows at the back of the stands to make room for their wanton offspring. "Six months ago they wouldn't sell my paper because I had nude pictures inside," says John Wilcock, the founder and one-man staff of *Other Scenes.* "Now they don't want me unless I put a nude on the cover."

The old lady was dressed in babushka, sweat socks, and battered black coat—classic vendor attire for meeting the Broadway dawn. Her hands were the purple-gray of a newsstand veteran—eighteen years, she said. Taking me for a swinger, she asked if I wanted the new *Screw;* when I said no, she countered with *"Gay Power?"* All the same, she was family folk, she said, like most of the other dealers.

"All of us are just trying to stay alive, and if Mr. Businessman wants to read dirt, I've got to sell it to him. Else he'll go across the street. You wouldn't believe the caliber of people who buy this stuff—I'm talking about your legitimate businessman. It used to be they at least bought the *Times* to cover up the sex stuff, but now they read it right out in the open. On the train! They buy five, six at a time, then run for their trains. I just put 'em out and they just melt away."

A few blocks up the street, another dealer refused to speak on the subject until I swore I was not a cop; he had been arrested twice this year, he said, shaking his head in disgust. "Look," he said, sweeping a hand across his entire stand, "this here's pornography, that over there's pornography, it's all pornography, I don't care how you spell it." I studied the display as though it were a collage, trying to make out a portrait of the literate New Yorker in the collection of magazines. There were more than a hundred publications for sale, and if they could be considered to be in combat for the hearts and minds of the people, there was no question at all that the people's choice was smut.

I bought a dozen sex papers on an eight-block walk and took them home for study. The worst of them were beyond even pity—mindless, artless, boring, all wrong in their idea of sex. Some were no more than collections of postage-stamp snapshots scattered through columns of ads for "swingers," bleak little messages that read more like confessions than boasts. But the best of the papers were surprisingly good, either for their humor or for their attempt at exploring a guiltless approach to sex.

Implicit in them all was the total devaluation of the tease, and in that I found a certain hidden moral. Page after page of unglamorous nudes and vivid, vulgar writing seemed to conspire in the thought that when we finally rid ourselves of impermissibility as a stimulant to sex, nothing will be left to us but love.

Everyone in the sex paper trade agrees that the market would die if everything were legal and permissible. Pornography cannot exist without taboos, as was shown in Denmark last year, when the absolute death of censorship drove all but the biggest dealers out of business. Pornographic booksellers (who also flourish in Manhattan) think of their customers as perverts and hope they stay that way, since only in stunted sex lives can they find a need to be filled. The underground press and the best sex papers take precisely the opposite view: being afraid of your body, they say, is the only real sin against sex.

\*       \*       \*

Now that they're no longer the dirtiest things around, the underground papers have had to rediscover themselves. *Rat* has become a guerrilla operation, taking up the cause of the Panthers and the Weathermen. *EVO*, with the most talented staff of any underground paper in the country, has become sounder and more thoughtful. Wilcock has decided to make *Other Scenes* into a mailed newsletter; he has spent fifteen years building a network of correspondents reporting on the Other Culture around the world, and he refuses to sacrifice it to the demand to get raunchy. "I don't want to put out a sex paper and I don't want to con anybody into thinking he's getting a sex paper because there's a nude on the cover. It's all crazy. The whole point in starting a paper that gives another version of life from what you get in the straight press is that once in a while you get a letter saying, 'Wow, man, you really lightened my load. I thought I was the only freak in Ohio.'"

To me, that seems a noble credo for any publisher, too valuable in its humanity to serve as no more than a valedictory for a good man's failed effort. It applies with special meaning to the sex papers, and one can only wish that they will come to understand it.

1969

# First Floor Rear at the Jungle's Edge

My wife and daughter are counting on me to take decisive action. I am trying to think of something to do. The police have just left our apartment and I have bolted the door to the hallway and come back to the basement room where the women are waiting. I offer them a morale-building smile, the smile of Gregory Peck. Last night, for the sake of our nerves, we all three slept together.

The police were here to investigate the third burglary we have reported in the past three weeks. As before, they poked around with no apparent interest, not bothering with their flashlights in the dark of the broken room. They are like Oriental actors, instructing us in pantomime not to get our hopes up. But we already know. There is no chance of recovering the things that were stolen nor any insurance to collect, this being a home in the high-crime zone, first-floor-rear in a brownstone on the edge of Spanish Harlem. The police come only to fill out the form that will permit us to claim a tax deduction. One fixes his eye on our Che Guevara poster; the other sits down to write.

The making of the list is an embarrassment. I am ashamed to tell these policemen that I had so much to lose. They have registered the political distance between us—in our hair they read volumes at a glance—so how can they help but hate me when I tell them that my skis cost $150? The list goes on and on. It carries our losses into the thousands. I am appalled to see the trouble the patrolman has spelling "portable electric typewriter."

I am also indignant, but I conceal this from the police, not wanting to betray the things I'm always saying. These burglaries are clearly the work of junkies, and my stand on junkies has always been elaborately sympathetic. They are sick and we are sicker for not reaching out to help. In conversation, I try to be as much like Gandhi as possible, given the handicaps of money and good food. But now I am not sure if I really believe my ideas or have only talked myself into them at a party. This is the doubt I hide from the police. It would give them too much satisfaction.

The first burglary was not so upsetting. I was far from the crime zone at the time, across the country in the model city of Palo Alto, California, just sitting down to a delicious lunch with friends when my wife called with the news. "Everything we've got!" she said, meaning typewriter, television, camera, tape recorder, radio, many things. Hearing her voice, I pictured her standing in shattered glass. Go to a friend's house and call the cops from there, I told her. Then I went back to the table, breathless to tell the news.

I might have behaved better if the story hadn't fit the conversation so theatrically. But we had been talking endlessly about the crime threat, and I was impatient with the decorous chatter of these eminently safe suburbanites. Their passion for a vicarious taste of the chaos made me jealous of my standing as the only one present who could see it every day from the trenches of his street. I had already told about the neighbor of mine who follows his wife with a butcher knife to protect her when she goes off to work at night.

Everyone was wonderful about being horrified. I bathed in their concern. There were efforts to misappropriate my story for use in support of local fears, but I squelched them by letting it drop that my precinct, the twenty-third, is the busiest in all Manhattan. But by the time lunch was over, my losses had been converted into precious social gains. The burglars had made me the only genuine invalid on the hypochondriac ward.

Since my wife was dealing with the police, the glazier, and the locksmith, I was free to plunge into a high-minded rejection of the "alarmed citizen" stance. I said I hoped the thieves weren't caught, since the intervention of broken-down justice would only make matters worse. Desperate men had eased their desperation by relieving my bourgeois apartment of its guilt-inducing richesse. There was a kind of ecological roundness to it.

Most of the missing items were replaced within a week. All that we lacked was faith in our doors and windows, but soon even that began to return. We made the acquaintance of our new possessions, reading all of the owner's manuals. The color TV was a big improvement on the old gray set. For a week we kept our bedroom dark, the better to watch the pink and green faces.

We went to Kansas for the holidays, taking care to lock our treasures behind a steel-clad door. And in Kansas, in Topeka,. we found fabled American calm. There was talk of dope in the high schools, of course, and some awareness of the local ghetto. But no one was thrilling to hints of the apocalypse, as in California. We went sledding on a hillside, we spotted a fox in the fields. I let myself be talked into telling the burglary story once or twice, but in this place of security and confidence the moral sting was gone.

The steel door was standing open when we came back home. The lock had been broken and everything was gone. We called the police, they came, they did their pantomime. The next day we went out to visit friends. While we were away the burglars returned to pick up a few remaining odds and ends. We called the police. They came.

They said we ought to move to the suburbs. I wished them good luck at the door.

Easy come, easy go, we say. We say we are invulnerable to burglary now that everything worth stealing is gone. We say these things as though we meant them, with the smile of Gregory Peck. But we know the time has come for mental toughness. We have found a stranger's knife in our rooms. The door between us and the jungle is getting so absurdly thin.

We have talked about a gun, a dog, alarms, new locks, but the defensive measure we can live with doesn't leap to mind. We cannot live behind San Quentin doors. We cannot encircle our lives with alarms.

For the moment we are too frightened to square our fear with our social attitudes. It is best, we say, not even to try. Instead, I tell myself that if I were to catch the thief red-handed, there wouldn't be time to worry about the system that corrupted him. I would kick him or trip him, I would make him drop my stuff. The thing to do is to set a trap, to be ready for his return. I tell my wife and daughter this. Next time I'll catch him, I say. My wife and daughter trust me. They do me the favor of looking reassured.

1970

# The Ghost of
# Shoplifting Past

I f the FBI wants to announce that shoplifting has increased by ninety-three percent since 1960, who am I to argue? I'll even go along with the retail merchants' claim that "shrinkage" this year will cost them a half-billion dollars. I think American merchants can be trusted to cover any two percent loss with a righteous three percent rise, and if J. Edgar Hoover doesn't find proof of our moral decline in the shoplifting figures, he'll only find it someplace worse.

But the other day a survey of shoplifting in a New York department store came out with a statistic that I greeted with a feeling of indignation that was only relieved by doubt. One out of ten shoppers, it said, manages to steal something before he leaves the store. As an old shoplifter of some fair standing in my hometown of Seattle, I was naturally repelled at the idea of so many people getting a successful hand in. One in ten might easily feel the urge to steal, might try to steal, might kick himself for not having stolen. But did one in ten actually have the heart? The hands? The good move out the door? I donned a coat of many pockets and went out to see for myself.

It was perfect shoplifting weather—cold and rainy enough for coats and scarves and umbrellas, yet not bad enough to discourage vast hordes of Christmas shoppers. I stood outside Macy's for a time and had a good long look at the customers and thieves as they came stampeding out doors to the sidewalk. If the ten percent figure was to be believed, I must have been seeing a thousand thieves a minute, but none came out running and none looked back. These were cool thieves—unless, of course, they were customers.

Inside, the thieves and the store detectives were doing the adagio I remembered, gliding around the aisles and fingering all the merchandise while secretly stealing little glances at each other. I cruised to the center of the store, coat flapping open, hands hidden in its folds.

It was warm in there, and what with the Yuletide decorations and the piped-in Christmas carols, I began to get sentimental about being thirteen years old in Seattle, when I could hardly get inside a store before I'd find something I desperately wanted sticking to my fingers like frozen steel, with no choice but to help it into a pocket and start drifting for the door. Then fear would take me by the nape, squeezing harder with every errant step and bursting into pure elation the second my foot hit the street. I became a glutton for that terrible sensation. I became a very busy thief.

I was not often caught, but the few times it happened were such searing humiliations that my memory of them has grown protectively dim. Vaguely, I recall being nabbed at the Pay 'n Save, with loot that included a squirt gun and a Japanese catcher's mask. I also remember how it feels to have a detective's hands turn your pockets out.

Still, I persisted in such escapades as stealing everyone a Christmas present, and I could put them under the tree with a real sense of giving. Buying a present, I told myself, meant budgeting your love with money. When you stole one, you were risking everything just to see new earrings on your sister's ears.

I must have been expert at throwing myself on the mercy of the authorities, because only forgiving justice could have kept me out of jail. The word *kleptomaniac* settled deep in my mind, and my family's optimism for me came to consist of hoping that my larceny and my acne were somehow related.

The twin curses finally faded some time after I left high school, but by then I had accumulated so much guilt that I thought of myself as a notorious felon well into my twenties. Then, one night at police headquarters, where I was working as a reporter, I slipped into the files and hunted up my record—the famous record that was going to haunt me for the rest of my life, the story as long as your arm. To my total stupefaction, only one permanent entry had been filed against my name. "Barry Farrell is suspected of breaking street lights on Queen Anne Avenue," it said. "He is 5'3", weighs apr. 100 pounds, and talks with a squeaky voice."

I was almost twenty years rusty now, and the vastness and complexity of this cornucopic store seemed to be putting me off my form. Back in Seattle, I had not encountered closed-circuit TV cameras, radio-sensitized dots hidden on expensive items to make them bleep for your capture as you carry them through the door, squads and squads and squads of plainclothes store detectives. Most of the nice little items, moreover, were now mounted on cards too big to fit into a pocket. It was a distinctly tougher league, I thought, adding to my doubts about the true number with the nerve to come up against it.

Not caring to contribute to the anxieties of some hapless thief, I decided to test the paranoia count by flushing out the detectives. I had no wish to steal anything, which made it easy to act suspicious enough to draw on some pursuit. And before very long I saw my man's reflection in the cellophane cover of a stationery box I was holding. He was dressed like a construction worker, but there was no mistaking his trade. He had that disengaged look, the look of the secret watcher. I thought I saw him signal a second detective, a pinch-mouthed woman who started to approach me. I floated around the counter. They were after me, all right, I was sure of it.

When I reached the door they seemed to lose all interest—perhaps they were thieves or shoppers after all. But the rush of anxiety I felt was real enough, and its sharp intensity unnerved me. I had nothing at all to be afraid of, and yet my heart had stopped on remembered guilt, somehow still intact after all these years. I was glad to be empty-handed when I made my move for the street. Somewhere, and not so far from the surface, the squeaky-voiced boy still lives.

1969

# The Repression in
# the Mirror

I have a friend who makes a big thing of being afraid to talk on
the phone. He calls up and says, let's meet someplace. Since we
never have anything at all seditious to discuss, his concern for security
is more a pretension than a precaution. But while I don't happen to
flatter myself that my phone is tapped, I would never discourage my
friend from thinking that his must be. He has been a pacifist war
resister since Abbie Hoffman was in high school, and there is little
enough for him to take heart in these days without my trying to
persuade him that the FBI probably doesn't even know his number.
So we meet in some cafe and exchange the usual gossip.

The last time I saw him was a few days after the explosion on
11th Street, the one in which the Weatherpeople blew up the fine
old Georgian townhouse while cooking down some dynamite to make
nitroglycerine bombs. Being a pacifist, my friend was naturally appalled
that his brothers in the revolution should be into making bombs.
"Custerites," he called them, meaning reckless fools riding to disaster.
But at the same time it was clear that he envied them their craziness,

29

as though he were no longer sure that his sense of moderation wasn't really a moral flaw. The bombers had raised the ante in the game he had been playing, so that calling himself a revolutionary now meant something entirely new.

I can remember times in the streets when he and I felt wonderful. We were shouters and paraders who thought that we could end the war and change the world. When someone wrote that Lyndon Johnson was the first American president to be brought down by a mob, we felt congratulated. And I remember how exhilarating it was to talk to my friend after he came back from the battle of Chicago: The frenzy of the opposition, he said, was proof we were on the right track.

Now he thinks we were nothing more than pawns in the series of events that gave us Nixon. The war drags on and spreads across new borders, and the movement against it has never seemed so frail and dispersed. There hasn't been anything like a successful demonstration since the Moratorium in November, and even that wasn't enough to distract the president from watching a football game on the White House color TV. Radical pacifism has begun to seem like an empty bag, and my friend says he has moments when he feels like moving up to the country and painting his mailbox blue.

My friend thinks these melancholy changes are explained by "the repression"—the idea that dissent is just what the country can't stand, the notion that silence and submissiveness are the new American virtues. The nagging thing about this sort of repression is that it is so selective and ambiguous that no force can be mustered against it. The Chicago Seven are sentenced to jail: repression. Yet here they are, out on bail, barnstorming the country. Timothy Leary is going to be an old man when they let him out of prison for possessing a gram or two of grass: call it repression. But Margaret Mead can still go on the talk shows to say it ought to be legal. It is the kind of "repression" that lets you buy guns and dynamite, issue revolutionary tracts, go where you want to go, talk to whom you like. But nevertheless you begin to sense that what you do and say may have consequences far more dire than before. You learn that the army is collecting dossiers on civilians, you see the police out taking photographs of faces in the crowd at even the tamest events. You begin to detect a certain loss of audacity in yourself. You go around obsessed with the feeling that the other shoe is about to drop.

So if you are a dilettante of the revolution, it is a good time to sober up. But my friend has his convictions and they forbid him from learning to live with the status quo. He has acquired a need to feel properly hated by the authorities, since not to be hated is only to be ignored. That is why he insists that his phone is tapped: If they aren't getting ready to kick your door down, they've written you off as safe.

My friend says he thinks the bombings might turn America into a police state. This is his most hopeful thought for the day. He can visualize it in the most encouraging detail. A *real* repression, the kind that comes with tanks parked on street corners, would speed up time for the revolution, giving the people no choice except to choose. The middle ground of liberalism and moderate dissent would be kicked away and with it would go the debilitating chance to get along in society when you're supposed to be struggling to change it. The moral task of being an American will be infinitely lighter then. Every time the secret police slam you up against the wall, you'll be treated to the kind of direct existential experience that frees you of your doubts. You'll find it easier to live with yourself, you'll cease to feel like an accomplice in all society's crimes. My friend painted a romantic picture. I could see very well what he meant.

Having lived for a while in Haiti, I have a very specific idea of what repression means. It means curfews, roadblocks, censors, spies, torture, disappearances, and deaths. But I also know it would be a mistake to suppose that there is nothing like a repression afoot in America merely because it hasn't assumed the classic grotesque dimensions. The authorities don't have to crack down on everyone: that is the worst way to do it. It is far more effective and pernicious when no one quite knows that it's happening, when you can never be sure that the chill you feel isn't just your own paranoia. For repression need be no more than a state of mind, however it is accomplished. If you think it is there, it is there: you can see it in the mirror.

But I'm afraid my nerves aren't up to seeing what revolutionaries call "the mask of democracy" torn away—even if it should turn out to be no more than a mask. I find my freedom, illusive or not, more agreeable than no freedom at all. I can't see how a crackdown would cause timid people to find their courage. The reverse is far more likely. It may be just paranoia, of course, but I picture myself alone in a room after curfew, wondering if my thoughts are still legal.

1970

# Some Notes on the Last Twenty Years

Admitting to a blunder can do wonders for a man, especially if he can arrange to do it on a Sunday evening, live from the Oval Office. Framed by his flagstands, shored up by his awesome desk, the penitent seems to float head and shoulders above the Great Seal as he solemnly faces the camera and waits for a little red light. When he sees it he remembers to hold his expression and count, *one-Mississippi, two-Mississippi,* all the way up to five. Then he attempts a fleeting smile. Then he begins to talk.

Yes, he confesses, some would say that he may have clung too long to his loyalties. He may have placed too much trust in trusted advisors, too much faith in overzealous aides. He may have been naive in his reluctance to kick men who were down. But tonight none of that matters. Tonight, as Chief Executive, *your* president, he alone must take the hard road into everybody's living room and find the personal courage to utter that humbling phrase: *frankly, it was a blunder.* Even when read from cue cards, it's a message that always comes across either brave or tragic, and one way or the other it's worth several points in the polls.

This could explain why, in a period when other nations were falling regularly under the boots of puppets, tyrants, senile father figures, members of misguided cliques, strongmen, madmen, sadists, and barking dogs, we in the United States have managed to keep a well-meaning blunderer at the helm for more than twenty years.

The Bay of Pigs, you may recall, was "a serious blunder."

Vietnam was worse: "a tragic blunder."

The Warren Commission's investigation of John F. Kennedy's murder was marred by "a series of honest blunders."

Watergate was "worse than a crime—it was a blunder."

In point of fact, presidential blunders are seldom worse than crimes, though often enough they appear to be identical. But the rule in confessing them is that the more one says about how terrible they were, the easier it is for the public to accept them as simple blunders.

Blunders evoke something innocent and forgiving in the American spirit, recalling the good, gone days when we loped around the world and were widely regarded as tall children, favored and foolish, twice too lucky and rich to require any culture or guile. When the pope held out his ring to be kissed, the Minneapolis druggist warmly shook his hand. The snippy French waiter turned up his nose when the vet from Iowa City tried to parlayvoo. Do you address all Oriental women as *mama-san*? Who knew? You'd get a picture postcard and write home, *I could have died.*

Today, however, with our innocence lost, the concept of blundering has been usurped for more important use. Lockheed blundered badly in bribing the Japanese. At Ford, the placement of the Pinto gas tank was conceded to be an engineering blunder. The eighteen-minute gap in Nixon's White House tapes was a secretarial blunder. The army, in an outrageous blunder, admittedly sprayed a bacteriological gas on the residents of San Francisco, producing both sickness and death. Teddy at Chappaquiddick might have committed a moral blunder, but it was of the kind, according to a family biographer, that "put the steel in his soul." Blunders, by definition, have always gone unpunished, which goes a long way to account for why the rich and powerful have taken them away from the common folk. To err may be human, but to blunder is divine.

It may not be the noblest work of statecraft to play upon the sympathy of the governed. But the governed will forgive you if you do. This is a time of such moral vertigo, such a numbing accumulation of disappointments and shocks, that it has become difficult to watch the evening news in the company of one's own children. Ashamed as we are of our own dismay, uncertain as we are of the future, it comes as a relief to provide the kids with a simple answer, however much we may doubt it.

*Hey, he goofed.*

Goofs, gaffes, snafus, and slipups: the American heart forgives them. And thus it has happened that every recent president, in times of grave national crisis, reaches at once for the blow-dryer and the eyeliner, whatever it takes to achieve that basset-hound look crucial to these confessions. We pull up our chairs and wait while he goes *one-Mississippi, two-Mississippi*. Then he starts talking and we listen, but we seldom understand. All we can feel is sorry—for him, ourselves, the kids. Elsewhere in the world, leaders may be feared or loathed or worshipped; here, in the world's most powerful nation, all they wind up with is our pity.

*That poor man.*

*Look how he's aged.*

You wake up, you read your paper, and the paper deprograms you from your dreams.

Your dreams interpret your memories.

But your memories rarely apply.

That is why it is so important to read the paper every morning and keep up with the news.

FBI ADMITS SPREADING LIES
ABOUT JEAN SEBERG

Have a cup of coffee and adjust to this. Read how our special agents sought to "cheapen the image" of the actress by dreaming up and planting with gossip columnists a false and anonymous tip that the father of the baby she was carrying in 1970 was a "high official" of the Black Panther Party.

Jean Seberg was married at the time to Romain Gary, the French author and diplomat, and when the stories appeared, she was seven months' pregnant. She had made an impressive comeback from her early failures in Hollywood, where at age seventeen she had come from her hometown in Iowa to play Joan of Arc in Otto Preminger's movie. She was the winner of a national talent search, gifted, golden, straight from the farmlands, an American dream if ever there was one. But things hadn't worked out as planned.

She lost her baby two days after the stories appeared. Then she took her baby's body home to Marshalltown so friends of a lifetime could file past to mourn and make sure that it wasn't black. Every year on the anniversary of her daughter's death, she tried to kill herself. This year, she succeeded. Her body was found in the backseat of her car, parked in a fashionable district of Paris. On the day of her funeral, in compliance with the Freedom of Information Act, the FBI confessed to its crime against her.

Hope was in sight, however.

The current director assured the press that the Bureau was "out of that business forever." It was just a blunder that belonged to the past.

A few years ago, I attempted to explain to my daughter why the CIA had thought it a good idea to dust the lining of Fidel Castro's shoes with a strong depilatory powder. Castro had come to New York for a special session of the United Nations, and after several members of the Cuban delegation were caught cooking chickens in their rooms at an expensive downtown hotel, Castro and his entourage had moved to the Hotel Theresa in Harlem, causing great merriment in the press. But that was the same special session where Khrushchev banged on his desk with *his* shoe, stealing the show and turning attention away from Castro's passage through the city until many years later, when the Church Committee uncovered the depilatory powder plan. I stormed around the house when I read about it. My daughter wanted to know why.

"What is depilatory powder?" she asked.

"It's to make your hair fall out," I said.

"But why in his shoes?"

"They thought he would leave them outside his door at night. To be shined."

"And they would sneak up and put the powder in?"

"Yes."

"Why, though? What good would it do if his hair fell out?"

"He's got a big beard, and his beard is part of his image, and they thought the Cuban people would think less of him . . ."

I could see her eyes glazing over. I have a beard, though nothing so powerful as Castro's, and in a flash of unreasonable sympathy for her it occurred to me that she might be worried that all dissident beards were now in danger. I decided not to tell her about the poisoned wet suit or the exploding seashells that the Church Committee reported our government had also concocted to effect Fidel's demise.

Paranoia approaches common sense as the world goes crazy.
—Norman Mailer

Back in the late '50s, I played softball with the Kennedys. Not touch, mind you, just softball. For touch you had to be family, but you could be a peripheral person and still get in the softball games.

I pitched a few innings for our side.

Jack caught a few innings for his.

Bobby played the whole game and ran out all his grounders.

My presence derived from my job as a speechwriter for a senator friendly to the Kennedys—not crucial, just friendly enough for softball.

While Jack was still catching, the boss came up to bat. The game was briefly halted so a photographer could step in front of the plate to frame a picture of the boss with his good softball buddy, JFK. The senator took a number of swings at phantom pitches that the future president strained to pretend to catch.

A few days later, a dozen or so glossies were delivered to the office, and we all crowded around to see. There were the two young senators, handsome and healthy and in full game form, displaying the vigor that would take them far. Looking at the pictures, it curdled my love of VIP softball to remember that no one had been pitching.

Years later, I had lunch with my old boss. We hadn't seen each other in a long while, and much had changed. He had become a high-flying hawk, perhaps the most powerful in the Senate. I was in town for a demonstration and had a gas mask and a helmet in the backseat of my car. The navy and air force were bombing Haiphong harbor at the time, and our conversation quickly grew shrill.

"When are we going to start the terror bombing?" I asked, meaning to be rhetorical, not knowing then that the terror bombing was only a few months away.

The senator fixed me with a patient look.

"When you're bombing," he said, "you've got the four P's."

He paused to tick them off on his fingers.

"You've got ports, power, petroleum, and population. Population is P-4, and you don't go to P-4 until you've knocked out the other three."

Never had I heard U.S. policy so nakedly defined.

Nowadays, I see the boss all the time on *Meet the Press* and *Face the Nation.* Except when he announces for president, everyone takes him seriously. As well they should.

Today, in Los Angeles, there should be no deep breathing. The authorities have called a third-stage smog alert, which means that even healthy persons in their prime should curtail all activities. No racing around. No agitation. No sending the children out to play.

The morning paper has the whole story.

WAR ON SMOG: A MURKY TRUCE

COSTS, CONFUSION SAP LEGISLATIVE, PUBLIC WILL

And it's true. Despite the nation's strictest air quality control standards, despite hundreds of millions of dollars spent studying and regulating poisonous emissions, despite all the technological advances in recent years, today is the worst smog day in almost twenty-five years. The battle we thought we were winning is actually being lost.

Hope is in sight, however.

A low-pressure front is said to be building off the coast. You don't have to understand precisely what a low-pressure front amounts to to know that its existence is good to moderate news. It's enough to know that officials are described as "cautiously optimistic."

Environmental and economic issues share a common dodge that makes them attractive to the new breed of politician: the sense that they are technical, immutable, impervious to all but the longest-range solutions. Back in Lyndon Johnson's day, the illusion was still strong of the U.S. as a Great Society that could accomplish anything with goodwill and heavy spending. Yet it was Johnson himself, in a bitter reflection on his failures in Vietnam, who coined the phrase that echoes through so much of the pessimistic chatter one hears these days—the U.S. as "a pitiful, helpless giant," now taking orders from the sheiks of OPEC, letting overseas money changers beat the dollar into the ground, fouling its nest, going on the dole, relentlessly slipping and sliding into second place or worse.

Militarily and in our merchant fleet, we're weaker than the Russians. The Japanese are whipping us every which way in manufacturing and world commerce. A dozen or more countries now enjoy a higher standard of living. While everyone else is making great strides, we are in an "era of diminished expectations." We must tighten our belts, drive less, be cold in winter and hot in summer. Inflation is here to stay. So is the poisoning of the environment. We are running out of everything. If we don't make all our demands more modest, show-down day is just around the corner.

But for all the complexity of what President Carter, in his television talks (*That poor man. Look how he's aged.*), calls "the crushing problems that threaten our society," is anyone convinced that our problems have actually moved beyond the range of remedy? Or is it just that the defeatist mood now at large in the country has created a new political lingo, along with a new set of dire threats?

Remember godless communism?

Bomb shelters?

Quemoy and Matsu?

Alienation and the generation gap?

Acid?

Amnesty?

SDS?

H. Rap Brown?

The old terrors read like names in a dusty dance program. But for as long as I can remember, we've always been involved in some hopeless situation, getting steadily worse. Crises are the natural resource of a crisis-management government. Without them the wheels will not turn.

In a problem-solving society, running out of problems is the one forbidden act.

If you had Hamilton Jordan's power and loose change, would you consider doing a little cocaine?

According to the news, Ham may have done a little cocaine at

Studio 54 in New York, and a little more cocaine at a party in Beverly Hills, and a little more cocaine back at his suite in the Century Plaza.

Ham's accusers are a seedy lot, but in this conga-dance culture you can't blame a man for getting around. Lots of the very best people do cocaine these days, and some even go to Studio 54. Disco fever. A little flash. Who wouldn't like to see Jackie O dancing with Truman Capote?

If Ham really did do cocaine on these occasions, his most obvious blunder was in his choice of friends. In the trust he placed in trusted advisors . . . and so on. No one alleges that he got even the slightest buzz on, or that any possible buzz was transmitted to the president, or that cocaine in any way influenced the conduct of official government business.

You have to read these stories all the way to the bottom to get to the good news.

Inescapably, undeniably, no matter how much you love it and don't care to leave it, this country has established itself as the world's number-one mischief-maker. No other country has killed more people since the Second World War ended almost thirty-five years ago. No one has sold more arms, launched more secret armies, invented more inhuman weapons, engaged in more "dirty tricks." It is all well and good to say that the real difference between our enemies and us is that in our open society the truth does out: no one else has a Freedom of Information Act. But it is well to remember that we ourselves created a government with an appalling capacity for wickedness, and that the truth of its secret actions had to be pulled like molars from the mouths of the men we put in charge.

God, this is depressing. Let's look at the bright side. We're tops in space, we're not at war, there is no draft, gas and taxes are higher in Europe, our athletes keep setting new records, lesbians can now hold hands while shopping in department stores. There have also been some important negative achievements: Nixon resigned, we learned a big lesson from the fall of the shah, a great many people have recently quit smoking. But that's about it. Politically, ethically, in substance and in spirit, there seems to me little doubt that our blunders in this era have made us smaller. What used to be called paranoia is now a settled street of middle-class thinking. Burglar alarm sales are going straight through the roof. Perhaps that's what happens when you lose a war: a tolerated decadence masks a crippled heart.

In 1965, I went to India to interview Prime Minister Shastri, who, following the death of Nehru, had become leader of the world's largest democracy. The thing about Shastri was his incredible humility. He dressed in a patched cotton dhoti and spoke in a very small voice. The best time for us to talk, he said, was after he finished tending his vegetable garden around 6:30 in the morning. He would only have a few minutes, but we could meet as many mornings as the interview required.

It wasn't a very good interview. A certain vanity and sense of self-importance is the engine that makes an interview move, and Shatri's serene engine was on idle. He'd just smile and nod his head to most of my questions. After a few mornings, I began drifting over to the New Delhi's government compound just as the sun was rising in the hope of catching Shastri in his garden. Sleepy guards greeted me and let me pass.

I didn't see the prime minister at first, because he was down on his knees sowing carrot seeds. Carrot seeds are tiny, and he had his nose close to the ground to make sure he was sowing them evenly. He was all alone back there, the leader of four hundred million people, dressed in the same mended clothes he would wear to his office after his gardening was done. I watched him for a while, then asked if I could make myself useful. He directed me to a patch of cabbage.

After a while, Shastri came over, inspected my weeding, and said I was doing fine. He wouldn't have time to talk, he said, but if I wished to I could stay in the garden and finish the weeding. I spent the rest of the morning there, as happy with my life as a reporter as I have ever been.

Shastri died a few weeks later and the government fell into the hands of Indira Gandhi, whose pride and hauteur brought to an end India's twenty-eight years of democracy.

Purloining the Pentagon Papers was perhaps the single most effective act of civil disobedience anyone committed in all these raucous years. It gave the lie to the notion that Vietnam was in any sense a blunder, a quagmire, something we hadn't intended. It was a tremendous service to the country. My only problem in fully appreciating it was that on my way home from India after Shastri's death I spent a few weeks in Saigon and there met Dan Ellsberg, who attacked me over dinner as a cozy Manhattan liberal and fashionable antiwar fool. An ex-Marine with connections to Rand and the State Department, he was so knowledgeable and persuasive that I naturally took him to be a CIA man. And now here he was, Public Enemy Number One at the Pentagon.

We change, of course, we all change, and it could be that had Ellsberg not given the war such ardent support well into the late sixties, his anger upon discovering the sham of it would not have been half so intense, and he would never have risked his career to take such drastic action. But then he had also married a millionaire and carried on in other ways that made me edgy about his status in the peace movement. I covered his trial, and when he and his co-defendant, Tony Russo, were freed following an incredible series of government blunders that led to a dismissal, I wrote a story attempting to weave together all the confusions and contradictions I felt the case revealed. Neither of those guys, or their lawyers, for that matter, have spoken to me since.

Imagine all you would have missed if you'd been tending to your garden all this time:

FRANCIS GARY POWERS SHOT DOWN OVER RUSSIA

CARYL CHESSMAN EXECUTED

JFK TRIUMPH IN CUBAN MISSILE CRISIS

JFK KILLED

WATTS IN FLAMES: BURN, BABY, BURN

PUEBLO CAPTURED

RUSS INVADE CZECHOSLOVAKIA

RFK KILLED

DE GAULLE DEFEATED

MANSON ARRESTED

HEYERDAHL CROSSES ATLANTIC IN PAPYRUS BOAT

ATTICA RIOTS

CALLEY CONVICTED

PATTY HEARST KIDNAPPED

NIXON RESIGNS

PATTY CONVICTED

PATTY FREED

Never mind that the only one of these great adventures worth repeating is crossing the Atlantic in Thor Heyerdahl's delicate boat.

One thing I have noticed about public life in America these past twenty years is what it seems to do to people's faces. I'm not sure if it's caused by flashbulbs or simple hysteria, but it's a process of balkanization in which the face splits up into city-states that break off relations with each other. The eyes are unaware of what the mouth is doing. The smile goes out of synch. Jacqueline Kennedy is the classic example, but you can already see the battle lines drawn in the face of Jimmy Carter. Even Tom Hayden is beginning to show some effects.

If there's one myth that has beguiled and sustained us through these years of lost illusion it's the Kennedy myth, the idea that those rakishly handsome millionaires were somehow of us and for us, no matter what they did. Since the deaths of John and Robert, we have learned that in private life one was an easily satisfied satyr taking seconds on a Mafia moll while the other was a truly unscrupulous schemer and dealer in the prurient proceeds of wiretaps and bugs. But never mind. Most of us would prefer not to know that while Jacqueline was giving tours of the White House and speaking her faultless French, the brothers were upstairs in the Lincoln Room, plotting the death of Fidel. Most of us would rather ignore the strong evidence that it was breakdown over her involvement with the martyred brothers that led Marilyn Monroe to her death. A few years ago, I spent a week or so interviewing a woman who claimed to be one of JFK's former mistresses. She told me all about shuttling back and forth between the White House and Sam Giancana's guarded compound in Chicago. She told me of meetings with Jack in New York, Palm Beach, Beverly Hills, meetings with Sam in Vegas. It wasn't a pretty story, but God help me, I believed her.

The only thing was: I never wrote the story.

"Executive action" is a phrase I wouldn't have understood in 1960.
I hadn't heard about government disinformation programs.
I didn't know the meaning of "nolo contendere."
Nor Zippo Squads. Nor "interdiction."
As our hopes grow poor, our language grows rich.
Or can you relate to that?

\*      \*      \*

A sense of passage through troubled times always carries with it a convenient loss of faith—convenient because it allows one to blame his own failures on history and never have to account for the distant memory of all that might have been. I remember the astonishing pride I felt to be marching along with my platoon when I was in the army—a pride that astonished me then, in the late fifties, and astonishes me all the more now. I feel a loss of faith when I think about this. But I must remember that there are those who, through it all, kept right on marching.

Sure, I could take the easy road. I could conceal my blunders or have them passed on to the courts for prosecution. But that would be wrong. So I must tell you tonight that I clung far too long to my loyalty to Adlai Stevenson, believing him to be the last, best hope until the day he collapsed and died on a London street. I thought for a while that the hippies had the answer, that flowers stuck in gun barrels just might work. After that, I took to carrying my gas mask in search of a demonstration. I thought that Jimi Hendrix was a genius who would live forever. I believed that Lee Harvey Oswald had acted on his own, and ditto for Sirhan Sirhan. I thought the ghettos would keep burning until racism was acknowledged as the nation's first, most immediate problem. I thought I'd grow old like my grandfather, saying, *If only I were young today!*

All of these notions have proved to be false or irrelevant.
*Mea culpa.*

1979

# Tragedies at Hollywood and Vine

My office looks out on Hollywood Boulevard. It's a third-floor corner room in an old building a block west of Vine Street. On all but the deadliest days, my two big windows provide a marvelous cross breeze. Sometimes being up here is like being aboard a yacht.

But not often. Usually, it's more like being holed up in an amiable asylum where they let you stay up all night and make your own coffee and light your own cigarettes. You can stare out the window all you want to. When you hear someone screaming in the street, you can rush to the window and look out.

I have things arranged so that while sitting at my typewriter I can glance up and scan the sidewalk without rising. But in six years of sitting here, I have become more and more discriminating. Today, only the most piercing screams, the most deranged shouting, and the siren song of real chaos can draw me from my chair. Even so, leaping up, rushing to the window, and leaning out constitutes my fitness program. I do it about twenty-five times a day.

I do it because my window is my mandate. Fate has directed that

I keep watch on the boulevard, and in my office it has given me what amounts to a box at the opera of Hollywood street life. Just now, by means of dangling a pair of office shears down to the sidewalk and pulling them back up with mailing twine, I have determined that my window sill is thirty-six feet, ten inches above the Street of Dreams. For a monitor of street life, this is the perfect altitude. Any lower and aimless chatter would intrude. Any higher and you'd miss the semihysterics. If I wasn't doing this work, who would?

The other day, after I had made the coffee and smoked a cigarette and was settling in for a serious stare, I heard a woman in the street cry out, "You're not leaving *me!*" Normally, this banal utterance would merit no more than a slight craning of the neck. But the day was young, and I thought I detected a note of psychotic promise in the woman's voice. I leapt from my chair, rushed to the window, and leaned out.

She was barefoot, she was blond, and her remarkable bosom was remarkably revealed by a shirt that lacked either buttons or button-holes. She was flailing at a dented Pontiac with a heavy purse. The Pontiac was painted Day-Glo orange, and across the trunk, in Day-Glo green, was written, "I Married a White Woman." As the car rolled away, a dark hand emerged from the driver's window and waved a mocking bye-bye. The woman stood at curbside, paralyzed by rage. Then an old convertible pulled up, and the man in the back scooted over and the woman climbed in and accepted a beer. The car ran down to the corner and turned right at Vine.

I have no idea what was said to induce the woman to enter the convertible, or why she was abandoned in the first place, or where anyone was headed, or what they found when they got there. That's where the thirty-six feet, ten inches comes in. Spared all the details, I can appreciate these scenes for their classic dimension: they are part of the tragic parade.

*　　*　　*

Benny Jones, who watched this same corner for thirty years from his shoeshine stand on Ivar Street, believes that Hollywood Boulevard turned tragic about the time they stopped making movies in black-and-white. That was in the late fifties, but the glory days were already over, the stars had moved on to Beverly Hills and Malibu, and all that remained were the old folks, the tourists, the drifters, the dopers, the runaways, the vice squad, and Marines on leave. There are shoppers, of course, and office workers, but few of them are true denizens of the boulevard. Only very seldom does an actual celebrity come down this street on foot.

But the boulevard has retained its allure in the minds of the dispossessed. It is an enduring symbol of the wonders that luck can bring, the last chance that no one would give at home. Every day the Greyhounds arrive at the depot on Vine Street with the gullible on board. Every day they depart with those not so gullible anymore. Those who stay are those who can't go elsewhere. They are obsessed with the dream. They are giving it a couple of months more. There's not much to go back to. They're too old to move. They love to see the palm trees sway.

I look out my window and see the palm trees sway. They are swaying in the courtyard of the Hollywood Plaza Hotel. The Hollywood Plaza used to be a grand address, with a band playing on the roof and gardenias floating in the lily pond. Today it is a bunker for the old, a retirement hotel.

Around the corner, across from Benny's stand, is the Hollywood Knickerbocker, formerly with a band on the roof and Joe DiMaggio in the lobby, refusing to sign autographs. Now the Knickerbocker, too, is a retirement hotel. The old folks drove Benny out of business. In his time, he shined the shoes of the great and the near-great. Joe DiMaggio. Jimmy Fidler. Jimmy Durante. Caesar Romero. In his last days at the stand, Benny was down to the likes of me.

He'd shine my shoes and we'd shoot the breeze, and he launched

me on my understanding of how fortunate I was to have a third-floor
office that looked out on Hollywood Boulevard. Once he saw Errol
Flynn riding a motorcycle round and round the block, wearing only a
bathing suit. Once he saw Carmen Miranda beating on a car with her
purse. He loved the past so much that he could see no charm in the
present. He would fall silent when I regaled him with the wonders I'd
seen from my window. I'd tell him that the current mix in the neighborhood wasn't all that bad. The moral tremor that occurs when an
octagenarian crosses paths with a transsexual can only do both of
them good; one is reminded of the varieties of life, while the other
comes to grips with the leavening of age. Benny would shake his
head and say nothing. I'd content myself with examining again his
autographed glossies of Rocky Marciano and Danny Kaye and Robert
Mitchum and the rest.

Benny packed it in about a year ago and closed his stand and
moved away without even saying goodbye. No one seemed to miss
him even a little. Before long a car stereo outfit took over his space.
I still hear the shouts, and the screams, and the sirens, and I glance
out the window, and everything looks much the same. The palm trees
sway in the abandoned courtyard. The tourists take pictures of each
other on the Walk of Fame. I look out the window with interest. But
frankly, I could use a shine.

1980

# On Flying First Class

I seldom fly first class. In fact, I never do. First class is for society swells, business dogs, showbiz wastrels. It's for people whose comfort really, really counts. When I step aboard a plane, I cast a scornful eye on the first-class spendthrifts as I make my way back to join the huddled masses flying coach. Unless they look like professional basketball players (whose long legs and long season make first-class seats only humane), I fix them with what I hope they take to be a Marxist-Leninist glare.

Yet today the winds of fortune deposited me on seat 2D on United's flight 656 from L.A. to Seattle, and I raised not a finger in protest. I probably don't have to tell you that seat 2D is a prestige address on a 727, being a window seat in the first-class cabin. To sit in 2D on this two-hour, 957-mile flight costs $180, or $35 more than it costs to make the same trip in any of the seats behind the curtain three rows back. It's a scenic flight, but the view is much the same from every window, and if all goes well the coach section lands at approximately the same moment that first-class touches down. So the

$35 is not money spent on transport or tourism but money spent to be pampered, indulged, and poured free drinks as fast as you can swill them. In the spirit of investigative journalism, I thought I'd give it a try.

Had I been a step more nimble at the airport, this probe into one of life's most dubious luxuries would never have occurred to me. I would have cashed in my ticket, bought a seat in coach, and cannily invested my savings in a fine old brandy or a fingertip massage. But I was traveling as a showbiz wastrel on money not my own, and my head was in the clouds well before I reached the airport. So instead of bothering with the line at the ticket counter I glided through check-in, was X-rayed and found innocent of iron, stood to the right on the people mover, and heard myself called "sir" six or seven times. In the boarding lounge, while others were left to amuse themselves as best they could in the last ten minutes before takeoff, I was urged aboard in order to be belted down and put on display by the time the gates were sprung for the plain folk. Seven other substantial citizens were in their places when I entered the cabin, and the most substantial of all was the fellow in 2C, an immensely fat young man with a foot that was heavily bandaged. When he saw that he would have to rise for me to take my seat, he paled visibly and shook his head in disgust.

While the fat man struggled to his feet, a stewardess helped me off with my jacket, employing a deft touch that made extracting my arms more awkward for me than a disco turn. With a mumbled apology to the fat man, wincing in the aisle, I slithered past with my briefcase and settled into the comfort of what felt like a very good club chair.

By then, the coach passengers were streaming aboard, and it was clear from the look of them that none mistook either me or the fat man for professional basketball players. Instead, they surveyed us for clues to our folly, appraised us for the source of our funds, shamed us with envy, with withering glances, with Marxist-Leninist glares. Only a few seemed to ignore us, and I felt a keen sense of relief when the sullen parade was over and the curtain between the classes had been mercifully drawn.

We were still climbing when the stewardess came beaming our way to ask what we'd have to drink. It was not yet 2:00, too early for serious drinking, so I ordered a vodka martini. The fat man wanted two gin and tonics, quick. In a trice, our eager attendant was back with tablecloths, and she snapped down my table before I could lift a hand, pinning my briefcase to my shoetops. Without causing further agony to my seatmate, there was nothing I could do to retrieve it until snack time was over and the table could go back up.

We were three drinks up the coast before the snack arrived—an icy crescent of pita bread stuffed with processed meat and cheese. Off to the side was a concoction the stewardess assured me was a salad: carrot remnants mixed with something vaguely green—premature raisins or decomposing grapes—on a bed of lettuce that in the coroner's report might be described as one (1) brown and green object smaller than a playing card and limper than a rag. God knows what was being served behind the curtain, but sampling the "cake" and sipping the insipid coffee left no doubt that the glory of this first-class snack resided completely in the tablecloth.

My disappointment in the fare led me to call for a fourth martini and attempt to calculate how many more I would have to drink if I were to get my money's worth. Back in coach, they were paying two bucks a pop; up here, at an added cost of $17.50 an hour, we were drinking free. If you allowed $2 for the bigger, softer chair, $1 for the better snack, and $5 more for the possible psychotherapeutic benefits of being strapped down and found guilty of coddling yourself by a large, informal jury of your peers, you still had to choke down fourteen drinks in order to come out ahead by the time you reached Seattle.

My briefcase was killing my ankles, but I was numb enough to endure it. The fat man didn't want to talk, and neither, anymore, did I. The West Coast from thirty-seven thousand feet is a sight of such absorbing beauty that it draws the imagination away from the trivial cossetting that airlines offer their passengers on both sides of the curtain. Better to forget the money and the wish for money, the booze and the wish for booze, better to lose yourself out the window, in the meadows and forests, the taming of the mountains, the miracle of Yosemite flattened by altitude and snow.

When we reached Seattle, the pilot cranked out a big mellow turn over the Sound that caught the city on a sparkling day, banking around boldly to show off the Space Needle and the big box that it came in. His landing was smooth and quiet. He taxied in what seemed like silence up to the terminal. There was the sound of hydraulic hissing. The door popped open. The flight was done.

We first-class passengers were off the plane first, which gave us longer to wait for our luggage. At the carousel, all of us, lords and peasants, stood together like brothers, waiting for the belt to roll, the spindle to spin. Our possessions started down the chute, their humble parcels, our handsome cases. We passed through the checkpoint and went out to get the rides that would take us home. We all needed cabs, buses, friends to come and meet us. Democracy, as always, was restored at curbside.

1980

# That Toyota of Mine

I 've just bought a brand-new car. It's got five-speed manual trans-
mission, steel sunroof, steering wheel that tilts, ninety true horses
under the hood. It's got rear window washer-wiper, lumbar adjustment
in the driver seat, digital clock, tape deck and four good speakers,
highway cruising range of almost five hundred miles. It's black and it's
just about perfect and I couldn't love it more if it were a Labrador
retriever.

I tell you this not by way of boasting, but rather to confess that
this new car of mine happens to be a Toyota, a Toyota Celica, a 1980
GT coupe, a car that was made in Japan. While American auto makers
lay off workers by the thousands, while American car dealers fall to
their knees to make a deal, here I go doing business with our number-
one economic enemy. The balance of payments will suffer. The dollar
will fall.

But to tell the truth, the fate of the dollar has never struck me as
my concern. The gnomes of Zurich will decide the fate of the dollar.
The news will be brought to us by a saddened president. He will cite

the findings of a panel of economic advisors who, in the eyes of overseas money changers, are not so much gnomes as dwarves. And if the price of gold should fluctuate to our disadvantage, who is to say that that is wrong? Caveat emptor, caveat vendor, and in the marketplace may the best man win.

So it's not the fact of buying a foreign car that makes me a bit uneasy—it's the fact of buying a car that is Japanese. I am just the right age (forty-five) to have remembered Pearl Harbor perhaps too literally, too vividly, too long. Longer, certainly, than the government. Longer than the first eager business dogs. I was six when the hand that held the dagger did whatever it did, and then two years later the man next door came home ruined by Japanese bullets, and by the time the war was over and I was ten, I had acquired from the movies and from my uncle and from my father an indelible belief that we were right and they were wrong and never the twain would meet.

I won't deny a long history of fraternization. When I was eighteen, I fell in love with a Nisei girl and I still call her up every December 7 to remember and to joke. On the twentieth anniversary of Hiroshima, I was in Hiroshima. And in December of that year, I spent two delightful weeks holed up in a Tokyo hotel. (When I say holed up, I mean quarantined. Having arrived from Saigon looking sickly, I was intercepted at the airport, scrutinized by immaculate doctors, and pronounced unfit to mingle with the Japanese. For fourteen days I was visited morning and afternoon by teams of doctors and nurses in sanitary masks, and on one of these occasions the doctor in charge displayed his command of things American by informing me that the day before, the Lambs had beat the Laiders.) After I was released, I bought a Nikon camera, and since then I have owned a Sony tape recorder, an Aiwa tape recorder, a Canon camera, and many small, subtle things only incidentally Japanese. A Japanese saw. Several Japanese chisels. A notebook and a purse and many stickers in the Hello

Kitty! line greatly loved by my daughter. My raincoat was made in Korea. I have a cap and a jacket made by the real Chinese.

But a car—a car is serious. You can buy a camera or a watch made by one or the other of the former Axis powers and not feel compromised. But just as a Volkswagen calls to my mind Hitler (who designed it and named it, after all), a Toyota reminds me of Tojo, causing childish emotions to well up, a child's voice calling, "Buy a Chevrolet."

I'm sure this residual prejudice is something that Toyota and Datsun and Sony and Sansui and all the other Japanese firms doing business in this country have studied and have learned how to cope with. And, to their credit, it seems to me that their strategy has been simply to be excellent, to be irresistible, to let craftsmanship speak for itself.

When you consider how thoroughly the Japanese, the Germans, and even the Italians have dominated us in technology and design since the days when they lay in rubble, it's amazing that we won the war. We won the war only to fall into decline, and today, if you want anything that works, it's not a bad idea to look to those old Axis powers. Cars and calculators and cameras—one or the other of our erstwhile enemies makes them better than we do.

Surely, this reversal will live in history as one of the compelling curiosities in the heave and thrust of modern nations. How it happened that a nation made great by its inventiveness and expertise subdued its enemies and then somehow bled away its genius, lost the art of being best. How we became the "pitiful, helpless giant" of Lyndon Johnson's phrase. How it could be that Detroit now runs a poor fourth to Tokyo and Turin and Wolfsburg.

Perhaps the answer lies in the submissiveness of the foreign worker—though, according to latest statistics, West Germany is more thoroughly unionized than we are. Perhaps the spark that ignites the imagination of an engineer requires more of a challenge than we have found in recent years. Perhaps, having won, we have elected no longer to compete.

But I fear that the answer may identify a social pathology all our own. American goods are often made in a state of rage. Rage against the system, against the boss, against the sense of decline. The man I bought my Toyota from was a refugee from a long career at General Motors. At first he struck me as the typical Hollywood showoff, letting me know how many cars he'd sold to the likes of O. J. Simpson and Steve McQueen. But then he told me a story that explained his new choice of employment as well as my new choice of car. In his last days at GM, he said, there was a big demand for Camaros, but none were to be had. He visited the big GM assembly plant in Van Nuys and complained about the shortage. The manager took him to a window that looked out on a lot where one thousand new Camaros were parked, all of them painted an appalling shade of pink. Someone had come to work cocked and loaded to the pee-oh'd position. He didn't like affirmative action. He didn't like what was happening to his check. He was the man in charge of the automatic paint sprayers, and he had just one way to express himself. So he painted one thousand cars pink. Nobody noticed, and it was only after the paint had dried that anybody cared.

My Toyota is sleek and black like a Labrador retriever. When you put the key in the ignition, it goes beep-beep-beep fifteen times to tell you to fasten your seatbelts. Then it shuts up. It goes down the road like a promise from a friend. It tells me that the war is over, and I wouldn't trade it for a Ford or a Chevy or even for the cars we all imagined years ago, the cars we thought that we alone could build.

1980

# Why My Friendship with Patricia Neal and Roald Dahl Ended

A fellow I know named Larry Schiller called up one morning almost two years ago and said he wanted to send me $2,500 in the afternoon mail. Sensing that he had caught my attention, he went on to assure me that I wouldn't have to lift a finger—all he wanted in return was an option on the motion picture rights to a book called *Pat and Roald,* written by me back in 1968. If all went well, he said, if he came up with the right script and a two-hour movie based on the book went into production, I could count on receiving $22,500 more the first day the camera turned. Wise to the ways of Hollywood and wary of Larry, I pondered this offer for several seconds. Then I said wow, gee, fabulous, thanks, and may God's love be with you.

Handsomely published by Random House in 1969, nicely reviewed here and there, *Pat and Roald* had foundered sadly in its second printing and gone on to be remaindered, recycled, smashed into pulp. True, you could sometimes find a paperback copy at the airport newsstand in certain mildly repressive Third World countries. You could luck into a first edition at a church bazaar. But the book was so deep in the grave that I had long since ceased to mourn it.

Naturally, I assumed that no movie would be made. Taking an option on a book implies the promise of a movie to about the same extent that taking a girl to a drive-in implies a wedding in June. So the $22,500 had to be considered only-if money, money best put out of mind. The $2,500, on the other hand, was found money, money floating in over the transom. I felt a flash of pride in those dear departed pages, which had brought me little but pain.

My agent, however, was not even ten percent as pleased as I was when I called him with the news. He reminded me that Larry and I had lately been speaking through lawyers, our friendship having run aground over rights to another story. Mightn't some vengeful motive have sweetened Schiller's pleasure in my prose? Could he have gotten wind of some other producer's interest? Wouldn't it be just like him to sucker me into leaping at this ruinous little windfall? I said I hardly thought so.

Schiller well knew that the heroes of the book—Patricia Neal and her husband Roald Dahl—did not care to see it exhumed. They hadn't liked it much when it was published and they liked it no better now that the passage of time had restored to them a measure of the privacy they had lost, or sold, after a series of strokes in the winter of 1965 left Pat in a long, deep coma, observed in what amounted to a world-wide vigil. Speechless, confused, half paralyzed, she awoke to find herself transformed into a saint of suffering; and in her struggle to reclaim her health and her faculties, the Oscar-winning actress won far more applause than all her movies could ever bring. Within two years she was making personal appearances and turning up on talk shows, and then there were movies billed as her comeback; medals and awards; finally, years later, even TV commercials. You may recall Pat's work for Maxim: "My husband is a *writah,* and he's terribly fussy when it comes to the coffee he drinks . . ." All that was behind them now.

Over the years, a dozen or so producers had confided in me their desperate wish to make a movie from my book. They would go off to England to discuss it with the Dahls, and then they would disappear, wordlessly, sometimes almost tracelessly, leaving only the faintest oil slick on my mind. Even Schiller, a man who had bagged such elusive game as Madame Nhu and Gary Gilmore, had tried them and had come away discouraged.

Nor were the Dahls conspicuously keen on the author of *Pat and Roald.* We'd met a few months into Pat's convalescence, when *Life* magazine assigned me to do a story on how she was getting on. Photographer Leonard McCombe and I rented a car in London and drove up to Buckinghamshire, where after some searching we found the lane that led to the Dahls' fine old Georgian cottage, covered with roses, surrounded by fields—Gypsy House, they called it. And there, waiting to greet us at the kitchen table, thirty-nine years old, seven months' pregnant, dressed in a housecoat, slumped in a chair, was the Oscar-winning Best Actress of the Year before, much impaired in mind as well as body. With her eye patch and her leg brace and the panic that showed when she smiled, she was too beautiful to look at for very long.

The next day I found a room above a pub in town, and for the rest of the summer I walked up the lane every morning, feeling useful and privileged. Pat was valiant, Roald was brilliant, and I was much in awe. Love and courage were what I thought I saw in the way he hovered over her, cornering her with his quirky erudition, getting the best of her, goading her on. Then he'd take a minute to teach me how to prune a rose bush, recognize a Chippendale, handicap grey-hounds, make mayonnaise. I went with them when it was time to drive to Oxford for Pat's baby to be born—Lucy, a perfect girl, un-harmed by her mother's ordeal. *Life* published my story to great effect. Prizes were won. Publishers were calling.

I spent that Christmas with the Dahls, and in the summer we

shared a vacation in France. When President Lyndon Johnson presented Pat with the American Heart Association's Heart-of-the-Year Award in 1968, I got to stand beside her in the Oval Office. It had taken us two years to agree that a book should be done, then me another year to write it. I rented a place a bike ride away from Gypsy House and stayed there through an English winter so cold and wet that I mastered the art of typing in mittens. Nearly every day Pat and I would talk, take walks, go through her drills and lessons. Roald and I would play bowls, feed the budgerigars, weed the lilies, drive down to London to bet on the dogs. The day I packed for home I felt as close as kin.

So it came as quite a blow when the Dahls read the book in manuscript and decided they'd been betrayed. They were outraged. I should have anticipated this if only because friendship never thrives on full disclosure; the last thing anyone needs to see is one hundred thousand words on how their faults make you love them all the more. Instead, mindless, I countered their anger with my own; and in our raging on the transatlantic phone I said some unfortunate things, such as telling Pat that she'd taken the fancy inscription on her Heart-of-the-Year Award far too much to heart.

Called in to serve as referee, my editor could calm them only at the cost of cutting paragraphs and pages. Drinking bouts, love affairs, follies, and trespasses—all the good stuff had to go. Doing the job, the editor said, made him feel like a vandal. I went cold on the censored words that survived, and I didn't much care when the book came out and then was gone, quiet as the passage of a cloud.

But the wound to our friendship continued to deepen and fester. We fell out of touch. Friends who happened to meet them came back with reports of how, having mentioned my name, they'd been regaled with accounts of my excesses when I was living in England, a bike ride away. Some of these stories would have flattered a man of twice my energies—how I'd spent the whole time lolling around with French actresses, haunting the casinos, draining every glass; how I'd wound up dashing off the book in a single manic weekend. I'd laugh, of course, but these stories didn't amuse me. They just informed me that the Dahls and I were through.

Knowing all this, Schiller still thought he could make a movie, and who was I to tell him he was wrong? Clearly, the right thing to do was to take his $2,500 and wish him the best of British luck.

Some weeks later, Schiller called to announce that he had signed Robert Anderson to write the screenplay. Robert Anderson, author of *Tea and Sympathy*. The man who wrote *The Nun's Story* and *I Never Sang for My Father*. Schiller was delighted with his catch, and not merely because he had brought to the project a playwright of talent and prestige; Anderson was also on the best of terms with a good many friends of the Dahls. Larry wanted to know if I could spare a few days to talk with Anderson in New York. Playing my excitement like a hole card, I said that I thought I could.

Mild, cultivated, handsomely into his sixties, Anderson welcomed me into his Sutton Place apartment and launched at once on a long ramble about his own loves and hurts. The more he talked, the more the story I'd come to tell welled up in me, and when my chance came to speak I leaped at it. Babbling at first, eventually blubbering, I told him about the loss of that irreplaceable friendship, the squandered feelings that had to be denied when my tribute was taken as a treason. Anderson fielded my gushings with psychoanalytic ease, nodding very wisely, taking microscopic notes. If my listener hadn't been so sympathetic, I might also have been embarrassed at how much it still pained me to tell.

Schiller kept calling with more good news. Anderson's script was wonderful. CBS wanted to go ahead with it, as did the sponsor, Procter & Gamble. He had given the script to the Dahls. They'd read it and failed to hate it, possibly encouraged by the friends they shared with Anderson. Then Schiller flew to England and returned with Pat and Roald's full script approval in hand. He'd signed Glenda Jackson to play Pat. He'd signed Dirk Bogarde to play Roald.

All of this seemed more than a little unreal to me; but I confess that in my disbelief, the $22,500 swam back into my mind. My old understanding with the Dahls, however, often abrogated, called for us to share equally in the book's earnings, so I would owe them $12,500, leaving me with $11,250 after my agent's tithe. But apparently this bonanza was a trifling sum to Roald, who meanwhile had talked Schiller out of another $50,000 to pay for this new loss of privacy. Asked in a newspaper interview about *The Patricia Neal Story*, Roald made sure there was no confusion about his high motives: "We're not in it for the money," he said. Nor were they in it because of any faith in the good intentions of the Hollywood types who were putting it together. "I hate the buggers," Roald said.

That sounded a lot like Roald, and so did the dialogue in Anderson's screenplay—much of it, I'm happy to say, taken from the book. Reading the script, I could hear the Dahls' voices, see the lane, remember the children playing on the lawn. Naturally, I felt there was room for improvement. For example, a character named Barry enters in the second act, flying the flag of *Life*, an ingratiating fellow whose every word is a kind of verbal curtsy. I would have made him tougher, stronger, wiser, better-looking, not so much a wimp.

I have no idea how *The Patricia Neal Story* will turn out. I hope the phone doesn't ring. I hope the Nielsens are good. I hope the Dahls' children see it and find in it good reason to admire their remarkable parents all the more. If all goes well, I'll even risk indulging in the wish that the tribute intended so many years ago will at last be understood and accepted.

1981

# Secrets of the Kite

I had about four hundred feet of number twelve coat and button running sweetly off my handmade Bombay reel, and my kite, an India Fighter, felt like a flying trout. The moving men had just emptied my apartment and driven off in their van, and I was across the street in Riverside Park, having a farewell fly. Looking up past trees that held the skeletons of a dozen learner kites, I could see my curtainless windows staring blindly down at me. It was late afternoon, and the sun, like the windows, was dim and orange in the smoke above the river. My kite was black and green.

Working into a corkscrew climb with a trick of thumb and finger, I looped up over the Soldiers' and Sailors' Monument, cutting back in an arc that held all the way to the penthouses on 86th Street, where the crosstown breeze tugged me out toward the Hudson. Conditions were sublime and I felt the familiar glaze of contentment settle over me. Tracing a diamond in the sky, I tuned my mind to the pleasure of an hour under the string.

\*　　\*　　\*

The glaze—it was like glaze, the feeling that I got in the park. My workouts there were supposed to be training sessions for the weekend kite flights above the Sheep Meadow in Central Park. The summer before, with only fifty or so hours of flying behind me, I had brazenly challenged both Bahadur and Frank, the rival bosses of the meadow, and was rewarded for my nerve with the loss of five kites, two to Bahadur and three to Frank. I knew Frank had me when I saw him preparing his cutting string, grimly massaging the line with a mixture of mashed cola bottle and diluted Elmer's glue. Frank was on me with karate chops before my kites were high enough to maneuver, his little white homemade fighter slashing down and around my hapless three-dollar birds, drawing the fatal cutting string across their taut and slender necks. Bahadur brought me down with classic high-altitude spins, circling tight around me until my string was entwined in his, then cutting me off so gently that he kept my kite in the air along with his and brought them both down unscathed, much to his girlfriend's delight. In the silly way that athletic rivalries get started, I made it my dream to cut Bahadur down.

Rehearsing for this combat, I sometimes sent a drone kite aloft, tethering it to a park bench and attacking from all angles until I'd perfected my kill. And though I was still no match for Bahadur (a professional kite merchant, by the way), I had brought down a few serious flyers, including the masterly, clerkish Joe, with his red-and-black Iron Cross special. But I lacked the necessary killer instinct, as I realized when I heard myself calling my workouts "seances" and "recitals."

These words captured the spirit of the thing better than I understood at first. It took a whole winter of flying, mornings and evenings, to cultivate the glaze enough to call it by its name, to pursue the winged enchantment for its own sake. Each movement of the kite transmits itself down the string and each movement of the hand sends a ripple shimmying up: the string coaxes my fingers, but the kite obeys my hand. Closing my eyes, I can follow it perfectly, feel the crisp flutter along its bamboo spine. The loops and rolls and arabesques are like a silent conversation; time passes and clouds change; the sun dies across the river.

"I used to fly kites here when I was a kid."

I looked down with a start to discover a man and his wife standing next to me, squinting up at my distant bird. "Oh, yeah?" I said. My voice sounded choked and foreign, as it does when I wake up from a nap. What I felt like saying was "So what?" My final trance in the park had been broken by this unsmiling kite inspector, a retired violinist from St. Petersburg, Florida, as he was already explaining. "We're just here another week, thank God. This neighborhood has gone to hell in the last forty years. It makes you sick. It used to be high-class, the best in town."

"Well, everything's changed," I said, as absently as possible. I liked the neighborhood as it was, full of old people's homes and delicatessens. The violinist pointed around the park with accusing pokes of his finger: a pair of brotherly drunks asleep on a park bench, a band of Puerto Ricans, boys and girls, playing roughly together—Keep Away, it seemed. An intense wave of affection for the park swelled up in me. It was there, along that concrete esplanade, that the secrets of the kite had revealed themselves to me slowly, deliciously, through two summers, a winter and a spring. I knew every tree between 85th Street and the monument, every draft and zephyr along the drive itself. Moving away only made it feel all the more like home.

To tell the violinist that I myself was pulling out would have won him his point, so instead I said something hotly patriotic—". . . Don't knock the neighborhood to me, mister. I live here and I think it's great." With that, I flipped over into a swooning sigh of a dive and drifted back out over the river. "Your kite could use a tail," the violinist said.

Telling an India Fighter kite flier that he needs a tail is equal to telling a diamond cutter that he needs an ax. The art, and certainly the sport, is in the wonderful lack of stability, the irrepressible wish to fly. Tying on a tail would be like tying a rag to a robin.

I admit that I am an occasional showoff—it was hot-dogging for passersby that cost me the kites in the trees, or anyway most of them. But the violinist was asking for it, so I came around fast in a series of rolling arpeggios, swooped down low over the park, stopped, hovered, spun, hung in there. Then I rolled over and up and traced a bullet streak across the spreading sunset. I was going for pure altitude now, and I reeled out line until my fighter soared up beyond the highest bird and was all but lost in the smudgy city sky.

It was an easy five hundred yards out over the Hudson when I saw the helicopter coming. Even before I made out the big orange NYPD stencil, I knew it was the flying police, cruising south down the parkway from the bridge. Glancing at the naked curve of my string, I also knew that my green-and-black hero, a veteran of Central Park, was in the gravest kind of danger. Coolly fighting back a flash of panic, I played out enough line to bring my nose over, then dove for the river as the killer blades approached. I screamed down like an eagle, like a gull . . . but not, alas, in time. As the cops flew past pretending not to notice, my fighter went limp and drifted dead into the river.

Omens are usually lost on me. A month or so before, in the Sheep Meadow, a mounted policeman's horse clumsily crushed my reel with his hoof, snapping the string and sending the kite straight into the bushes. "Police brutality!" I shouted but only as a joke for Frank. Kite flying is a lot like cockfighting—you can't get sentimental every time you lose a bird.

But to be chopped out of the sky by an official city chopper was an "accident" too obvious to ignore. Taken together with the fact that I had just quit my job, canceled my lease, and bought a ticket for Europe, it meant that my days in the park were finally over. I felt like telling the violinist, but he and his wife were already walking away.

1967

# dances of

# death

# In a Let-Burn
# Situation

W atching their pyre burn until the sky went black, one had to wish those still alive inside the important consolation of a TV set, bringing them live pictures of the fabulous send-off they were getting. The anchorman called it "the greatest domestic firefight in the history of mobile television news coverage," but if the six who were to die failed to hear those words, failed to see the doomsday look of the powers arrayed against them, their grand delusions must have quit them just as they were coming true. Unaware that the combined forces of the FBI, the Los Angeles Police and Sheriff's Departments, and the California Highway Patrol could find no way to subdue them short of paying them the homage of a coast-to-coast auto-da-fé, the Symbi-

---

*The Symbionese Liberation Army seized the attention of the national media in February 1974 when three of its members kidnapped Patricia Hearst, granddaughter of William Randolph Hearst, the famous tycoon. After a month in captivity, Hearst publicly denounced her ruling-class past, announcing that she had taken up her captors' cause and changed her name to Tania. On May 17, 1974, six SLA soldiers—about half the "army"—were surrounded by police in a small house in Los Angeles. All six died in the ensuing shoot-out and fire. Hearst was arrested by the FBI in September 1975.*

onese gunners likely died in some despair, believing themselves
defeated.

Six lesser deaths, or six less widely witnessed, would doubtless
have put a discouraging twist on the saga of the SLA, that reckless
band of overbelievers who went to such lengths to animate their
country's winter and spring. Still more dismal would have been cold
surrender, the disarmed dream taken handcuffed past the cameras,
wincing at the lights. But to die in a flaming house with a flaming
palm above you and something resembling the Americal Division
crouched in the street outside is not exactly what it means to be
defeated, not when it happens in plain sight of millions of viewers,
among whom an unhealthy number may be presumed to have been
inspired by the show. The police had come away the empty-handed
winners of a fight they could hardly have lost, while the six inside the
house had died the only death that could give full meaning to the
idea of being a "terrorist." And now that word, so long in finding an
American application, was a word that carried with it a dangerous
undertow.

Because gunfire from the windows of the yellow stucco house
had led the police to launch their assault on the familiar assumption
that anyone inside had to be Vietcong, the coroner's announcement
that Patricia Hearst was not among the dead had been greeted at
headquarters as a public-relations godsend. Unhampered by the need
to mourn the death by fire of a millionaire publisher's daughter, the
mayor could praise "Operation SLA" for its clean, professional character. Press conferences could feature the theme of law enforcement
dealing insurrection a mortal blow in the battle of 54th and Compton,
where decisive police action had reduced the famous Cinque from
terrorist leader to terrifying sight, the same hard fate that had consumed half his outragoeus army. The police could admit to a work-
manlike pride, as if the cinders that reposed in Dr. Noguchi's morgue
were just the kind of trophies they were after in their war with the

SLA. No regrets were expressed that none of these most-wanted persons would henceforth be available for questioning, clear though it may have been that a certain interest still attached to a number of questions only the dead could answer—how they had turned Patty into Tania, for example. In the flush of combat victory, such matters were waved aside.

What absorbed the authorities instead was the military merit of the May 17 campaign, a question of performance, not intent. With more than five hundred officers on hand to secure the perimeter and keep the ghetto crowds at bay, with helicopters lacing through smoke and gas to coordinate movement and direct fire, with ammo wagons and M16s and German-made MP40 submachine guns, the flak-jacketed Special Weapons and Tactics teams had conducted themselves as in an exercise at Quantico or Benning, pouring twelve hundred rounds into the target without bringing death or injury to anyone outside. Only twenty-three SWAT-schooled officers had actually engaged in the shooting—five of them FBI men, the rest from the LAPD—and only one of all the hundreds in camera range had been seen on TV displaying less than the desired level of deliberation and comportment, a shirtless volunteer in Bermuda shorts waving a large revolver. When he turned out to be an off-duty interloper from some department in the suburbs, unclouded satisfaction became the order of the day among officials at Parker Center, and their blameless critiques gave little cause to quarrel with what seemed to be the central claim: nobody caters a firefight quite like the LAPD.

But then the body count got bungled. Then documents, photographs, and keepsakes belonging to the dead were found in the rubble by scavengers after the crime lab had raked through it for days, employing an electromagnetic metal detector and other eye-catching devices. Children had to be warned not to play with live rounds found scattered around the neighborhood—they might be SLA bullets, spiked with cyanide. Thirty-five persons filed $150,000 in claims against the city for damage done to buildings and cars by bullets and fire. Tania and her accomplices slipped from sight after making a dozen appearances all over town in a succession of stolen vehicles, causing the police to lurch about in pathetically heavy numbers, as if five hundred to six were the tightest odds they'd go. The aura of clean professionalism began to dim. It began to appear instead that the police had been flaunting their mastery in battle as a mask for their sour luck in crime detection.

The first note of official displeasure with the ferocity of the assault came within a week, when a city councilman refused to join his colleagues in voting to honor the police with a special commendation. Sensing that they were about to be had as usual, the police reponded sharply in the press, pointing out that the property-damage claims could nearly all be traced to the sightless fusillade laid down by the unisex guerrillas. Moreover, the fire that took the target house had been purely accidental, touched off by exploding Speedy Heat Jumbo tear gas grenades or by bullets striking one of the Molotov cocktails the terrorists no doubt had inside; and since the fire hadn't discouraged the gunners at the windows until the whole house was ablaze, would any sane person have risked his life to douse it any sooner? The police vocabulary included a term for precisely this kind of showdown—"a let-burn situation." It was no more than a technical term, normally unfreighted with the vivid pictures of suffering it happened to call to mind now. But it was still a troublesome phrase to hear spoken, one that seemed to express a definite combat nostalgia.

Forced further back on the defensive by some unfavorable TV coverage (these terrorists had clergymen and doctors for fathers, and their anguish had been widely shared on the network news), the police maintained that they had attacked the house instead of laying peaceful siege to it only because the onset of darkness made them fear that the terrorists might escape, spreading gunplay through the neighborhood and endangering innocent lives. Since millions had observed the shoot-out in progress and come away with the impression that the house had been rather well surrounded, it was surprising that the police would resort to this argument from weakness, especially when a more sympathetic, less preposterous explanation had presented itself so clearly on TV: the humor of the crowds behind the barricades. As always, the police were in the ghetto on a limited visa. They could not bivouac there. A strange exhilaration in the streets around the shoot-out told judicious commanders that darkness would bring trouble in many forms. When the ACLU and several black community spokesmen charged that the attack would have never occurred had the terrorists holed up in Beverly Hills or Brentwood, the police would have done well to fall back on the All-Purpose Law Enforcement Answer—silence steeped in integrity. Instead they countered hotly with an eerie promise. If duty compelled it, they stood ready to waste the finest hootch in town.

Inasmuch as Donald David DeFreeze had been a whiner and a snitch before he became a general field marshal, and since he was also strongly rumored to have worked for a time as a paid informant for the intelligence division of the LAPD, it was probably inevitable that sinister inferences would also be drawn from the annihilating force of the attack, from the apparent desire to erase all traces of the gang instead of trying for at least one prisoner. Few radicals had ever been able to make much sense of the SLA, and the only ones who had were those who saw Cinque as a provocateur gone hog-wild. DeFreeze's walkaway escape from Soledad last spring was often cited as a proof of this hypothesis, as was the SLA's decision to introduce itself last November with the murder of Marcus Foster, Oakland's first black superintendent of schools and a liberal ally of the militant poor. At first considered no more than routinely paranoid, this view gained some respect as the 190-day "manhunt" dragged on for the wildly theatrical guerrillas. The police have Cinque in their sights, it was reasoned, but are waiting to strike until he is positioned for the kill. Two weeks before the shoot-out, stories of DeFreeze's possible involvement with the LAPD appeared in the press, alongside the chief's flat denial. But when the chief went on to denounce DeFreeze as "a cheap, undependable, turnover punk," he seemed to be admitting to exactly the kind of acquaintance the paranoid view described, and his denial of the rumors was seized upon at once by all who chose to believe them.

The police were once again disadvantaged when Dr. Noguchi announced that "psychological autopsies" had been ordered on the six in the hope of learning more about "compulsive" elements in their refusal to surrender; never in all his years of practice, the coroner said, had he seen evidence of such unyielding behavior in the face of flames as his study of these corpses revealed. Earlier, it had been possible to ascribe the guerrillas' failure to emerge from the flaming house to panic, confusion, incapacity, or death, to the simultaneous collapse of all alternatives. But when the coroner's reading of seared tissues taken from the terrorists' lungs disclosed a degree of commitment to the fight that surpassed his understanding, a new interpretation of the shoot-out seemed required, one that implied that the police had merely outdone themselves in obliging the terrorists' kamikaze intentions.

The fatal incaution of the SLA's May Day flight from its sanctuary in San Francisco to the mercury-vapor fields of fire it discovered in L.A. could almost be comprehended in this light. So could Tania's tendency to tattle, General Teko's absurd theft of a pair of 49-cent sweat socks while shopping for cold-weather gear in a sporting goods store, the whole gang's zany recourse to offering strangers hundreds of dollars to lodge for a night in places where the neighbors might stop by to marvel. It must be said that the sweat-socks factor is a universal among people on the lam—somebody always has to give the game away. But what directed the police to the free-fire zone on Compton Avenue was not the shoplifting fiasco (which led to Tania's baptism as an automatic rifleperson: spraying the front of the store to aid the shoplifter's escape). What attracted the police was a telephone call from the grandmother of some little children who were frightened to come home and find the Malcolm X Combat Unit camped out in their living room, engaged in the fondling of bandoliers and guns. Since this was a narcissistic folly indulged in by every member of the innermost cadre, it seems fair to assume that some aberrant group impulse had gotten the best of the terrorists' dedication to their fundamental rule: "Keep your ass down and be bad." Making themselves conspicuous, imploring trouble to hurry to their door, they were seeking a shortcut to the dream of a revolutionary D-Day, the day the street fighting finally begins. The police were being beckoned, one might say.

If all this was so, then Cinque's suicide represented no failure of nerve. Having provoked the authorities into arranging for his televised immolation, he must have been aware that death was offering him better terms than many general field marshals have to settle for. With his comrades dead or dying and a firestorm upstairs, he must have felt he had earned the right to slither down into the crawlspace, press the pistol to his temple, and depart this life on a swoon of highest Hitlerian rapture.

Thus the laws of paradox were invoked in many ways to confuse the moral content of this climactic encounter between the police and the SLA. The same pattern had obtained from the beginning, as though each side was impelled by larger forces to move in ways that could only work to serve the purposes of the other. The SLA, with its miserable pretensions, its rummy love of slogans and guns, had done no more for "the people" than to cause some food to be flung at them from trucks. The language of its communiqués, reeking of Vietnam and the cellblocks, conveyed a bitterness and confusion that estranged even persons usually disposed to searching for high motives in low acts. Such "counterrevolutionary" antics as winging passersby on the way out of bank jobs and issuing murder warrants against "fascist insects" who turned out to be old friends gone stale on the dream had made the SLA the pariahs of the Left, assailed by the

Movement's most radical voices. Because of the SLA, the police were enjoying a credibility that hadn't been theirs in years. It would be harder than ever to do time in the California prisons, more dangerous to call oneself a revolutionary. And for all the terrorists' talk of raising the fighting consciousness of the people, their one great accomplishment had been a kind of countermiracle—restoring to a flattering light long absent the image of the well-enough-meaning white American daddy.

The police, however, were equipped to perform even greater feats of transmutation. In the words of Randolph Hearst (who, as the principal target of the SLA's propaganda section, was now a beloved figure despite his father and his father before him), the police had used their vaunted firepower to turn "dingbats into martyrs." The police had the good taste not to respond to this familiar accusation; the men of the LAPD are so accustomed to holding their silence while eulogies are spoken over the graves of the "perpetrators" they kill that their badges might as well be inscribed *"De Mortuis Nil Nisi Bonum."* But death is a marvelous restorative in affairs of this kind, and a death like Cinque's could do more to improve a man's grasp on the reins of revolution than a long life spent hiding in rooms with *¡Venceremos!* written on the wall. Because of the shoot-out, and for no other reason, many would be driven to acts of emulation. Many would feel a need to express their "solidarity" with the fallen commandos of an idea not long ago despised. The shoot-out validated the SLA's otherwise empty claim to relevance. In effect, it came as the crowning move in a process of authentication that began last November with the killing of Dr. Foster and the first communiqué.

Although the school superintendent had the support of all who spoke for the interests of Oakland's vast ghetto, the police did not strongly resist believing the claim that his parking-lot murder was the work of Third World revolutionaries. "Death to the Facist Insect that Preys Upon the Life of the People!" said the SLA's "Warrant Order," employing a phrase of Eldridge Cleaver's. This was the kind of lingo

the police had primed themselves to pounce on back in the days
when many wore "Pigs Eat Panthers" buttons. They seemed keen to
hear it again, as though too finely trained to snap at the sound of it
to be put off by its incoherence in this instance. Neither the police
nor the media could immediately trace the SLA to any known quarter,
yet neither showed any reluctance to acknowledge its self-image as a
liberation army.

In December, when the House Internal Security Committee issued
a three-volume report on revolutionary scheming inside the prison
system, the SLA failed to get a line. But within a few days of the
kidnapping, the committee came out with a thirteen-page study of the
SLA that became a sourcebook for many of the lazier press accounts
that followed. The study gave Chairman Richard H. Ichord the opportunity of becoming the first man in Washington to grant the SLA the
quasi-legitimate status of an urban guerrilla army, one that would be
going for our hearts and minds, "obviously emulating the Robin Hood
tactics of the Argentinian terrorists."

Nearly everyone close to the case was convinced by this time that
when you talked about the SLA, you were talking about no more
than a dozen persons. But police intelligence and the HISC study had
already linked SLA members to the Venceremos Organization, the
Revolutionary Union, the United Prisoners' Union, the Vietnam Veterans Against the War/Winter Soldier Organization, and the Prison Law
Collective, as well as to such prison-based groups as the Polar Bear
Party, the Black Guerrilla Family, and the Black Liberation Army. Even
the SLA's seven-headed cobra was perceptively observed to have been
lifted from the cover of an old Jimi Hendrix record. With so many
subversive connections established in the minds of its chief pursuers,
the SLA's credentials appeared very much in order, and the obscure
Cinque was swiftly promoted into the ranks of such certified revolutionary nuisances as Bernadine Dohrn and the Weather Underground
(whom the police hadn't been able to catch, either).

                    *       *       *

The charade that led to the shoot-out could never have endured so long or captivated so many if the SLA's choice of kidnap victim had been any less inspired. It might be said in fairness that the theft of no one else's daughter would have persuaded the Hearst newspapers to go along with calling Cinque a general field marshal and not putting quotation marks around it. But since abridging the SLA's fierce etiquette was always seen as endangering Patty's chances, the press at large followed the careful tone set in San Francisco, seldom letting slip any word that Cinque might find insulting. Reporters assigned to the case were compelled to suppress numerous bits of information they dug up, not because the details would have been useful to the outlaws, but because they would have embarrassed the Hearsts or the SLA. When Hearst himself went to the state behavior-adjustment center at Vacaville to ask a lifer called Death Row Jeff to appeal to Cinque for the safe return of Patty, the *Examiner* identified him as one of the architects of the SLA philosophy and allowed his message to begin as if from political exile ("First of all, I want to extend my very personal greetings to all the poor and oppressed peoples of the world . . ."). Rarely in the history of confinement had the bars proved quite so resonant.

As long as Cinque had the world's ear anyway, the media might have done better to have pretended to a still-greater thirst for his teachings, causing the man to deplete himself in the struggle to find the words. Instead, Cinque could always lapse into provocative silence and count on a chorus of police officials, politicians, and rewrite men to do his nattering for him. One imagines the grandeur that must have enveloped the plum-wine drinker as he lolled around the safehouse waiting for the six-o'clock news. One imagines how Nancy Ling Perry must have surged with wonder to hear herself described as the enemy's "chief theoretician," a title last held by General Giap, now bestowed upon this child of Santa Rosa whose past seemed most intriguing when condensed to the phrase that usually followed—"former Goldwater supporter and topless blackjack dealer." One also imagines that Tania's exorcism of her Patty past could not have been accomplished in less light; for while guilt and sex might have done the job alone if cunningly mixed together, a true American brainwashing would need to see itself confirmed on television.

By the time the SLA made the covers of *Time* and *Newsweek*, it was clear that the minuscule army had touched upon the sorest of American vulnerabilities, the temptation to see in new calamities the appearance of new entertainments. But the notion that the media somehow overplayed the story or romanticized the guerrillas could not be more mistaken. The sense of abiding menace that gave the story its sting derived not only from the perils of Patty but also from the many false alarms set off by the authorities, ever ready as they are to announce that the enemy has landed. Since the SLA's "actions" were all specifically criminal, there was never a sound police reason for the gang to be approached as a terrorist organization. Cinque & Co. were wanted for prison escape, murder, kidnapping, bank robbery, arson, auto theft, the illegal possession of weapons, and forty-seven kinds of conspiracy, more or less; it ought not to have mattered that much that they fancied themselves an army. But it did matter. It gave the police occasion to imagine themselves engaged in a higher, more historic struggle than their normal war against the rats. It turned the law-enforcement mind to new hardware, new specialties, to techniques often practiced but seldom put to use. It induced politicians of the most remote and extraneous variety to jump aboard the case, some scolding the police for their "timidity," all of them enlarging the fear of these home-grown *fedayeen*. Finally the police took to explaining themselves too loudly and too much, letting their frustation show, losing that implacable look so important to their work; and all of this was tinder for a let-burn situation.

Speculations as to the moral tone of the chord that is struck in the American people by excitements of this kind have a way of draining meaning from the language. This was a psywar face-off occurring deep in the national consciousness, a father–daughter dialogue much abetted by money and guns. Nowhere on this earth dwells a people too high-minded to respond to its allure. The six-month rise and fall of the SLA followed the typical course of all such "reigns of terror," and the silence that follows the shoot-out crescendo is classically uninformative. It may be true that the country's infatuation with violence, or its guilt over war crimes, or its decline into self-doubt, had something to do with the spell the guerrillas cast here. But to say these things is not to name the nerve so deliciously twanged by the worst of the nightly news.

The psychoanalytic approach, always subject to the fallacy of inferring general madness from the madness of a few, is further complicated when so many of the patients have been killed. The fact that the gang's members were a conspicuous juxtaposition of bad-assed blacks and young white lesbians has led to the surmise that its appeal was essentially sadomasochistic, and a number of commonly observed reactions to the news seem to correspond to this idea. The unwholesome amusement in Patty's metamorphosis. The sharp, unexplained impatience with anyone caught vaguely in the middle (Patty's boyfriend, for example, the aptly named Weed). The absurd ring of any voice not speaking the dialect of maximum involvement (as when Patty's younger sister urged her to surrender for the good of her cause "if you really feel the SLA is your thing"). But the S/M interpretation of the SLA will have to await the witness of Tania—if she can be taken alive; then, perhaps, it will be discovered that her venom in renouncing her past only betrayed the desperation of her wish to foreclose upon the future, that what her tapes were really saying was "Spank me if you can."

Yet one resists these terms, turning instead to the untilled middle, to the forlorn sound of the father's voice as he tries once more to be reasonable. Poor Hearst! What a service he could do if only a flash of divine exasperation would sear his wounds and drive him out to confront the twenty-headed microphone cobra one last time; and there in the clear air of Hillsborough, calm eyes raised to a camera's stare, to speak in measured tones the words his brooding country needs to hear—"Tania, go fuck yourself." Deaf Ears to the Fatuous Ingrate that Preys Upon the Hearts of Her People!

The interests of Los Angeles County have required that portions of Cinque's brain, skull, heart, and liver, as well as his fingertips and teeth, remain with Dr. Noguchi. But apart from these deletions, the man is dead and buried, gone for good. Refusals to mourn have been heard from every quarter. Even Tania's taped elegy, found in an alley two weeks after the shoot-out, fails to capture any hint of the charm he must have held for her, this one-time robber of prostitutes who taught her that "to live was to shoot straight"—a disheartening lesson, it would seem.

But there was one thing about Cinque that makes it certain he will not be soon forgotten: he was the infinitely replaceable man. Cinque was possessed of the most widely shared delusion in prison life today, the belief that by the authority of their suffering alone, convicts make natural revolutionaries. The radical Left, ignoring Marx and Lenin in favor of Jackson and Cleaver, has done much to encourage this belief in recent years, and although Cinque was dismissed as an embarrassment while alive and at large, in death he becomes yet another black martyr whose story will be told to further this cruel flirtation. Men who survive long confinement with strength enough left to be angry almost always lack the ability to estimate the meaning of a fight outside the walls. They have lived with such diminished chances that few risks seem too great to them. They think everyone wants to pick up a gun. They think everyone wants to die as bad as they do. A life and death like Cinque's can be made to seem a triumph over destiny, and there is no doubt that his example will be followed many times. The authorities are aware of these "politicized" prisoners, and most agree that the convict-led, eight-to-twelve-person revolutionary combat team is the "grave new threat" that will haunt the streets for many years to come.

It took a month, but the city council finally got around to commending the LAPD for its courage and efficiency in "freeing this city and the nation of an unconscionable reign of terror imposed by wanton, misguided revolutionaries." This helped preserve the illusion of victory, and unless one counted the bombing of the state attorney general's Los Angeles offices claimed by the Weather Underground, the streets were indeed free of terrorists. The police gave no credence at all to General Teko's suggestion in a taped communiqué that "B Team Leader" of the Symbionese antiaircraft brigade deserved credit for downing a police helicopter with a Russian-made missile seven days after the shoot-out. It was true that a chopper had crashed northwest of the city on that day, killing the commander of the SWAT team and injuring two of its members. But there was no reason to believe that the crash had not been accidental. The pilot, it appeared, had simply flown too close to the ground while the officers were practicing a skill to be held in readiness for future let-burn type encounters. They were learning to hit ground targets from a moving gun platform.

1974

# In Hollywood, the Dead
# Keep Right on Dying

" **Y**ou wouldn't believe how weird these people were," the detective said, not for the first time. We were talking about the most dreadful murder in Los Angeles memory, but the detective's fascination for the lives the victims had led kept intruding on his interest in the case. Our lunch grew cold as we talked, staring out the windows of the police cafeteria.

The murder was still etched across every conversation three months after the event, with the killers still at large to make nightmares for the city. Yet the police seemed to take a strangely philosophic tone, as though the feeling that the victims were not like the people next door had put a few nicks in their keen edge of indignation. The detective, in fact, could almost find a parable for law and order in the

---

*Sharon Tate, Jay Sebring, Abigail Folger, Voityck Frokowski, Steven Parent, and Leno and Rosemary LaBianca were murdered the mornings of August 9 and 10, 1969. Charles Manson and four of his followers—Leslie Van Houton, Susan Atkins, Patricia Krenwinkel, and Charles "Tex" Watson—were convicted of the murders in 1971. All five were sentenced to life in prison.*

killings: "If you live like that, what do you expect?" Sharon Tate, Jay Sebring, Abigail Folger, Voityck Frokowski—these were not *people,* these were *weird people.*

They were weird because they used drugs and "messed around with sex," weird in all the fashionable ways, weird as in the new movies. Their circle may have been friendly enough to protect them in their lifetimes, but now, in their posthumous notoriety, rumor had revealed them to all as connoisseurs of depravity, figures torn from a life that was pure de Sade, with videotape machines in the bedrooms.

In respect for the dead, and for Roman Polanski, Sharon's husband, it should be said that the truth is disappointing—that their wild dope parties usually ran to endless evenings spent boring each other into such a reach of mindlessness that it would finally seem a brilliant idea to watch the test pattern on color TV. By the standards of modern Hollywood, they were only a step or two faster than the horde, predictably loose, predictably stoned, too afflicted with money and success to be dedicated degenerates, let alone retrospective heroes in the suicidal-romantic tradition.

But the truth in such affairs is only so many entries in a detective's notebook. What counts is the folklore, the expanded, popular version that everyone believes. The victims could have been any kind of moral vagabonds, but in fractured, menaced Hollywood, people can think of any number of good reasons for killing whatever they were.

Everyone sees the murders in his own light. Every story casts an interchangeable demon into the same blank scenario. Speed freaks or fags or Mafia contract men or black terrorists or witchcraft nuts or vigilante rednecks enter the house, do the job, slip away. The same abject details are cited again and again, always proving something different, until one collects an impression of the victims murdered again and again by relays of fresh marauders.

The most persistent theory describes the crime as an act of revenge for a sexual humiliation, a homosexual misunderstanding driven to the extreme erotic conclusion. Since all rumors have the same validity as projections of one's own fears or hates, there is no good reason to believe this account over any other. Yet something about it appeals to the popular imagination, and it still holds sway, even now that the coroner has revealed that the bodies showed no signs of torture or sexual mutilation, as was widely reported at first.

The rumors read like a graph of community paranoia. Every story promotes the murders into assassinations, crimes of logical consequence in which some vision of the victims' way of living makes them accomplices in their own deaths. It is as if no one is satisfied with the crime until it can be perceived as a political act—the murder of a lifestyle.

One soon learns to recognize an entire social attitude from speculations on the murders. Those with positive knowledge that the blacks did it are those who feel most threatened by the blacks. Those who identify most closely with the victims' way of life tend to see the hand of fascist America, snuffing out its young. Each new rumor works within its own vortex of fear, swirling around in uncollected fragments until it finally winds up proving, one way or another, that the jig is up for us all.

The sense of the apocalypse has always flourished in Hollywood, but these killings and their reverberations have made it more palpable than ever. So many anxieties have emerged from so many different directions that one feels the chill of alien cliques shutting in upon themselves. Nightfall on that random, smoking landscape can bring on a vivid impression of guarded bonfires burning against the hostile dark. The price of an attack dog has reached $1,500; in the chitchat columns, celebrities brag about their bodyguards.

Absorbing all this talk stills the visitor's emotions, creating an all-horrors composure that leaves him standing there politely with a drink in his hand, talking to bodies blessed with the gift of speech, while death rattles and agonies float through the ears unwinged.

The police are still on the case, of course. Their task force of nineteen detectives is the biggest one assembled since Bobby Kennedy was shot. Occasionally, there will be some new word from headquarters, such as the recent announcement that a careful analysis of a pair of eyeglasses found at the scene suggests that one of the killers had a volleyball-shaped head. But the folklore has so outstripped the few little items the police have been able to add that one is left only to hope that the story will somehow find a merciful conclusion on its own.

That frail hope perhaps explains why I couldn't help but detect monstrous notes of reassurance here and there—as one night at the Factory, last year's discothèque, when I saw that the face hanging in the smoke across the table was moving its lips my way. I cupped my hand against the music and leaned close to hear. "Let's hope Roman has enough sense to sell the rights to somebody good," the face was shouting. I searched the face for some sign that it was joking. But no. The face was serious, sincere.

1969

# California Inquest

As I examined the document under high-intensity light through the lens of my Agfa 8× magnifier, I began to form certain doubts that its author was Charles Manson. The two-page letter had been discovered in a large cache of mail sent to the Los Angeles County Jail in the spring of 1969—four months before the murders that made Manson famous—and although I had long heard rumors of its existence, it was not until a few weeks ago that a copy came into my hands, the gift of a friend who confessed he feared the worst of it.

Looked upon as a handwriting specimen, the letter could not have been more enticing. Between salutation and pseudonymous signature were 101 words employing all the letters of the alphabet except $q$, $x$, and $z$; in the date and the ZIP code on the envelope, the numbers 2, 3, 6, 8, and 9 appeared. Since I happened to be in possession of a number of Manson documents whose authenticity I had no reason to question, I was able to spend several hours at my desk, absorbed in the fascinations of graphology.

The basic flow of the writing looked much the same in each of the scrawled pages before me. An eccentric use of capital letters, an irregular spacing of words and lines, and the diminished size of the capital *I* (thought to betray a menaced ego) were only a few beguiling points of similarity. The stroke and design of the letters *h* and *r*, however, seemed much too far from the Manson hand to be explained by his possible use of drugs or drink or by other factors that might have altered his script on that "beautiful day" in Beaumont referred to in the letter. Nor was there any accounting for the middle initial *A* in the return address: C.A.M., General Delivery, Beaumont, Calif. 92223. I was aware that Manson was a man of many identities who, even now, in the sanctuary of his gang-locked cell at Folsom, was calling himself "Sunstone" and signing his letters with a mystic seal. But nowhere on my copy of his five-page rap sheet was there any indication that he had ever used a middle name other than Miller, Milles, Mills, Millis, William, or Willis at any point in his eighteen-year criminal career.

The letter was postmarked April 28 P.M. While my chronology of Manson's movements around that time was by no means exhaustive, I knew it to have been a period during which he made several fast runs between his outpost in the Goler Wash region of Death Valley and his base camp at the Spahn Movie Ranch, a few miles outside L.A. Given Manson's weakness for taking back roads and assassins' routes on his flights across the desert, he could easily have shown up in Beaumont, a roadside town of six thousand in the ridge lands west of Palm Springs. Still, it seemed most unlikely that he would have stopped there long or often enough to bother with the ZIP code.

Yet if by the remotest chance the letter were to prove genuine, its disturbing implications would demand to be explored. And I could not deny that there was something about its benevolent tone that carried a distinct "family" flavor. This is what the letter said:

*Dear Sirhan:—*

*Just these few lines this Morning. Its a beautiful day up here in Beaumont. Do you know that many of us wish that you were free*

*to enjoy it. But who knows perhaps that day is not too far off. Things*
*that are worth striving for is worth haveing. Now here is a sample*
*of a written letter as addressed to one of that Jury. It is the very*
*substance as to that given verdict to you by many. So will close for*
*to-day. From your Sincere friend*

*—Beaumont*

*P.S. Be sure Sirhan to look for that Rain bow in the Sky.*

The attempt to find politicial links or spiritual affinities between
Manson, Sirhan, Juan Corona, the Zodiac Killer, and the rest of the
ranking heavyweights of homicide who animate, as well as extinguish,
life in California was an obsession of mine, one I thought had been
cured by years of persistent failure. But California was still a place
where the ancient quest for the origins of Evil could be undertaken
with an almost medieval intensity, so strong was the temptation to
believe that a single hidden answer would explain the state's peculiar
ability to provide the setting for the country's most enthralling murders.
The police, who alone were disposed to deal strictly in the random
facts of violence, would joke about the Curse of the Donner Party
and go on about their work. But long after they had closed and filed
their casebooks, the unifying monster called California Evil was still
being sought by a posse of writers, psychiatrists, private detectives, and
anti-occult divines, along with a variety of slandered Satanists eager to
clear their names. I had ridden long and hard with this bunch and
looked back upon the experience through a haze of remembered
hysteria. Yet now, holding the letter in my hands, I became aware of
how thirsty I was for the bogus thrill that enslaves so many investigators, the feeling that you and you alone are on to something.

The letter's strange allusion to jury tampering and the reference
to the guilty verdict that had been handed down to Sirhan eleven
days earlier were not at all uncharacteristic of Manson's way with the
language. Nor did the writer's failure to grasp the seriousness of Sirhan's situation differ in the slightest nuance from the family's glad

manner two years later when their own murder trials were drawing to a close. Nothing could ever make them take their eye off the Rain bow. These insubstantial parallels in literacy and style would mean very little to the police, but they were certain to intrigue the posse. It was only a matter of time before other copies of the Beaumont letter would reach this watchful crew, and many among them, overcome by a morbid wishfulness or by dread of the absurd, would see it as a documentation of devils marching arm in arm.

A number of "investigations" had already found their way into print, and, with credulity running high in the population, the most outlandish among them tended to be most widely believed. The most recent had "positively tied" Manson to Naval Intelligence—Oswald's old outfit!—and arrived at a "matrix" of matching admissions and curious facts that showed how all major recent Western murders were part of a scenario planned and executed by a secret organization of military intelligence and right-wing police. The Corona operation two years ago, in which twenty-four itinerant farmworkers were slashed to death and buried in a peach orchard, was just the government's way of talking to Cesar Chavez. And, for the first time, the Tate-LaBianca murders could be said to make some kind of sense: Manson was a government fall guy, set up to discredit hippie lifestyles and LSD.

The daily press never took any interest in conspiracy theories or other political explanations of the horrors it reported, but the best and biggest papers in the state were colossal suckers for any invocation of Satan's name that was uttered by someone in handcuffs. Police and prosecutors, who saw an insanity defense in the making whenever persons charged with murder spoke of infernal commands, were always incensed to see such headlines as

ORANGE COUNTY DEVIL KILLER ADMITS "SACRIFICES"

when, they felt, something more on the order of

TWERP WHO KILLED TWO SAYS DEVIL MADE HIM DO IT

would have been more reasonable and accurate. But the allure of anything witchy, when trumped with a bloody death, made the willing suspension of disbelief almost automatic at the soberest city desks. At times, the press appeared to be a claque for all the state's worst actors. At other times, its cynical zeal led to acts which were themselves little murders—as when the Manson women were conned out of the curli-cued letters and diaries that held the last threads of their illusions.

Repelled as I was by these unhealthy proceedings, I could not deny having taken a certain hand in them. And although I had retired from the hunt convinced that there was no way to clarify the carnage, I did not feel ill disposed toward those who remained in the field. The quest for coherent Evil, no matter how lurid or paranoid, is a drive fueled by religious yearning and should therefore enjoy immunity from ridicule, if not from exasperation. But I confess that I did feel some impatience with the Evil-obsessed sleuths I had come to think of as the Gothic posse, and it was forcing me to consider my obliga-tions to my own grim ideas, which a highly suspicious string of pleasant events in my private life had allowed me to forget. After a day's hesitation, I did the only right thing. Picking up the telephone, I dialed Sheriff's Robbery & Homicide.

Sheriff's Robbery & Homicide was my favorite haunt when I moved to Los Angeles three years ago. It was not so much the dank and sinister premises in the old Hall of Justice that attracted me (al-though I did like the dank and sinister premises). What kept me going back there on increasingly trivial errands was the chance to listen to the talk of the best detectives and bask in its wonderful calm. The calm of these detectives went deeper than the calm that obtains when nothing surprises anymore. Everything surprised these detectives, but always to the same mild degree. Insanity, depravity, absurdity, dis-grace—they were glad to listen to any raving, so long as it had to do with an unsolved homicide in the unincorporated portions of the county. For this reason, they were much preferred by the posse to their colleagues down the hill at Parker Center, the *Dragnet*-depicted detectives of the LAPD. At the LAPD, a military rectitude tended to inhibit conversation between officer of the law and psychoneurotic volunteer crime analyst; Sheriff's Robbery & Homicide, on the other hand, was a marketplace where fantasies and delusions and arcane readings in the lore of the occult could sometimes be swapped for suspect names and addresses.

Since the Manson trial was nearly half over by the time I arrived to cover it, I was at some disadvantage when it came to the search for that larger moral pathology of which the inscrutable defendants were thought to be only the most obvious carriers. I was hundreds of hours away from acquiring even the minimal proficiency in local crime mores that is available only in newspaper morgues. I had the whole Black Dahlia tradition to absorb. After the day in court, I would make it my business to attend happy hour at Li Po's, the Chinatown bar favored by Sheriff's Robbery & Homicide. Then I would set out on my motorized rounds, and if midnight didn't find me touring the city with maps in lap, searching out murder sites and murderers' old milieus, it was only because I had chosen to pass the evening in the green basement quarters of a young assistant coroner who had taken me under his wing. It wasn't long before I was acknowledged by all as a working member of the posse, and when a homicide detective would toot his horn and wave as our cars passed in some uncertain district, I would feel braced for all forthcoming horrors, a definite beneficiary of the buddy system.

But much as I was concerned about my lack of a master plan in case persistence or luck should direct me to the monster, there was no use pretending that my calm accomplices in their blatantly inconspicuous county cars knew much more than I did about what it was we were after. All that was agreed upon was that the state was experiencing an unnaturally high number of savage murders, murders no one quite understood, and the likes of which few had seen before. Poor shards of bodies would wash up on beaches around Los Angeles and Santa Barbara, or be discovered by hikers in the Santa Cruz Mountains, or be found stuffed in car trunks or bureau drawers or castaway suitcases. Some bodies bore more than two hundred fifty stab wounds, and while there was seldom any sign of robbery or sexual attack, there were decapitations, dismemberments, eviscerations, and, occasionally, instances of cannibalism. In a single year, medical examiners around the state noted at least two dozen murders in which there had been an exceedingly rare concentration of knife wounds in the throat and upper chest—rare because a single puncture of the trachea or the carotid artery produces a result that will almost always cause a killer to bolt.

The police spoke of these murders as "overkills" and could be counted on to shake their heads or whistle through their teeth when describing them: a guy's got to be nuts to do something like this, they would say. But because the police were concerned with specific cases inside their own jurisdictions, they were not quick to perceive how many killers in nearby places were going nuts in remarkably similar ways. When the hunt for the Tate-LaBianca killers led state authorities to draw up a list of recent unsolved murders in which bondage, mutilation, or excessive stabbing had occurred, there was general amazement that there had been thirty such crimes in just two years. Only then did police around the state begin wondering if something might not be in the air, and when they did, many started calling these killings "LSD murders."

It was true that many young killers were projecting acid-casualty images, sometimes discernible under psychiatric examination, but more often apparent only in their clothes and haircuts, in the way they flashed peace signs at photographers and rambled on about astrology in their murder confessions. The police were inclined by their hatred of drugs to take psychedelic confabulations somewhat too literally, or so it seemed from the matter-of-fact tone they adopted when discussing the visions reported to them by killers they had caught.

Few psychiatrists could be found who claimed to have observed predictable effects arising from the use of LSD, and even when defense attorneys had the wit to elicit the best clinical testimony, it always seemed to have a tentative, inchoate quality completely dwarfed by the ghastly facts at hand. The normal psychiatric practice was to look first for organic brain disorders in killers charged with acts of "inappropriate" brutality; failing to find demonstrable morbidity, or evidence of a psychosis deep enough to permit fugues of unrestrained violence, the psychiatrist in the courtroom was left to rely on hypothetical estimates as to how much of which drug would have to be ingested in order to achieve the cascading loss of impulse control such an act required. It was never a good show, and the juries didn't like it.

The posse didn't like it either, conceivably because not a few of its members dropped the odd tab themselves from time to time, but also because the LSD analysis failed to come to grips with the localization of these crimes in California and the West. Or did it? Could it have been that some miserable lab in Long Beach was cooking up just enough murder acid to circulate at home? The police did not ignore this possiblity and could often be induced to tell of green-speckled sunshine pills, little blue-and-black mini-bennies, caps of fake mescaline that looked like brown sugar, and other underground pharmaceuticals that kept turning up in all the worst pockets. But there was never anything conclusive in these findings, and a good many detectives shared the posse's belief that there had to be some further explanation, something culturally over the heads of the police and remote from the psychiatric imagination, something that pertained most acutely to life as it is lived at the Western extreme. For most of the posse, and even for a few detectives, this line of reasoning led directly to the cults.

The routine discovery around the state of beheaded goats, skinned dogs, and other magic animal remains lent an undeniable credence to the idea that there were Satanists about whose services did not stop short of bloodletting. And if these same groups were bent on attaining the highest magic powers that come only with the ultimate offering, then the "overkills" could be "ritual murders" in which the element of excessive stabbing resulted from many hands taking their turn at "unleashing the fiend." Rumors abounded of screams heard near beach fires where charred human bones were found the next morning, of Wednesday-night ceremonies in a Brentwood home where corpses were provided by the wealthy host. The fact that no band of necrophiles or occultists had ever been caught *in flagrante delicto* did nothing to discourage the posse. On the contrary, it only went to show how clever the Satanists could be.

But apart from Sirhan's Rosicrucianism and the eclectic Manson's borrowings from Scientology and the London-based Process Church of the Final Judgment, the state's leading killers were not known for their affiliations. Death row had housed members of the Satan Slaves, the Straight Satans, the Jokers Out of Hell, and the San Jose chapter of the Gypsy Jokers, but these were bike gangs whose manly ethics forbade any truck with the kind of pale-lipped Luciferians who would murder a dog or goat. Even killers who had claimed devil worship as their trial defense were unable to show past involvements with any traceable group, and the two "devil killers" I was able to speak with at San Quentin and Atascadero State Hospital both fared less than well when subjected to an occult IQ test I had devised. What is the name of the magical language used in Satanic rituals? Who represents the powers of darkness? What are some of the infernal names? They did not know.

Since so many "overkills" were unsolved, however, the fact that no one in custody for similar crimes seemed to be a certifiable Satanist did not mean all that much. There were just enough claims and confessions and uncanny little facts to keep interest alive, and it took me almost a year to tire of talking to persons who wished to be addressed as "Caliph" or "Exemplar," stubborn as I was in the belief that if I steeped my brain long enough in their lingo I might eventually recognize secret dialects in the conversation of killers, captured and at large.

It was not always easy to explain to my editors why the long-simmering California murder story required another trip to Boston for further consultations with the adepts of the inner plane, nor to explain to myself what I was doing spending so much time with people I couldn't stand. One couldn't help but pick up a lot of new information in the course of talking to occultists, but most of it had a way of lying dead in the mind the moment it was learned.

The third major theory to preoccupy police, press, and posse was the notion that the impulse to murder without motive was governed by the landscape. Murder maps were compiled that seemed to indicate that zones of special danger existed in the state, but even with these maps, observations on the geography of homicide often took the form of bromides on the importance of seclusion. That deserts, canyons, and ocean afforded matchless impromptu graveyard facilities was clearly not to be argued; but whether or not the absence of a close horizon, the Santa Ana winds, certain phases of the Western moon, or the uncertainty of life along the San Andreas Fault might account for many "overkills" was never much more than a guess. Those who did believe that some antimagnetic effect of topography or climate was deranging to the murder-prone had no trouble at all locating ground zero. Ground zero was at Santa Cruz, sixty miles south of San Francisco.

Once they were solved, the Santa Cruz murders did a great deal to demythify Manson. While they were in progress, however, the killings caused a dense fog of dread to descend upon the pretty town and the wooded hills around it. Between the fall of 1970 and March of 1973, twenty-six persons died there in "overkill" murders, some as horrible as any reported before. An almost equal number were killed in similar fashion in the neighboring counties. Two teenage girls on a picnic, stabbed three hundred times. A priest slashed to death in his confessional. Hands and legs found by the roadside. A doctor, his wife, two sons, and secretary, bound, gagged, executed by pistol shot, floating facedown in the swimming pool alongside their burning house.

But as the killers were caught and photographed and interviewed and brought to trial and sent to prison and asked if they felt like writing books, a kind of normalcy born of nausea returned to town and county, allowing the murder rate to settle back to the basic seven to ten a year. Many felt that the Santa Cruz killers would have achieved greater fame if the public hadn't been so weary of Manson at the time they came to trial, and it was true that they were not entirely an unprepossessing lot, as murderers go. John Linley Frazier, who killed the doctor and his family, was an ecology guerrilla who left behind a murder note saying "Today World War III will begin as brought to you by the free universe," signed with the names of tarot cards. Herbert Mullin, who killed thirteen people, including the priest, said he was trying to save California from an earthquake by making sacrifices to "the voices." Edmund E. Kemper III, a six-foot nine-inch 280-pound giant, feared the police were closing in on him for the six murders he had committed since his release from the state hospital, where he'd been held since the age of fifteen for the murder of his grandparents; finally, turning to his mother, he had chosen to "bear the burden of killing her as well, to avoid her suffering any embarrassment."

Contemplating the depths of these delusions was an experience of such intense bewilderment that it would finally be impossible not to embrace whatever barren landfall was suggested by the few facts at hand. So it would begin to seem important that Mullin and Frazier (both users of psychedelic drugs who also dabbled in the occult) had probably drifted into Santa Cruz and stayed there because of its physical setting. There were little dairy sheds all over the county, abandoned years ago when the pastures were taken, and there were also many dilapidated auto courts built in the thirties and forties, run-down old resorts left over from the time when Santa Cruz was famous only for its boardwalk. Frazier had lived in a shed for $5 a month. Mullin was paying $24 for a one-room place by the beach. No one could deny it: here was a common denominator.

Talking to the killers themselves was always more rewarding than seeking to understand them through the records of their lives and crimes and trials. But this was only because talking to them served to diffuse any impression one might have had that they belonged to a single caste. If they shared anything beyond the bars of their pathetic dwelling places, it was only a kind of passivity, a tone of voice, a tendency to speak of their crimes as acts of capitulation. Many were practiced in the popular shell games of self-analysis and could be maddeningly philosophical about the act of murder, particularly after Manson started the tautology craze that swept the cellblocks during his trial. The karma's coming down, man. Your thought is your karma. And if death is your thought, man, death is gonna be your karma. It sometimes would occur to me that one obvious thing these celebrated killers had in common was the spellbound attention of many persons like myself, and when I saw a couple of familiar faces in the flush light of a TV special devoted to the murdering mind, I realized that I had come to think of murderers as cruel and frail young men who had succumbed to the most abject of American desires, the wish to be introduced on television as Truman Capote's friend.

The idea that some coffin-oriented aspect of the culture was imploring the weak to murder returned my thoughts to the Beaumont letter. For if the morbid obsessions of the death-dealing society had made the heavyweight championship of homicide indeed a prize to be won and worn, what better way for Manson to touch gloves with the reigning Sirhan than with this jive fan letter? I could picture him skidding up to that cinderblock post office in Beaumont, then loping back out to the girls in the dune buggy with no less a trophy than Sirhan's friendly reply. I had this tableau in mind when (having finally gotten through to Sheriff's Robbery & Homicide) Sgt. Paul Whiteley came on the line. Whiteley and his partner, Charles Guenther, had been the first detectives in town to start thinking about Manson for the Tate-LaBianca killings, and both were respected mentors at Li Po's, the calmest of the calm. I may have been a little guarded about stating my hunch that the Beaumont letter was genuine, but Whiteley spared me the need to explain myself and told me to send it right down.

The police always took their time performing any task that required expert analysis, so I knew that for a week, or even longer, I could consider myself on quasi-official standby to Sheriff's Robbery & Homicide. I had a strong urge to make the most of it immediately, to put on a suit and go downtown and drink with the detectives. But the thought of walking into Li Po's almost two years rusty was all it took to restrain me. The detectives I knew did not exactly converse; they trafficked in conversation, and unless you had something for openers, something you'd read in an autopsy report or been told by someone in jail, you couldn't even ante. So before putting the Beaumont letter back into the mail and thereby rejoining the posse, I called around and made a few appointments.

It had been a while—a month or more—since the papers had carried any news of dismemberments or multiple stabbings, and thinking that the pace might have slackened, I visited the state's leading authority on such matters, the Los Angeles County coroner, Dr. Thomas Noguchi. Dr. Noguchi was known to shoulder his responsibilities with an enthusiasm some people found unnerving, especially upon hearing him testify in court, where his painstaking reports were delivered in a thick Japanese accent whose macabre associations caused even judges to smile. He was, it was said, a specialist in the unspeakable. Handless and decapitated homicide victims who arrived at his door tagged Jane or John Doe held a special attraction for him, calling upon the most refined techniques his office had developed for making identifications. Once, he had succeeded in giving a name and address, and thus a fate-sealing death certificate, to a left clavicle found in some pulverized remains in a canyon north of the city.

On the day I saw Dr. Noguchi, he was distracted by the presence in his office of some officials from Hawaii who had just flown in with a decomposed body they wanted him to see. I was distracted by the presence of a twenty-four-inch closed-circuit television monitor that flashed an endless chain of two-second snapshots of corridors and loading bays deep in the morgue. Even so, he did manage to say, and I to comprehend, that the trend toward gratuitous violence in the act of murder was still plainly visible in the cadavers coming through; that the mutilation of bodies was now "quite common," though perhaps more vividly sexual than in Manson's day; and that torture-murders (as opposed to postmortem desecrations) appeared to be subtly on the increase. The trend-setting nature of these murders continued to puzzle him, Dr. Noguchi said, but there was no question that homicide styles were born in California, then repeated across the nation.

A few days later, I penetrated the elaborate screening apparatus at the LAPD and made my way up to the big and noisy offices of Robbery & Homicide, where the mention of Noguchi's name brought a current case to the mind of Lt. Robert Helder, the chief of the detail. It appeared that a gang of hard-leather sadists was presently at large in the city, a gang that had left the scattered remains of at least six young homosexuals on local beaches and parkways in the space of the past twelve months. These murders had been marked with an especially grotesque turn or two, such as hiding a severed head in a place where some poor devil was sure to come upon it jack-in-the-box style.

But Lt. Helder was as calm a detective as any in town, and he cautioned me against reading any cultural imperatives into these crimes. They were novelties, rough-trade pranks completely outside normal homicide patterns. No, your classic L.A. murder was still bang-bang across the living room, with the ricochets busting the bottle of muscatel. "Almost eighty percent of our cases are what we call the mom-and-pop type of homicide, basic self-solvers on the surface," Lt. Helder said. "Unless you count the Tate-LaBianca, which was seven in two days, L.A. has never had a mass murder."

The bleak facts of homicide could never be made to square with its vicarious appeal, nor could the country's unblinking attention to it be explained by the cold actuarial fact that homicide ranks almost even with congenital anomalies as a cause of death. It could also be said that Detroit, Dallas, and Washington, D.C., had murder rates almost twice that of San Francisco or Los Angeles, and that right through the worst of the Manson era, California's murder rate was never more than half that of South Carolina. The police took great solace in these figures, as though the burden upon them was lightened by the statistical relentlessness of life and death.

But homicide prevention was not the business of the police; catching killers was, and no numerical breakdown could disguise the fact that their luck wasn't improving. Self-solvers were one thing, but when it came to the kind of random, brutal murders that terrorized and titillated, they trusted more than they knew to the killers' compulsion to confess. Of the thirty murders on the list that started everyone talking about "overkills" in 1969, twenty-six were still unsolved more than four years later.

During my wait for Whiteley's call, the Zodiac Killer broke a silence of thirty-four months with a new letter to the *San Francisco Chronicle*, this time claiming credit for thirty-seven deaths. The police had conceded him no more than seven in the course of their eight-year manhunt, but in one of his last communiqués before dropping out of touch three years ago, he had announced his intention to adopt a new style of killing even harder to detect: "I've grown rather angry with the police that are telling lies about me. So I shall change my way of collecting slaves. I shall no longer announce to anybody when I commit my murders. They shall look like routine robberies, killings of anger, and a few fake accidents."

The Zodiac had established his bona fides with the police by mailing in such relics as a bloody scrap torn from a victim's shirt, so they did not take his letters lightly. The search for him had continued throughout the long silence, aided only slightly by the use of computers to crack his double codes and by the publication of a uniform "Zodiac Manual" for the use of police in all the Western states. If they were alert, the police paid special attention to all suspicious persons who fit the Zodiac's general description: male Caucasian, thirty-five to forty-five, five-ten, one hundred ninety pounds, crewcut reddish brown hair, plastic-frame eyeglasses, paunchy stomach. If such a person said anything funny, the police would make sure he wasn't wearing size-11½ shoes. And if he was, the search would begin immediately for his Marine combat boots, his 9-mm Browning, his machete. None of this had worked.

It did not escape my attention that the Zodiac had written his new letter on a day when every newspaper in the state had banner headlines telling of the point-blank sidewalk executions of five people on a single night in San Francisco. Nor that the next night, with the Zodiac back in the headlines, three were slashed to death in an Oakland mortuary. The streakiness of murder was the one thing about it that expressed its emptiness of meaning, and a dozen apparent coincidences immediately came to mind. Corona's vast graves were discovered just as the Manson trial was coming to its end. Frazier had appeared within days of the Zodiac's farewell. Kemper started his string of killings as soon as Frazier was sentenced to death, only to be knocked off page one in the climactic days of his trial by the mass murder of nine in Lodi. It was as though the end of one misadventure was the provocation that led on to the next, with each new killer driven on to new extremes in order to surpass the great feats of homicide already accomplished.

In some excitement, I compiled a calendar of celebrated killings and murder trials, a chronology of California deaths. My data was too scant to be conclusive, but the patterns were unmistakable. The moment one top killer was ushered out of the limelight, unseen forces would summon another to take his place. Murder inspired murder, and if the nature of that inspiration could be understood and anticipated, a kind of seismology might come into being sensitive enough to monitor murderous pressures on a doped-out drifter in a dairy shed. When Whiteley called to say that there was no way Manson could have written the Beaumont letter, I felt the tingle of exhilaration that comes when you have important new information to pass on to a detective. I asked him if he'd be dropping in at Li Po's soon, but Whiteley said no, he'd cut that out some time ago.

1974

# Merchandising Gary Gilmore's Dance of Death

G ary Gilmore sat alone in his special cell at Utah State Prison, facing the most important decision of his life—should he sign with Schiller or with Susskind?

Not that Schiller and Susskind were the only ways to go. Two of the networks and at least four film studios had expressed interest in the Gary Gilmore story. Paul Anka, of all people, had called Gilmore's Uncle Vern at his shoe repair shop in Provo and offered $75,000 for the whole Gary Gilmore package—the TV movie, the movie movie, the book, whatever was there. The *National Enquirer* was willing to pay $55,000 for the one-time-only North American rights to print a 15,000-word article based on interviews with him by its "team of writers," presuming time enough remained to crowd them in. A filmmaker-pathologist had called from Los Angeles to ask whether the

---

*On two consecutive nights in July 1976 Gary Gilmore murdered Bennie Bushnell and Max Jensen, two young Mormon fathers. Less than three months later he was found guilty of first-degree murder and sentenced to die. At his own insistence, he was executed by firing squad on January 17, 1977.*

right offer might possibly induce Mr. Gilmore to forgo facing the firing squad in favor of being executed by injections of various deadly viruses and truth serums: science could gain valuable insights by observing the progress of his death, especially if Mr. Gilmore would submit to having an auxiliary pituitary gland painlessly grafted to his armpit.

But Gilmore and his agent weren't taking any more calls from gruesome doctors. Or religious nuts. Or the lady in New Jersey who claimed to have proof of his innocence. The Board of Pardons would meet in forty-eight hours in a prison conference room already being rigged for microwave relay and live TV. And after the hearing, if Gilmore got his way, it wouldn't be more than a week before they stood him up, aimed, and shot him. The hour was fast approaching when it would be too late to reconsider. Everyone agreed that the ultimate decision was his alone to make. He had to decide between Schiller and Susskind.

Susskind was a name he vaguely knew. David Susskind, the old guy on TV. Susskind had come in at first with an offer Gilmore now understood to be paltry: $20,000 on signing and $15,000 more on the first day of principal photography. But he'd kept sweetening the kitty until now he was bidding something close to $150,000 up front against a fifty-fifty split of net profits. Telegrams and phone calls from Susskind in New York were coming into Provo every day. Uncle Vern could have sworn he heard David say the equal split of profits would run up to $15 million.

Uncle Vern was Gilmore's agent now. They had signed an agreement a few nights before giving Vern twenty percent of all income from whatever deals they made. Gilmore knew he'd let Vern down in the past. In April, when he came home on parole, Vern and Aunt Ida had put him up in a spare room and tried to help him out with a job in the shoe shop. And of course he'd blown up on them right away, not even lasting two weeks on the job. By the time he was arrested for the murders in July, he'd done just about everything he could think of to demonstrate the oldest fact of his life—give him enough beer and reds and there was no telling what he'd do. So while Vern Damico, his shoemaker uncle, might not have struck some as a serious choice of agent on the sale of a property as big and multifaceted as his story, Gilmore trusted him, even loved him in a way, and it made him feel good to be finally in a position where he could do something nice for the family.

Gilmore's agency agreement with Uncle Vern nullified the verbal contract he'd made two weeks before with Dennis Boaz, his former attorney, the fourth attorney he'd fired since the first of the month. He and Boaz had agreed to split everything down the middle, an arrangement that would compensate Boaz for his services both as lawyer and as writer, while also protecting Gilmore's interest in his one and only asset—The Gary Gilmore Story.

Boaz saw his duty to his client in terms as simple as they were unique: to get Gary Gilmore before the firing squad as soon as possible. He didn't have to bother much with legal research; the Utah attorney general's office was glad to assist him with points and authorities asserting a condemned man's right to die. But his involvement as Gilmore's biographer was a subtler, more creative task, and it seemed to absorb him to the exclusion of other cares. Once or twice a day, he would drive the twenty miles south from Salt Lake City to the prison at Point-of-the-Mountain, undergo a skin search and sit with Gilmore for two or three hours, taking notes for the book, the teleplay, the movie. Interest in the condemned man who couldn't wait was mounting around the world, and without even trying, Boaz was able to make a couple of deals to cover expenses—$500 from the London *Daily Express* for a telephone chat with Gilmore, another $500 from the Swedish labor paper *Aftonbladet* for an interview with Boaz. This was the first hard-cash proof Gilmore had seen that his story was worth money. But after costs and expenses were taken out, he wound up with only $125, not counting the $100 bill he'd managed to hide in his mouth and pass on to his girlfriend Nicole in a goodbye kiss.

Boaz had been leaning heavily toward Susskind—in fact, Susskind's offers were the only ones he conveyed with real enthusiasm. He liked the way Susskind saw the Gilmore story as one man's struggle against society. He liked the five percent of profits he and Gilmore would share, the $10,000 consulting fee that would be his alone. Most of all, he liked the screenwriter Susskind had dispatched to Salt Lake in anticipation of closing the deal, Stanley Greenberg, author of *Pueblo* and *The Missiles of October*. A formidable docudrama man. Gilmore, too, was impressed that Susskind would demonstrate his earnest by finding such a high-priced talent to hole up in the Salt Lake Hilton and start to work on the project without waiting for any papers to be signed. He didn't need Boaz to tell him that Greenberg was good— he'd seen his TV work in the joint.

But Uncle Vern seemed less attracted to Susskind than to Larry Schiller, who had come to Salt Lake on his own and made a point of getting around to meet the family. Schiller's advice to one and all was to hire a lawyer, and when the lawyers were hired they found in Schiller someone who could talk their language, who knew all about court-appointed guardians and trusts, who carried with him a briefcase full of elaborate contracts for the rights to stories even more spectacular than Gilmore's. The man was apparently something of a carrion bird: already he'd done business with Susan Atkins, Marina Oswald, Jack Ruby, Madame Nhu, and Lenny Bruce's widow.

Gilmore decided he would have to hold his own council. However it turned out, the Gary Gilmore story was what he'd be remembered by, and he didn't want to trust it to others. He was not holding out for more money—since the negotiations began he had tried suicide and done all in his power to have his death sentence carried out. Money didn't mean that much to him. Wrung numb by Fiorinal and fasting, made hostile and skittish by the empty-eyed closeness of his guards, he saw that his only course was to remain resolute. He would fast until they let him call his girlfriend. He would insist on his right to be shot. He would not sign away his story until he met the man who was going to produce it.

Dennis Boaz had a whole new life in mind when he moved to Salt Lake City in September. Powder skiing. Indoor tennis. A raft trip. He was leaving almost $15,000 in debts behind in California, where his bar dues had lapsed and his law practice had trickled down to odd jobs serving as counsel to a few Bay Area gurus. Boaz had eased away from law to take up freelance writing under various pen names— K. V. Kitty, Lejohn Marz, S. L. Y. Fox—but he had yet to make his first sale. In Salt Lake, he hoped to recoup by writing, editing a transit workers' newsletter, and teaching a college course that would be a blend of Sufism, numerology, astrology, a little *I Ching* and the *Tao*. The rectitudinous mood of the Mormon capital did not oppress him— you could sit in the window of Fred's Family Restaurant downtown and watch a higher percentage of beautiful women walk by than in any city he knew. Many of those women, he reflected, wanted to meet Californians for the fresh taste of evil they carried with them. "There are millions to be made here importing California consciousness," said Boaz, who also had a sandal franchise in the back of his mind. At the time he first took an interest in Gilmore, however, his only serious project was writing numerological tracts to go along with the custom jewelry sold at a friend's gift shop, the Cat's Meow.

"The first time I saw Gary was on TV," Boaz told reporters. "They were asking him, did he kill a person. And he said he just stood there, pointed the gun, and pulled the trigger. It was heavy. He and his lawyers differed on his wish to die, and I thought I really ought to write the man. I spent about fifteen minutes on my letter, basically saying, I agree with your right to die. We have that choice. And certainly, under the circumstances, facing the hideousness of life in prison, I found his position reasonable. And there were his attorneys on TV saying insulting things about his sanity. I told him I wanted to interview him.

"Gilmore wrote back at once. But the day before his letter arrived, the prison chaplain came by and said that Gary wanted to see me. Later that same day I went out to the prison and met him. He asked if I would represent him, and I naturally said I would. He said he had considered throwing my letter away several times, but there was something in the first paragraph that made him change his mind."

The next day Boaz appeared before the Utah Supreme Court to argue Gilmore's right to die "like a man," saying this was "not a case where my client has some kind of suicide pact with the state, or perverse death wish, or is in an irrational state of mind." Craig Snyder, one of the two Provo lawyers who defended Gilmore at his trial, was there to argue to the contrary, but when Gilmore accepted Boaz as counsel, the court had relieved Snyder, and the young lawyer was smartly rebuked for his efforts. "You're no longer in it," one of the justices told him. "You've been relieved, supplanted. Why don't you accept in good graces his firing you like he's accepted in good graces the responsibility of the court?" It was Boaz's first court appearance in four years, but it could only be judged a quick victory: The court ruled that Gary Gilmore could become the first person executed in the United States since 1967.

Boaz had failed utterly to impress Snyder, however, and when a week went by without his making an effort to examine the record and learn what transpired at the trial, the local lawyer began to wonder whether the Utah bar had looked into the Californian's credentials. "If you're going to get involved at the point Boaz did, you've got an obligation to contact the former counsel and find out whether or not their work was any good," he said. "Maybe we screwed up. Maybe there is something in the case that would give Gilmore an absolute out. But Boaz has never called. He's never contacted us. I've never spoken to the man. Aside from that, and the publishing agreements he's made which fly right in the face of the Canon of Ethics, I think there's a serious question as to whether his support of Gilmore's supposed wish to die satisfies the code of professional responsibility."

Gilmore's trial in early October was, in fact, precisely the kind most intriguing to legal opponents of capital punishment. Despite a poll that showed that ninety percent of the jury pool had heard of both murders Gilmore was accused of, a change of venue motion was denied and he was put on trial for one of them. Jury selection took a day. The trial took a day and a half. There was no defense. Gilmore was mute. The jury spent ninety minutes finding him guilty. Gilmore had taken Fiorinal all through the trial, and his cold, impervious stare was as much of an impression as the jurors got of him. He testified for thirty minutes as the jurors considered what penalty to hand down, but failed to show sufficient remorse to sway them. It took them three hours to decide on death. A few cried.

Gilmore said he thought that his trial was fair. He took responsibility for his crimes and wanted to atone for them in blood. But was there any justice in expecting something better than murder from a violent and suicidal thirty-five-year-old ex-con coming into a tight little Mormon town after spending eighteen of his last twenty-one years in prison? The man's wish to die was clearly pathological; indeed, there were those who said that his murders were provoked by his knowledge that in Utah you get a macho exit—it is the only state in the union that has a firing squad.

Boaz did not rise to these speculations. "Gary doesn't want to appeal, do you understand that?" he would say. "Gary wants to die. I'm representing Gary, not the whole fucking legal system. He's accepting responsibility. He's dead on the facts, really. One can get carried away on the idea of looking for errors. He gave himself up by his actions. Even if he got a new trial, he'd be convicted again, anyway."

Not many days passed before it struck the assembled press that, as a literary property, Gilmore was worth far more dead than alive. If by some fluke or unwanted commutation his life were to be spared, he would slip into the crowded death-row limbo, where others dwelt with stories of their own to tell. This line of reasoning led some to wonder if Boaz's alacrity in supporting Gilmore's death wish might bear some hint of taint. They began to press him. "Where you from, Dennis? Where were you were born?" "I was born in Bakersfield, which is a good place to be born," he would say. "But, fortunately, the next day I moved to Ventura. And played at the sea." Few pens would continue scratching through this kind of filigree, but that was the counselor's true flavor, and the press was stubbornly wrong-headed in sizing him up as a slightly wacky con man in town to exploit Gilmore. The opposite was much closer to the truth. Gilmore was a highly intelligent psychopath who, in the words of one of his doctors, had "the ability to get ahold of one of us healthy neurotics and yank us by the strings." Boaz was suggestible and naive, Dennis in Murderland, and while one could grow impatient with his lighthanded treatment of state-ordered death, his most conspicuous failing was his incomprehension of what the Gilmore story might eventually be worth.

When Schiller learned that Boaz had sold a Gilmore interview for $500, he knew he was dealing with an amateur. Schiller had come to town flying the flags of Warner Bros. and ABC, but his real strength was not so much in his backing as in his front. He had a long history of walking past SWAT teams, getting deathbed confessions, finding his way into the tightest corners in the news. In the ten years since he became known as a photographer for *Life* and *Look* and *Paris-Match,* he had forged a new identity as a mogul in the making, with fifteen books, several television hours, and a couple of movies either done or in the making. After a brief lunch with Boaz, he decided to maintain cordial relations with the lawyer while privately developing what he intended to become a larger relationship with Vern and Ida Damico, and with Mrs. Kathryn Baker, the mother of Gilmore's girlfriend, Nicole.

Schiller also got in direct touch with Gilmore by sending him a four-hundred-word telegram and, the following day, a letter enclosed in his latest book. The letter contained a code; if Gilmore trusted his Uncle Vern, he was to instruct him to report back to Schiller, "Gary got the book." Vern had the message right when he came out from visiting Gilmore in prison the next day, and from then on Schiller began feeling like a winner.

But Schiller saw Nicole's signature on a legal release as even more important than Gilmore's—"that's the number one release, the release that you want to get right, that never goes back, that's going to stay alive." Nicole and Gilmore had already been retrieved from comas following their suicide attempts, but Nicole had sunk much deeper and was now committed to a state hospital. It would take at least two weeks to appoint a guardian, but Schiller assured the lawyers he wasn't in a hurry.

At the distance of New York, Susskind meanwhile had restructured his original offer, so that now he was asking for Nicole's signature as a condition for paying off on Gary's. This was Schiller's signal to get on the phone to ABC and convince them he could do a whole story even if he were missing one of the releases.

"If you got Gilmore without Nicole," Schiller said, "you could do a story on the guys who volunteered for the firing squad, all right? You could do capital punishment, the right to die, okay? You could do a whole picture. If you got the girl and you didn't get Gilmore, you could do the struggle of these two sisters, Nicole and April, the whole love story, the first husband and children, her coming upon a man who's a criminal, him passing through the life of a girl who herself for many years had wanted to die, all right, but yet presenting a certain amount of hope, you know? I'm not saying this is right or wrong. I don't pass judgment. I just said you could pass Gilmore by in about twenty-five percent of the movie and make it a woman's story. Or, the other way around, stay away from the suicide, the love pacts, the girl hitchhiking to see him in the prison, know what I'm saying? You could stay with either Gilmore or the girl was my message, and I went right to top management with that."

The phone rang in maximum security—Johnny Cash for Gary Gilmore. Johnny Cash was Gilmore's favorite singer, and Boaz had gotten word to him that a call would do much for Gilmore's morale. The correction officer answering had to tell the singer that Gilmore couldn't come to the phone, but he'd sure let him know that Johnny Cash said take care. When the corrections officer went to death row to deliver the glad tidings, he found Gilmore in a sorry state. They rushed him to the hospital, pumped the Seconal out of him, saved his life, and afterward said it was a damn lucky thing that Johnny Cash had called just then.

At home in nearby Springville, Gilmore's girlfriend Nicole lay dying, having dropped almost twice as many reds as Gary. She and Gilmore had a lovers' pact: They were going to meet on the other side of the veil. Nicole had been frightening people for days with her talk of suicide. Just the night before, talking to a reporter for the *National Enquirer* who had bought her story for $2,500, she left such a disturbing impression that something told the reporter he'd better look in on her first thing the next morning. When he arrived at her apartment, her three-year-old son opened the door. Nicole was lying on the couch, naked to the waist, clutching a glossy of Gilmore and fading fast. Three days later, when she awoke in a guarded room at the hospital, she learned that her life had been saved by the *National Enquirer*.

This surprised Nicole, who thought the reporter had said he was from NBC. She was only selling her story to earn money to pay for her funeral—but she hadn't meant to sell it to the *Enquirer*. She didn't want her life to look lurid. The reporter felt terrible about not letting Nicole know whom he was working for. He hung around the hospital for days, looking contrite, and the *Enquirer* sent $160 worth of flowers.

Tamera Smith of the Salt Lake *Deseret News* also sent flowers. Tamera was the youngest reporter on the *News,* a cheerful and ambitious twenty-two-year-old Brigham Young University journalism graduate who, until a few months before, had been the paper's Provo stringer. When Gilmore was arraigned for his murders in July, the story looked too routine for the *News* to bother sending a staff reporter the forty miles from Salt Lake to Provo. So Tamera got the assignment, and while she was at it, she struck up an acquaintance with Nicole. Four months later, when Gilmore became a story of another dimension, Tamera got back in touch with Nicole and eventually was able to read and copy more than one hundred of the condemned man's letters. They were eloquent, powerful, extraordinary letters.

Although normally a staid, Mormon, afternoon home companion, the *News* saw the excitement in Tamera's story and ran it big on page one, under a copyright. For two mornings running, Tamera's stories were held up for display on the *Today* show, and Tamera herself was interviewed on local TV. She had the biggest scoop of the whole extravaganza, and the *News* was able to sell the articles to at least eight buyers here and in Europe, at $850 a shot. While Nicole's life was in doubt, the *News* gave some thought to using the money to start a trust fund for her two children. But then she got well, and the plans fell into doubt. Tamera was not at all disturbed that the paper had earned more money from her scoop than she herself had been paid since joining the staff in August. She was content with her cub reporter salary. She was in love with her job, in love with the paper, and, as a serious Mormon, was also proud of the good progress she was making at storing away food to last a year. She wasn't looking for more money—on the day her big story appeared, she was carrying ninety pounds of honey in the backseat of her car.

Gilmore wasn't pleased to see his letters published. They were meant for Nicole's eyes alone, as were the poems he'd written or copied. In *Newsweek*'s Gary Gilmore cover story, lines such as "Say, maiden, wilt thou come with me" were attributed to the killer-bard. This embarrassed Gilmore, who feared that people would take him for a plagiarist.

Geraldo Rivera, the TV news star, came to town and turned Dennis Boaz on to some Thai stick. The Thai stick released Boaz's pent-up emotions: he broke down and cried as he said that he couldn't support Gilmore's wish to die anymore. "Will you say that on television?" Geraldo asked, and the next morning Boaz did so, on *Good Morning, America.* The following day, Boaz woke up thinking that his TV appearance had been a mistake, and he wrote a long letter to Gilmore, who was just getting out of the hospital:

"On Wednesday morning, on *Good Morning, America,* I stated that I could no longer participate in the process of execution. That was a selfish, emotional, foolish, unprofessional act and unfair to you as my client. It was Soap Opera News . . . I hope that you can forgive my hyper-emotionalism. It was definitely not a cool thing to do."

But Gilmore never quite forgave him. The next time Boaz saw him, Gilmore said, "I'm having second thoughts about our relationship." "Okay, Gary," Boaz answered, "go ahead and fire me, but just remember that as soon as you do, all the things you've told me go out on the open market. Everybody gets to take a crack at it."

David Susskind said he saw the Gilmore story as "a dramatic indictment of the penal system." It was "a many-faceted story," the story of "a Jekyll-and-Hyde," a "disturbing commentary on capital punishment." That was why Susskind was offering $150,000 or so to package it, why he sent Stanley Greenberg to Salt Lake, why he was willing to split the profits fifty-fifty with Gilmore. Susskind didn't feel he was obliged to make any provision in his offer to compensate the families of Gilmore's victims. "That's Mr. Gilmore's concern," he said. "What he chooses to do with his equity is strictly his business." Nor was Susskind disturbed to learn that Larry Schiller's offer included an immediate payment to be shared by the victim's families. "Any contest between me and Mr. Schiller," Susskind said, "would be like the Dallas Cowboys playing the local high school."

The moviemakers who were in Salt Lake drank in the peculiar flavor of the place. There was a Swissness in the air, a suffocating sense of *us,* and you could feel the stunning impact you'd get from panning down the complacent valley, past the mobile home parks, the doublewide expandos, through the heavy pall kicked up by "the Provo steelmaking team," letting the camera glimpse the mountains and meadows until, gray and lifeless in the foreground, you came upon the prison where Gilmore wanted to die. Gilmore had put a crazy-house focus on life and death, right and wrong, denying his executioners their righteousness, making them collaborators in his suicide. The radio provided just the right surreal soundtrack: "Dr. Christian says Gilmore can return to death row if he continues to improve."

Two days after Gilmore threatened to fire him, Boaz told Gilmore that they ought to split whatever money they got from the Gary Gilmore story with the families of his victims. He said he was going to give the two widowed mothers half the money he got, but Gilmore would only say he thought they deserved "a substantial percentage." Relations between them had cooled to the point where Boaz began to suspect that Larry Schiller had blindsided him by getting to Gilmore through Uncle Vern. He was right.

The next day Gilmore fired him: "Gary came out and said hi. I said, 'I understand you want to fire me,' he said, 'Uh, right.' I said, 'I think that's a good idea.' Which really blew him out of the saddle. I told him, 'Look, I don't want to see your execution now, either.' I was pissed. And I knew that would bother him a bit. Then we talked for about an hour. He said, 'I hope this isn't going to interfere with our friendship.' I said, 'Of course not, I still dig you. I can see what's happening.' So Gary said, 'I'm just a businessman. I decided I had to go with family. But I don't want to leave you out in the cold.' He said, 'I don't like to write, but I'll write the last quarter of the story and send it to you certified mail.' I know there'll be limitations, but Gary's going to put a provision in his contract that I can write about him—not for movies or TV, but some other way. I'll still come out of this with something. I may just use all this in a couple of chapters in a novel I'm writing. Or I may do a piece for *Rolling Stone*. It's a great story. We'll all be able to appreciate Gary if I can write it.

"I called Susskind and let him know that I was fired. He said, 'You botched it up, Dennis. I spent all that money, it's all a waste, and it's your fault. It's a mess.' Then I got a great classic comment from him. He said, 'If anything happens, call me, but don't call collect.'"

The famous lawyer Louis Nizer called Uncle Vern's lawyer in Provo.

"This is Louis Nizer calling from New York. In case you don't happen to know who I am . . ."

Uncle Vern's lawyer said he knew who Louis Nizer was.

"I'm calling on behalf of David Susskind. In case you don't happen to know who David Susskind is . . ."

But Uncle Vern's lawyer knew who David Susskind was, too.

The day before the Board of Pardons met, Schiller got through to Gilmore. The Uncle Vern connection had paid off, after all. Gilmore told Schiller he thought Warren Oates might be good for the title role in *The Gary Gilmore Story*. Schiller said he wasn't too sure about Oates. That was the right answer; Gilmore had been testing him—in fact, he hated Oates. Sitting eight feet apart, regarding each other through heavy glass, talking on phones, the two hit it off right away, and Gilmore wound up signing for less money than he could have had from Susskind. There would be $40,000 for the victims' families, $60,000 for Gilmore, and $25,000 for Nicole, with Gilmore paying the lawyers and Uncle Vern, and Nicole's money entrusted to her mother and paid in three stages. "There is the word *duress*," Schiller had told the local lawyers. "There is the word *mental incompetence*. And I don't want those words cropping up after we sign contracts." It was an impeccable deal.

Now Schiller had a vested interest in the man who insisted on dying, but he recognized that Gilmore was a public figure who couldn't be put under wraps. "I had to ask myself, do you fool with history?" Schiller said later. "So when the press got a court order forcing the warden to let Gary be interviewed, I didn't try to step in the way. I just told Gary, remember, you've got an asset to protect. And Gary knew exactly what I was saying. He was perfect with the reporter who got in, saying just so much, okay, not getting deep into the personal stuff, holding back a little, know what I'm saying? I think he made a great impression."

Gilmore also made a strong impression at the Board of Pardons hearing. Sarcastic, tough-minded, seizing the moral advantage that derived from his will to die. "It seems the people of Utah want the death penalty but not the execution," he said, touching the central nerve of the whole debate. The board voted to let the sentence go forward, and the following day the judge who presided at his trial set his execution at dawn, December 6, two days after Gilmore's thirty-sixth birthday.

Forty-four men have been executed by the State of Utah, and all but six have chosen the firing squad over hanging. They have gone out in all degrees of courage and dignity, including none at all. The first two, in 1854, were Indian raiders—Antelope and Longhair. Men were shot for killing their wives, their bosses, for killing sheriffs and policemen. Joe Hill, the Wobbly organizer, was convicted of an improbable murder and shot in Salt Lake City in November 1915, despite a clemency appeal from Woodrow Wilson. Among Hill's last messages was a telegram to his fellow radical, Big Bill Haywood: "It is 100 miles from here to Wyoming. Could you arrange to have my body hauled to the state line to be buried? Don't want to be found dead in the state of Utah."

The urge to go out grandly runs strong and deep. To wave away the blindfold. To shame the men who shoot you with an icy quip. There is an allure to firing-squad folklore unmatched by legends of life in prison. The last man to face a Utah firing squad was a uranium miner named James Rodgers, in March 1960. When asked his last wish, Rodgers said, "I told you, warden—a bulletproof vest." Rodgers' execution left two men on Utah's death row. One committed suicide two years later, beating his execution by a day. The other, a boy of eighteen at the time of his murder, is a little fat man now, frightened and broken, a creature of the system.

The more you think about it, the more difficult it is to know just what is meant by cruel and unusual punishment.

1976

# The Court Said the
# Victims Invited the
# Trouble

If the tag on the young lady's toe bears a good local name, and the clothes they take off her are decent clothes, and her family and friends don't happen to betray her in the grief they express to detectives (She was so friendly! She saw the good in everybody!), the modern police science of victimology can suddenly give way to the old-fashioned idea of innocence—innocence pure and complete: the kind that puts blood in the eye when it is discovered raped, murdered. That one can hardly bear to see lying sprawled in the coroner's pictures. That causes detectives working the case to let themselves be heard saying what they'd give for five minutes alone with the lunatic who did this. No other crime inspires the police to attack their work with stronger feelings of nausea and outrage. They know that somewhere out there is a real sicko, a sicko who goes after good, clean kids.

But if the toe tag says Jane Doe, or the clothes are bad, or the girl was known to hitchhike, or instead of impressive struggle marks the coroner notes a butterfly tattoo, those damp ringlets across the forehead, the chipped polish on the nails, the pierced ears, the poor dental work, even the victim's vapid goodbye grin can begin to look a little whorish to the professional eye. Somebody from homicide will still show up for the autopsy; but while one man cuts and sews and the other stands by clucking, doctor and detective will reassure each other in the calming belief that the lady must have died as she lived— asking for it. In which case, God only knows who killed her.

Nowhere today is the concept of "a girl's reputation" so vividly alive as it is in morgues and squad rooms. All along the chain of criminal procedure, in conversations with patrolmen, detectives, prosecutors, and judges, one hears sentiments expressed and sees inferences drawn that seem rooted in nostalgia for a time beyond recall. A twenty-four-year-old rape victim, one is told, was "already putting out." A waitress with two jobs and no car to get to them is described as "a chronic hitchhiker" after she disappears; when her body is found a few months later, mention is made of her black bikini panties. Doubts develop about the character of a college student found raped and murdered after detectives interview her boyfriend: the kid has a beard and admits they smoked pot together.

The Victorian flavor of this thinking can cause great alarm when it emerges in judicial opinions—as, for example, last month, when in the course of reversing a rape conviction the California court of appeal stated that if a woman hitchhikes alone "it would not be unreasonable" for the man who picks her up "to believe that the female would consent to sexual relations"; by standing in need of a ride, she "advises all who pass by that she is willing to enter the vehicle with anyone who stops," that she "has less concern for the consequences than the average female." The opinion, written by Justice Lynn D. Compton, was widely attacked at once as a frightening new sanction of violence against women; and many saw in its apparent shift of blame to the victim a close parallel to the recent scolding a Wisconsin judge gave a sixteen-year-old girl for appearing at school in sweat shirt and jeans and thus enticing the three boys who caught her in a stairwell and raped her into "doing what comes naturally."

But even though the court later succumbed to political pressure and struck the offending language from its ruling, the original un-amended opinion was in fact no more than a mild statement of what police take to be an accepted fact: when a woman enters a stranger's car, a sexual current passes between them that she cannot help but recognize. The confidence a modern woman might have in her ability to deflect such a current and get on down the road in peace and safety is lost on the authorities. They see it as a new kind of social recklessness, and police detectives, almost to a man, believe it to be the reason why the rape and murder of women along the highways— an infrequent crime ten years ago—has become so commonplace in California. Some women are willing to enter the vehicle with anyone who stops. Some women have less concern for the consequences.

The police are not in business to insult women, dead or alive, and their exasperation in dealing with crimes against female hitchhikers is based at least in part on their helplessness to prevent the horrors no one but they have to see. Homicide detectives are almost figures of fun among their colleagues for their obsessiveness, their tendency to agonize, the grief they leave scattered around the place, their habit of going haunted on you after a couple of beers. Some of them have plainly seen too many sparrows fall, and if they stop caring the same about each of them, it may be only because they've reached a point where they have to budget their pity.

Even so, it must be said that disgust for the victim of crime is a routine police attitude. As applied to people who leave their keys in the car or get rolled by men they thought were women, it even makes a kind of hasty sense in the course of a hard night's work. But when the crime victim lies by the roadside in silence and ruin, guesses colored with contempt about how she got there are guesses that can grossly misdirect the hunt for her killer. And in light of the abysmal luck the police are having in solving these highway crimes, it seems worth asking if their attitude toward the victims might be getting in the way.

The detective standing over the body must attempt a few guesses. Ordinarily, he has nothing else to go on—no witnesses, no physical evidence, no personal motive, no crime scene, no weapon, no past associations between victim and killer, no knowledge of where or when they met. So he turns his eyes to the victim and tries to picture her as she was before.

His judgment will almost certainly reflect the peculiar blend of cynicism and chivalry which police work seems to encourage; this will not serve him well, being the aspect of his personality which most likely would have kept them strangers had he and the victim met. He may feel sickened or oddly disgraced or even aroused at the sight of her. He may stare at her closely or have to turn away. Prude, square, swinger, wife beater, whoever he is and however he feels, he embarks on his investigation with what amounts to a moral appraisal of a corpse. And by the time lab work and file checks and other procedures add substance to that appraisal, the victim's epitaph will probably be written to the satisfaction of the police. She was either a good, clean kid who was raped and murdered or a tramp who met her fate.

However coldly or mistakenly it may be accomplished, however it may reek of sexist incomprehension, the point of appraising the victim's character is not to judge the seriousness of the crime. Rape by itself may not always be rape in the eyes of the police, but murder is always murder, and every murder that remains unsolved is supposed to be a war without armistice. The point of judging the victim is to gain intuition about the person who killed her, to look at the pillaged woman and imagine the pillaging man. The police play the percentages, and the percentages tell them that certain kinds of women get raped and killed by certain kinds of men. Sometimes, by some act of ritual or staging, the killer will provide a helpful self-portrait. But in the typical case there is nothing to consider but the castoff body, and in looking it over the police are hoping to learn something of the man they're after: is he some kind of a sicko or just an average Joe who must have lost his cool?

Clean kid. Tramp. Average Joe. Sicko. At the start of an investigation, the police tend to paint in bold strokes. As they look deeper, they become aware of more subtle shadings. It will turn out that the victim really wasn't that much of a tramp. She was more of a ding, a happy-face. The odds will then say that an average Joe didn't kill her. She wouldn't have set off an average Joe. It was probably more of a creep. Not an old creep, though. She could have handled an old creep. Which leaves us looking for a young creep, a shy young creep with a car.

City police and sheriff's detectives in the fifteen California counties traversed by the major coast roads presently have open in their files about eighty unsolved murders—all committed in the last five years—in which a woman or girl was either last seen or found dead not far from the highway. With few exceptions, the victims whose final hours could be reconstructed disappeared while hitchhiking or waiting at a bus stop. Almost all were between sixteen and twenty-three. Most had pierced ears and shoulder-length blond or light-brown hair. All but a few were sexually assaulted, many after death. About half were found within yards of the highway, almost always to the east of the road.

Although isolated highway killings of women continue to be reported almost monthly somewhere along the thousand-mile coast, many recent cases have occurred in clusters: three last year in Humboldt County and another just across the Del Norte County line; eight in the two years before around Santa Rosa; two in Orange County in the space of five weeks; six last year between Oakland and San Jose; two south of Mendocino late last summer; four near Santa Barbara since last November; three in San Diego since the start of the year. Taken together with the sameness in choice of victim and dumping site, these outbreaks led some detectives to wonder if a large number of the crimes could be the work of the same man—a man, or group of men—with the ability to move inconspicuously in and out of any area up and down the coast.

For a while, the police turned their attention to long-distance truck drivers, traveling salesmen, and others whose home was the highway. But then an arrest somewhere would clear a case that had seemed to fit the pattern, or another killing would occur that seemed to break it. Some of the victims were strangled, some stabbed, some shot. Some were mutilated or tortured. Some bore wounds inflicted as if according to ritual. Some had rope or tape burns that told of their having been held captive for a time. And while some bodies were virtually flung out on shoulders, others were painstakingly concealed. As the number of rape-murders grew, so did the conviction that all they had in common was the highway.

The California coast roads are rim roads of hazy expectation for nomads from all over. From Mexico to the Oregon border, they describe the arc of hope for many who have never seen them. Highway 1. Highway 101. In all parts of the country it is taken on faith that no one can know what mellow is who hasn't traveled these highways. So, drawn by rock dreams, drawn by ocean and sun, fresh faces appear daily at roadside—heedless thumbbunnies, brand new to the coast, hitching rides in places where others like them disappeared a few days before.

But the victims' insistence on replenishing themselves is not the only feature that makes the police look with dread on these highways as beautiful killing zones. Like all major roads, they are rivers of forgetfulness, where the passage of each car is erased by the passage of the next. Sunlight glances off the windshield. Long easy miles are accomplished in a trance. A car is noticed pulling off on a shoulder. A figure approaches it at a trot. Then you pass, and they vanish from sight and mind. They are gone in the general hum and blur. No one is witness to anything. No one can recall what was seen. The car moves up the highway with its new passenger, perhaps to turn off at a canyon road within minutes and twist up into the solitude of the century before.

But the rape-murders are not simple crimes of opportunity; they have a pathology all their own, which leads some investigators to go further in attempting to identify specific qualities of the coast roads that might hold unknown attractions for those who troll along them. Among these experts is Robert Morneau, a recently retired FBI agent who for many years was the Bureau's top sex crimes expert.

"There's something about that whole area, from Ventura up through the Monterey Peninsula and up into Santa Cruz, something really peculiar," Morneau says. "A lot of symbolism is involved in sex crimes, and I've got to believe there's something about the way the fog rolls into the canyons, or the pounding of the surf, something about that area draws people to commit strange acts.

"In every major series of sex crimes, you'll find a thread of uniformity. The time of day, the phase of the moon, the clothing. But here, what is it? Maybe something symbolic about the wind howling through the canyons. Maybe the canyon becomes somehow vaginal to these people when the wind blows hard. Or it's the ocean, the water, the Freudian idea of water representing a return to the womb. There's just something about that area that impresses people. Hard telling what, exactly—you always have to ask the sex offender what he thought was so exciting."

Out of recklessness, or boastfulness, or sadism, or self-loathing, the killer left the woman's jacket in plain sight, off to the side of the canyon road, not ten steps from the body. Two hikers came across it the next morning and noticed the blood. Before the morning was over, the body had been found. Shot once in the head. Raped, or sexually molested. Bent into a posture of maximum defeat.

That was Patricia Laney, twenty-one, a student at UC Santa Barbara, a poet and amateur cellist, an accomplished juggler, an actress, a mime. She had been on her way to mime class the last time anyone saw her alive, waiting at a bus stop on Hollister Avenue in Goleta. Since Hollister Avenue was the same street from which two other women had disappeared during the two preceding months, the discovery of Laney's body prompted an immediate search of the steep and desolate brushland in the canyon where it was found. By nightfall the next day, a search dog had located the remains of Jacqueline Rook, twenty-one, another UCSB student and the first of the three to vanish. She was too long dead for her body to reveal much of what had been done to her; but she, too, had been shot once in the head, and the killer had arranged her clothing and posture to shock the finder in the same way as had been done with Laney.

Detectives from the Santa Barbara County Sheriff's Office sifted the earth where the bodies were found. They took photographs and smears, drew diagrams, paced off distances, placed items of interest in evidence bags and sealed them with their signatures. They took impressions of random footprints and tire tracks. They plotted the sites of the abductions and the places where the bodies were found on maps, then searched for some telling vector. They compared the times of the abductions against tide tables, weather logs, paydays, holidays, phases of the moon. They interviewed people who knew the victims or thought they'd seen them passing through. They ran license checks on cars they saw stopping for hitchhikers. They put out decoys, leafed through mug books and MO files, staked out Hollister Avenue. It was the biggest investigative effort in the history of the department.

At first it seemed that the killer might have left a trail. Both Laney and Rook had disappeared from the same busy intersection, and Mary Ann Sarris, nineteen, a Goleta waitress, whose body was later found, was taken from a spot just a few blocks up the street. Sarris and Rook had both been hitchhiking, one headed toward the student town of Isla Vista, a mile or so west, and the other toward Santa Barbara, ten miles east down Highway 101. All had disappeared during the afternoon of warm and sunny days, and all bore a striking physical resemblance—they were heavyset, with round, full faces and shoulder-length hair parted in the middle. The canyon where the first two bodies were found, Refugio Canyon, fifteen miles up the coast from Goleta, was as remote as any in the Santa Ynez range, and the choice of it as a dumping ground suggested that the killer was a local man.

The detectives, led by Sgt. Mike Kirkman of the major crimes detail, tried to build revealing scenarios from what clues they had. Since all three women were taken in places a killer would not choose if his approach depended on pulling a gun, it was assumed he was someone capable of a polite, reassuring approach—someone disarming. Laney had been aware of the disappearance of the others and had even joined in efforts to alert campus women to the perils of hitchhiking alone. She had made arrangements with her boyfriend to meet her in his car at the bus stop and take her to the mime class—but the boyfriend couldn't be sure that he wasn't a few minutes late. Had Laney been anxious enough about getting to her class on time to discard caution and accept the first ride that looked good? The police consulted the appraisal they'd made of her character and decided that she'd probably stuck out her thumb.

"The problem here," Sgt. Kirkman said, "is that we're dealing with an accumulation of social changes that has created a new MO. Only recently has it become acceptable for young ladies to hitchhike. They come up here to the university, and they can't afford a car; that means they have to rely on the bus or some friend. To do that, they have to give up their independence. And that's the one thing they can't stand giving up. They'd rather just run the risk of being hurt."

To illustrate his point, Sgt. Kirkman recalled the case of Noel Rascati, twenty-three, who was seen hitchhiking on a Highway 101 spur road in Goleta near nightfall on the day Laney's body was found. A sheriff's deputy had pulled up and lectured her about the risk she was running. The next news of her came ten days later in a story from Los Angeles—she had been found in Elysian Park, near Dodger Stadium, nude, raped, strangled.

The Santa Barbara sheriff's detectives were under pressure from an alarmed community, and they went to great lengths to calm nerves while pursuing their investigation. A car was sent when a woman called in to report a man smoking a cigarette at a bus stop. A report was taken on a possibly significant dream. When members of the women's movement on the campus staged rallies and issued broadsides describing the fate of Rook, Laney, and Sarris as expressions of "rape culture," the police did not ignore them. Maybe the way to solve these crimes was to look at them from that perspective, to consider the possibility that the women were killed and raped not because that fugitive sicko was still out there, but because some violent average Joe was grappling with what he took to be the mandates of manhood. But no. That didn't lead anywhere, either. Sarris's body was found by a hunter in another canyon six months after her disappearance, but even then, after thousands of hours of work, the police were still stuck for a lead. About all they had was a psychological profile of the man they were seeking, composed with the assistance of the FBI, and drawing on all the clues, all the wisdom, all the fictions they possessed.

The suspect is believed to be white, in his early twenties, never married, and definitely a psychopathic personality. It is further believed that he is unable to carry on a normal sexual relationship with women due to emotional and sexual immaturity, and may suffer from a mother fixation and sexual impotence. The suspect is thought to be a loner and probably works at menial tasks.

In other words, a sicko. A shy young creep. A loner. A loser. A casualty of Mom. There wasn't much in the profile you could tack up on a post office wall, but could so many psychological insights be inferred from the clues the sheriff's detectives had in hand? Did an absence of semen prove his impotence, a shard of fingernail or scrap of soiled fabric suggest his menial work? Or were the police merely hoping to taunt him into coming out into the open by hitting all the standard psychopathic sore spots with a clever string of insults? Sgt. Kirkman would not say, but for a week after the profile was broadcast and printed in the local papers, he and his men had heavy stakeouts on all the trolling zones.

The conventional wisdom about violent sex offenders was neatly packaged in the profile. But as criminals go, they are such complex men that not much can be said that applies to the group at large. In confinement, sex offenders generally are a sorry crew, often so wrapped up in themselves that only psychiatrists can stand them. Partly this results from their place on the bottom tier of the prison caste system, but it is also true that they live in shame and preoccupation, endlessly prowling the quirky terrain of their inner lives.

Even as free men, sex offenders tend to retain the qualities that set them apart in prison: inwardness, self-pity, mildness, lack of humor. Too secretive and self-absorbed to acquire the talent for friendship, they are likely to lead private, retrospective lives, collecting comic books on Saturdays, going to the zoo on Sundays, trying to dwell in the calm masochistic harbors only their own company can provide. All these features make them difficult quarry for police. Whenever one is captured, chances are that a compulsion to confess caused him to mark his trail carefully, like Hansel dropping bread crumbs through the woods.

The study of the crimes they commit is a somber business, unrewarding without the criminals' commentaries: All there is to contemplate is a ghastly residue. But comparing series of sex crimes for the purpose of detection is quite another matter, and until two years ago it was pursued with energy in California. Then, in one of the small economies of the Brown administration, the Homicide MO Desk at the State Department of Justice was eliminated—the one place where a statewide murder watch was kept, where reports of unsolved homicides of all kinds were examined and compared. The crime analyst at this desk was the first to observe patterns emerge in reports of rape-murders along the coast, and in February 1975, he sent the state's 1,075 police agencies a confidential study detailing his findings. No arrests resulted, but the report is still the most comprehensive analysis of the killings available to police. Many detectives continue to refer to it as if it were the latest word, even though about forty-five similar cases have been reported since it was published.

Today, there is no official means for homicide detectives to share information with their colleagues in other agencies around the state, and they rely instead on personal contacts with each other. They have formed their own professional society, the Homicide Investigators Association. Like life-insurance underwriters or powerboat dealers, they meet at conventions; instead of yachts or actuarial tables, they talk about new MOs.

Rape-murder on the highways, of course, can no longer be considered a new MO. Yet the understanding of it is as incomplete today as it was years ago. No other form of homicide is as grim and thankless to investigate, and none has a lower solution rate. With a choice of murders to unravel, the police yield to percentages and go off to solve the mom-and-pop case downtown. They'll go looking for that goddamn sicko, they promise themselves, when time again permits.

Off to the side of the highway, man of menial tasks waits to be cured of all ills by cute hitchhiker, huffing up the shoulder with her backpack, blond and bouncy in his rearview mirror. Watching her run to him, he rises to imagined excitements, stuff that would kill his mother. Then she's there, framed in his window, flushed cheeks, breathless—he is stunned to see that she could want it this bad. A bubble pops high inside him and he fumbles the usual blah-blah, but it doesn't matter. She likes shy men, she trusts them, she hops right in. He puts a good move on the wheel and hits the highway while she tells him things he's too busy to hear. It looks to him like she digs his driving. Already he's in love with her nipples and knees. He makes a little jerky conversation. She asks him if she can play the radio.

Who's running this show? he thinks. She takes his tight smile for permission and starts messing with his dials. These hippie chicks can get pretty independent if you don't know how to treat them, but he'll teach her a trick or two. She gawks out the window. She hums out of tune. He asked her a question, but she doesn't answer, or she beats time on her beautiful knees. Now she won't even look over at him. He yells hello at the top of his voice. She looks over and tries to smile, he thinks, puts her eyes back on the road. If he wasn't in his rotten work clothes, she would probably be in his lap. He begins to feel stupid about stopping. He begins to feel robbed by the promise he had read in her thumb.

What happens next? He drives on in a sulk and takes her where she's going. Or he frightens her with his driving and idle shouting but doesn't try to prevent her from jumping out when they come to a stop. Or he pulls off the road and tells her she's got two choices, one of which is walking. Or he tells her he won't hurt her if she goes along with him, so she goes along with him. Or else she doesn't, and he loses heart, kicks her out, and drives away. Or he whips up a lonely road with her, rapes her, and leaves her there. Or rapes her, apologizes, offers her money, rides anywhere. Or rapes her, then kills her to cancel his shame. Or kills her, then rapes her to ease the pressure.

One obvious possibility is excluded from his grim selection: that the woman takes control of her fate. Even when an encounter with a rapist happens enclosed in the steel shell of a moving car, a woman is not without resources, and there are many who have come away unscathed because by force of confidence and wit they tamed the cowardly lion at the wheel. Edmund E. Kemper III, who killed six young women hitchhikers around Santa Cruz five years ago, kept count of all the women he'd picked up during an eleven-month span when he had nothing but murder on his mind—one hundred ten women in all, most of them college students. Kemper, who is six-foot-nine and so powerful that his friends used to call him "Forklift," was clearly no one to tangle with physically, and yet there were one hundred four potential victims who stepped out of his car with nothing to report on but a ride.

The women Kemper did kill struck him all alike: highborn, educated, spoiled, too pretty, the kind who were cruel to him in high school. The others, he said, just weren't his type—he just didn't feel like killing them. In no case did the cause of death have anything to do with the victim's behavior once the killer was launched on his fugue. The cause of death was her choice of a sweater, her way of smiling or saying hello, the way her hair caught or did not catch the sunlight. These perceptions came from so deep in a private abyss that no one but Kemper could hope to decipher them, but that is the feature of his murders that makes them typical of the highway homicides. They are crimes of almost perfect randomness, mechanized crimes of passion between total strangers that involve unknowable combinations of man, woman, car, stretch of road, attack, resistance, surrender. And for the police to think of the victims as types that can be classified into levels of vulnerability and provocation is as dangerous an error as for women to suppose that a roadside guess will always keep them from harm's way.

The rapist behind the wheel has an overwhelming advantage over even a strong and alert woman, and by the same logic that often makes timid men aggressive drivers, men who look upon women as paraphernalia—average Joes and sickos alike—are all the more inclined to do so when in control of a car. A car lends them a feeling of allure that they might otherwise lack. It permits them to cruise the streets and highways and examine the women they pass with a sexual frankness they would not risk on foot. If a woman rejects them, it is a double insult: Both man and driver are diminished. When they happen to see a happy-face standing there with her thumb out, they think it means whither thou goest, sweet daddy.

So, evidently, does the state court of appeal, whose first, frankly stated opinion on the risks a woman assumes when she hitchhikes may be read as a manly license by every sexual shopper with a car. Men with rape in their hearts read the newspapers, too: at least someone on high is telling them that what they see getting into their cars is precisely what they're entitled to get. One imagines Justice Compton quoted in some heat by all variety of men who can't accept the bad news that the hitchhiker sitting beside them only wanted a ride—*I thought you had less concern for the consequences! I thought you were advising all who pass by that you were willing to consent to sexual relations!* It would all be a very fine farce if only sex crimes had no victims. But in a state already plagued by men who plunder women, it is at best an act of judicial abandonment to draw away from the victims' loss and, in the process, encourage its repetition. Women would be safe, of course, if only they stopped accepting rides from rapists. But even the police will tell you that it sometimes takes a close encounter to tell a sicko from an average Joe.

1977

# Stalking the Hillside Strangler

**W**ight drove down to the wharves and parked where he wouldn't be seen from the guard shack. It was just past 5:00 but already dark and cold, with a winter wind blowing rain squalls in off Bellingham Bay. Nobody else was around—only Wight, the sergeant he'd brought with him, and this character, Ken Bianchi, who was waiting inside the shack.

Wight had met Bianchi once before. He'd gone to arrest a thieving door shaker at an outfit called Whatcom Security, and there in the office on Iron Street was captain Ken Bianchi, the new man in charge, wearing a brand-new uniform. The dark blue pants and jacket, the captain's bars, the badge. You had to look twice to see that he wasn't a real cop.

*From October 1977 to February 1978, ten girls and young women were raped and murdered in the Hillside Strangler serial killings in Los Angeles. Kenneth Bianchi and his cousin, Angelo Buono, were arrested for the crimes ten months apart in 1979. In return for a life sentence, Bianchi agreed to testify against Buono, who was convicted on nine counts of murder and sentenced to life without parole. Bianchi also received a life sentence, but will be eligible for parole in 2005.*

Bianchi was cordial and helpful, and Wight was much impressed. He made a mental note to tell Randy Moa, Whatcom's owner and a former partner on the Bellingham police, that he had a real sharp boy running his business for him. Moa appreciated hearing that. He'd hired Bianchi as a security guard when Ken was new in town, then lost him after a couple of months to Fred Meyer stores. Bianchi did great there—the guy could pick off a shoplifter like lint from his lapel. But now Moa had him back for a few more dollars plus the captain's bars and badge, and he only hoped he could hang on to him a while. No one who had held Ken's job before had bothered with a uniform—"captain" being just a fancy way of saying "office manager." But Moa decided that dressing Ken up in a captain's suit was a darn good way to "take advantage of the PR aspect of having him around."

It didn't surprise Wight that this same Bianchi now looked good for the murder of the coeds. At thirty-six, Wight had fifteen years of police work behind him, and there wasn't much left that struck him as off the wall. Besides, he wasn't the only one who'd been impressed by the man. After only six months in town, Bianchi was up on the eligibility list for the Bellingham police, having scored high on both the written and the orals—which proved that even the brass had seen some promise there. All that mattered now was that Wight knew what he looked like. That was why he'd volunteered to bring him in, even though it was quitting time and that meant first calling his mother out on this filthy night to pick up his daughter at a basketball game.

Wight figured that Bianchi would be armed. He had a permit to carry a concealed weapon, and as a prospective member of the Whatcom Country Sheriff's Reserve he also owned a full set of police gear—the belt, the cuffs, the gun. You had to take him seriously as a professional. He'd left work a few minutes after the bodies were found, probably because he'd heard the news on his police-band scanner. If that was true, he might readily guess that the radio message instructing him to drive to the guard shack and wait for a call from his office was a ruse to position him for an easy arrest. All the same, in a deal like this, it wasn't the best idea to come with the SWAT team and panic the guy, and Wight was sure he could take him one-on-one. So he told the sergeant to hang back by the car and keep him covered. Then he took out his revolver and walked up to the shack.

Ken always left the bodies in plain sight. Sometimes just dumped out at roadside. Sometimes naked and spread-eagled. Once, in L.A., with the V of the legs sort of framing Parker Center. Something for the boys to consider. A counterintelligence joke. Usually, the bodies were found at daybreak by a paperboy or jogger or somebody walking the dog. Here it had taken almost twenty-four hours. It didn't matter. Hiding the bodies just wasn't something he did.

But it was obvious as well that the younger girl, Karen, had disobeyed his instructions not to tell anyone about the house-sitting job, and that gave him some cause for alarm. Ken knew Karen from his days at Fred Meyer's, where she had worked the front counter, a pretty, talkative blond. He got nowhere trying to flirt with her—she had all the boyfriends she could use. Still, of all the girls he'd met at the store, Karen was the one he liked best.

He'd thought of her again after going out to the Catlow house on Bayside to set up a vacation-watch contract for Whatcom. Bayside is in the Edgemoor section, a new neighborhood of winding roads and good houses, and the Catlow house is among the best. Catlow wanted it patrolled and checked for frozen pipes while he was away on a California trip. And while showing Ken around the place, he had remarked that with all the trees and the distance from the road, the house was so secluded that someone could come in and haul away his furniture and no one would ever know.

Ken had to call around for Karen's number, but, when he got her on the phone the next day, he had no trouble setting things up. He told her that the burglar alarm system at the house needed some work and the insurance company was willing to pay him $300 to keep the place secure while the job was done. He offered her $100 just to sit there for two hours, and when Karen asked if she could bring along her roommate, Diane, Ken said sure—he'd even give Diane another $100 and just keep $100 for himself. Karen had been excited, of course—too excited to keep her word.

Still, Ken had done a good job on the cleanup, and the cleanup was what counted. A few weeks before, he'd attended an FBI sex crimes seminar, and, when someone brought up the Hillside Strangler murders, the agent conducting the class said that what stymied the police in L.A. was the absence of any crime scenes; all they had were bodies, and bodies told less than one might think. Right there was the genius of the thing: eliminating the crime scene. And now, in Bellingham, he'd done it once again.

After the girls were dead he collected their books and tossed them into a plastic bag along with the rubber gloves, the cord, the Ace bandages. Then, leaving the girls behind, he'd driven off in the Whatcom Security pickup he'd tricked one of the guards into letting him use, tossed the bag in a trash bin behind a junior high school, gone over to the street where he'd persuaded Karen to park her Bobcat, switched vehicles, gone back to the house, loaded up the bodies, made sure the place was clean, driven to a cul-de-sac on a building site not yet cleared for houses, parked the Bobcat, walked to his truck parked about a mile away, dropped by the office on Iron Street, gone home, watched a little TV with Kelli, the woman he lived with, brushed off his clothes, and gone to bed. No muss, no fuss.

Around midnight, Randy Moa called. He wanted to know how Ken had spent the evening. Ken reminded him that Thursday was sheriff's reserve night. Randy seemed satisfied. But then Ken got to thinking—possibly because he saw the blue-and-white car cruising slowly past his house. For Randy to call, Karen must have told someone about the house-sitting job. So Ken called Whatcom and learned that the police had been asking about him. Getting the jump on his pursuers, he called the police and set up a meeting for 2:30 A.M. at the Iron Street office. He was waiting when the police arrived.

He got the ball rolling by admitting that he'd lied. He hadn't gone to his reserve meeting. Instead, he'd spent the evening driving around, trying to get his head together. At first he denied knowing any Karen, then suddenly remembered her—oh, *that* Karen! Sure! She used to tell me how her boyfriend beat her up all the time. I was her confidant. The police seemed to go for this. After an hour or so, they let him go back home.

The one thing he'd forgotten was the other girl's coat, left behind at the house on Bayside. So when he heard on the scanner that the bodies had been found, he went over to the house, picked up the coat, and was on his way to get rid of it when the call came telling him to go to the guard shack. He drove straight to the wharves, giving himself time to bundle up the coat and hide it before the police arrived.

He had no reason to panic. This wouldn't be the first time he'd been face-to-face with some detective investigating the murders. In L.A., he'd sent them packing twice, and those guys were real pros. Up here in Bellingham, the cops were fishermen and farmers—six detectives were all they had.

When Wight was just a few steps from the shack, Bianchi drifted over to the window as if to peer out. Wight rushed the door, coming in fast behind his .357. Bianchi stayed calm. He went up against the wall and let himself be searched; he wasn't armed—and he wasn't disarmed, either. "He was very self-assured about the whole thing," Wight said later. "He was positive we weren't going to be able to prove a damn thing. His attitude was, Well, you guys just made a mistake, and I know you'll get it straightened out pretty soon, so I'll just go along."

In most cities, a report that two college women, both unmarried and both adults, were two hours late returning from an evening engagement would not get much of a rise from the police. In Los Angeles, for example, anyone over ten must be missing for twenty-four hours before the police will even fill out a report. But Bellingham is still the kind of place where oddities are noticed and individuals count, and the night shift had barely started before the police made it a priority matter to look into the disappearance of Karen Mandic, twenty-two, and Diane Wilder, twenty-seven, her friend and roommate.

Karen, they learned, had arranged with her boss at Fred Meyer's to take a long lunch break that evening—from seven until nine—and when eleven came and she still wasn't back, he called a boyfriend of hers, Steve Hardwick, who happened to be a police officer on the Western Washington University campus, where both Karen and Diane were enrolled. Karen had told Hardwick about the house-sitting job, and, when he asked why on earth she was being paid so much, she said it was because a friend knew that she needed the money and was trying to help her out. Hardwick couldn't remember the friend's name or the exact address he'd been given. But when he called the police to report that the women were missing, he said that the house was down by Bayside and the friend was someone Karen knew from work who was now with Whatcom Security.

Sgt. Donald Miles got on the case at once. After waking Moa and hearing back from him, Miles called the reserve captain and learned that Bianchi was lying about the meeting. Without delay, he put out a radio bulletin instructing patrol cars to be on the watch for the two women and the car. When Bianchi called back to arrange the meeting, Miles took another sergeant along, and both came away with the impression that Bianchi was a frightened, transparent liar. Moa's faith in Ken remained unshaken until he heard that he told the police that he'd spent the evening driving around. That sent a chill through Moa, and he passed through what he remembers as the worst and longest moment of his life.

When morning came, Miles briefed Chief Terry Mangan on the night's events. Already the police had searched the city's parking lots and downtown streets, and Miles passed along to the chief his hunch that something serious had happened. Mangan and detective supervisor Duane Schenck drove over to the house the women had shared. The first thing they noticed was that the porch light was still on. Then they noticed that the cat had not been fed. That was enough to convince Mangan that the case should be approached as a possible homicide. By all accounts, these women simply weren't the kind to go off on some adventure and forget about their cat.

Mangan's men often described him as an intellectual, and it was true that he collected books and could keep you up till morning talking Sherlock Holmes. But police work engaged him in spirit before intellect, for Mangan was a former Catholic priest who had marched in Selma with Martin Luther King and been wholly content with the pastoral life when a conflict arose that led him to give up the priesthood for the police.

As the eldest of seven children in a traditional Irish family, Terry didn't have much choice. He went from Holy Ghost Prep to Saint Mary's College to Saint Mary's Seminary to Saint Albert's College, emerging at twenty-seven the fulfillment of his mother's last wish: Father Mangan. With a master's degree in divinity, he joined the faculty of Junipero High in Monterey, where he taught religion and creative writing, and in his third year at the school he was named dean of students. But by then it was 1966, and in the nearby town of Seaside the police were having their troubles. Seaside had grown by more than double in a few years' time, and most of the new faces were black; tensions grew, and the old storefront police department suddenly found itself in need of sensitivity training. Mangan's time in the South made him a natural choice for the job, and with the blessing of his religious order, he became so involved that eventually there he was in uniform, a reserve officer, out in a patrol car almost every night.

Mangan rode with the police to get a notion of life as they saw it, but the police themselves were what wound up striking him most. "It was very humbling for me to see the patience and the dedication and the generosity of these men, and then go back and do some soul searching and ask if I saw the same patience and generosity among my own peers," he says today. Neither Mangan nor his superiors in the church were troubled by the possibility that some police encounter might compel him to use his gun; although slightly built and standing only five-foot-eight, Mangan found that force of personality was almost always force enough. But then a papal representative visited the diocese, and the papers were writing about the "Pistol-Packin' Padre," and Rome was not amused: according to canon law, a priest may not bear arms. Forced to a choice he had never anticipated, Mangan asked to be laicized. "After I left the priesthood," he says, "I had the same feelings and all the same friends. I still went to Mass. I maintained contact with many of the nuns. I hadn't left for the reason of getting married or anything like that, so it wasn't really that big a split. And I did as much counseling as a police officer as I ever did as a priest."

When Mangan took charge in Bellingham in the summer of 1976, he was the first outsider to command the department in more than fifty years. On paper, he looked wonderful: great education, six years on the Seaside police, four more as a public safety director (in Lakewood, a gerrymandered city squeezed between Bellflower and Long Beach), good experience in the street and also at city hall. Yet here he was, a New York–born ex-priest coming in from southern California, a little guy, the smallest man in the department. Mangan expected some serious hazing. But there was none of that. Instead, he was well received and quickly enough was able to wrangle the funds to refurbish the station house, upgrade the blue-and-white cars, and generally improve both efficiency and morale. When he walked past the locker room one day and heard someone shout, "Chief's on the floor—no more short-guy jokes," he knew that he'd been accepted.

So there was no hesitation to act when Mangan said this looked like it might be murder. A statewide teletype had already gone out, and by noon Mangan himself had called all the local radio stations with a description of the women and their car. Police in four-wheel-drive vehicles were combing dirt roads and trails in wooded sections of the city, and supervisor Schenck had turned the case over to his two most seasoned detectives, Fred Nolte and Terry Wight.

Nolte and Wight were both Bellingham boys with long years in the department, and they usually worked together when major cases came along. Nolte at forty-one was thoughtful, shambling, paunchy enough to inspire his wife to give him a treadmill for Christmas. Wight, a handsome, brooding man, lived in town with his sixteen-year-old daughter. On his off-duty days he ran charter boats around the San Juan Islands, and he sometimes used his vacations to work on commercial fishing boats on the Alaska run. Nolte and his family lived near the water at Gooseberry Point, and for years he too had been an avid boatsman, the former commodore, in fact, of Wheel and Keel, a local powerboat club. Now what he loved was the desert, and, when vacation time came, the Noltes usually took off in their motor home for Utah or Nevada. Nolte's specialty was bad checks and credit-card fraud. Wight was the narcotics man.

Among the department's six detectives there was none whose specialty was homicide. The year before the two women were strangled, one person had been murdered; a homicide man would have starved. The forty-six thousand people of Bellingham had a healthy capacity to lie, cheat, and steal from each other, and often enough they stepped over the felony line. Occasionally, someone would swoop in off the interstate and stick up a 7-Eleven, or the fur would get to flying at the Fat Cat or the Flame. But by and large the city was calm and sane, and all it took to keep the peace there was a friendly force of sixty-eight men, one woman, and four dogs.

No one in memory had ever been strangled there. When someone did get killed, it was almost always a self-solving mom-and-pop affair, with the murder weapon a shotgun or a rolling pin or a knife. Murder was rare, and when it happened the whole department felt the outrage. "We get a homicide, it's big business," Nolte said a few weeks ago in the quiet of his basement office. "Everybody goes out and we all start digging. It's big stuff—my goodness, somebody got killed in our town! Homicide! We hit it hard and fast and quick."

The Bellingham police made it their practice to videotape all major crime scenes. The tapes served to document their field procedures as well as to make vivid in the eyes of juries the victim's injury or loss. Only a week before the killings, Whatcom County prosecutor David McEachran had met with Bob Knudsen, the department's evidence supervisor, and they had hit on the idea of calling in a fire truck with floodlights mounted on its boom when a case required working outdoors after dark. So when a citizen who had heard the radio bulletin called in to say she had seen a green Bobcat parked in a cul-de-sac, the first officers to arrive kept their distance until Knudsen, McEachran, Mangan, the coroner's men, and the fire truck were all in place. Then the floodlights came on, and in the sudden brightness the men went forward to see what they had found. The bodies were curled together, Karen on top of Diane.

Bellingham's setting could hardly be lovelier. The hills rise out of the water and the mountains rise out of the hills, green-on-green going to white-on-white. The harbor is a fjord. The hills are rich in pastures, rivers, and lakes. The breeze comes fresh from the ocean, and morning only begins when the sun lifts over Mount Baker and the Cascades. But in the name of Cha-wit-zit, the all too friendly Lummi Indian chief who in 1852 showed the white men where to put down their stakes, Bellingham is a blight on the horizon, an unfortunate tangle of three old towns that could only have been accomplished by men absorbed in other things. The courthouse alone denies all the natural graces. The streets are mainly bleak and dim. Much of the waterfront has been carved away to make effluent ponds for the pulp mill. The sky is vandalized by what Georgia-Pacific calls steam. And when, as frequently happens, some chemical event at the mill sours the air with the scent of the planet dying, the locals gamely say that that's how money smells. Down through the years, Bellingham has been a homely stepsister to Seattle, ninety miles to the south, but today there are two major oil refineries, a big aluminum plant, a university with ten thousand students on campus, and a lively tourist trade composed of skiers, boaters, and Canadian shoppers, for whom the city serves as a tame Tijuana—many bargains but not much fun. The Lummis who survive live on a reservation and tend to get in trouble when they come to town.

Even so, Bellingham looked just fine to Frank Salerno and Dudley Varney when they rolled into town in a rented car two days after Bianchi's arrest. Both men were homicide detectives—Salerno with the Los Angeles Sheriff's Office and Varney with the LAPD—and both had been members of the Hillside Strangler Task Force since its inception almost fourteen months before. The task force was so big and unstinting that it had long since outstripped its own bookeeping powers, so that no one could say anymore just how many hundreds of thousands of man-hours had gone into the hunt for the killer (or killers) who in a span of one hundred twenty-one days in the winter before had left at least ten women and girls dead on hillsides and roadsides in and around Los Angeles. At the height of its activity, the task force had included more than one hundred thirty investigators, and the feeling among them that an army had been mounted led many to speak of the hunt as a war.

Imagine—one hundred thirty detectives all working the same case. Cliques forming. Feelings getting hurt. The buddy system put to a terrible test. More than ten thousand clues poured in and were logged in the biggest law enforcement computer in the West. The county's top forensic pathologist, Dr. Thomas Noguchi, had a surfeit of specimens in his lab. There was a bank of twenty-four hotlines, unlimited overtime, the metro squad on call. In haircut money alone, the task force had outdone anything ever dreamt of by your average police department.

And yet for all of that and more, it had come up empty, and the frustration of having failed was made all the worse by the annoyance of working within a system so top-heavy with authority that it brought to mind the comic image of the Brazilian army: all gold braid and parades. Journeyman detectives were reduced to the role of "clue investigators," and to keep security tight their superiors made a point of keeping them ignorant of any detailed knowledge of how the murders were done. If this was war, this was Vietnam.

Of course it didn't help to be working in a city as crazy as L.A., where in the course of a quiet year about two dozen people wound up getting strangled. That was twenty-four out of the eight hundred or nine hundred murdered annually in other ways, so in a sense the task force had to be considered a PR move, a reply to media pressure that consumed much time and talent that could otherwise have gone to catching killers. Nor did it help to be working in a climate of such hysteria that every time the phone rang it was some woman saying, My boyfriend's weird; here's his name and address. And it certainly didn't help to be working in a city so estranged from the police that people who could have been helpful were hostile instead. All in all, it was a sorry call to duty, and it was hard on the troops involved.

Things might have gone smoother were it not for Daryl Gates. Gates had taken personal charge of the task force when he was still Ed Davis's loyal adjutant, and, when two months later the chief retired and Gates himself took over, he was so eager to make his mark that hardly a week went by without his calling a news conference—"a crowded news conference at Parker Center"—to announce some significant development, some promising arrest. Twice someone was arrested, called promising at a news conference, then released, and on a third occasion a dead man was named as a suspect. The Brobdingnagian task force lumbered along under the glare of the spotlights, under the pain of the work. Marriages suffered. The kids felt the strain. But nobody caught the strangler.

Then Bellingham called. Bellingham called not because the task force was sending bulletins and fliers to all Western states—security was far too tight to permit that. Bellingham called because, at 2 A.M.

on the night of Bianchi's arrest, Mangan and his detectives wrapped it up, and he went off to an all-night diner to talk things over with one of the men. Mangan recalled having met one of the strangler's victims. Mangan had been visiting a nun who was principal of the school the girl attended, and the father had happened by. After the girl was killed, the nun had written a sorrowful letter to Mangan, saying she wished that he was still in southern California and could do something to help. Now Mangan had seen two more victims, and the manner in which they were killed told him that Bianchi was no beginner. There was the absence of trauma, the cleaned-up crime scene, the bodies stuffed in the back of a car. In point of fact, the cul-de-sac where the bodies were found was actually on a hillside, and Bianchi had come to Bellingham not long after the last of the hillside stranglings. It was a long shot, and the men were tired, but before they went home, Mangan left word to get in touch with the task force first thing in the morning.

When the call came, it brought joy but little pride to the task force to discover that this same Kenneth A. Bianchi was listed in the computer as a suspect under clue numbers 6,111, 6,458, 7,598, and 7,745. The task force had received a tip a year before that Bianchi had a badge and handcuffs and lived near two of the victims; no one got around to checking it out. Another tip advised that Bianchi knew one of the victims, had been a neighbor of two others, and was a bitterly disappointed LAPD reject; the detective who interviewed him closed his report with "nothing to connect." The day after Kimberly Martin disappeared from the Tamarind Terrace apartments in Holly-wood, the detective who interviewed the building's tenants spoke to a man in apartment 329, Kenneth A. Bianchi, but neglected to follow the standard procedure and check his ID. Had he done so, he would have noticed that Bianchi's driver's license would have shown an address across the street from an earlier victim, and a check with the Department of Motor Vehicles would have yielded another address which the state now claims was the site of nine of the ten murders in which Bianchi was involved. The fabled computer, as it turned out, was just a storage bank, an electronic file cabinet, programmed to index information but not to analyze it. Unless one thought to ask Have we heard of this man before?, the computer would not say.

So Salerno and Varney didn't feel exactly like the New York Yankees as they pulled into town to compare notes with the pint-sized Bellingham PD, which, meter maids and all, could hardly have staffed the task force night shift. "I hope they didn't get the impression that we were the big guys coming up from the big city," Salerno says, remembering that day. "We were just there to get our feet on the ground and see what they had. And they had all the bases covered."

The task force detectives wound up spending much of the winter and spring in Bellingham, flying up the coast five or six times and generally staying a week or more. On their second visit, KVOS had their pictures on TV, and after that people waved and smiled when they saw them driving by. It was incredibly refreshing. They loved the people, loved the town, talked about retiring there some day. And of course it also felt good when the Bellingham detectives, searching Bianchi's house, came up with a ring that had once belonged to Yolanda Washington, the first of the Hillside Strangler victims.

The case against Bianchi had come to resemble a house with no windows. Nolte and Wight had statements up and down the line showing how he'd spent days setting the whole thing up, lying to this one, tricking that one, leaving his name and number, calling back. They had eyewitnesses who could put him at the house on Bayside and at the cul-de-sac about the time the murders were done. They found Karen's name on a note at Ken's house, and Ken's on a note at Karen's. They found Diane's coat hidden in the grass near the guard shack. At Bianchi's house, they found a list of nude models filched from the campus art department. They had a girl from the list who would say that, shortly before he was arrested, Bianchi called and politely canceled their evening appointment. The hillside stranglings hadn't stopped; they'd just moved north.

But the real mortar of the case was in the physical evidence, and that was Knudsen's triumph. A big, blond, assertive man, Knudsen at forty-seven had twenty-one years on the job, and the list of courses he'd taken around the country in the various investigative sciences was almost two pages long. He was the fingerprint man, the ID man, the evidence man, the crime-scene boss, the one who trained the others; and at the FBI crime labs in Washington, where Knudsen was a constant correspondent, he was thought to be as solid as they come. His domain was a basement evidence room that he himself had designed, and he kept it sealed tight as a bathysphere.

At the cul-de-sac, Knudsen made sure that freshly laundered sheets were draped over the gurneys to catch hairs and fibers when the bodies were lifted out of the car. At Bianchi's house, one of Knudsen's investigators took clothing into evidence, not failing to remember the lint brush. In the police garage, when he and Nolte went over Karen's Bobcat, Nolte noticed a fresh dent in the gas tank. It wasn't a scrape but the kind of dent that might result from the car's coming down on something hard and sharp, and since it wasn't caked with mud like the rest of the undercarriage, it must have happened on the car's last ride. Two men were sent out to the Catlow house to search the driveway, where under a cover of heather they found a large chunk of broken rock. The striations on the gas tank were a perfect match to the rock.

Knudsen then dragged Nolte back to the house to do a Knudsen-style hairs-and-fibers search. Because the ligature marks on the women's necks suggested that the strangler had been standing above and behind them, the detectives reasoned that he must have struck while following them down the stairs. He'd probably brought them in one at a time, telling the other to stay in the truck in case anything came over the radio. He'd killed them first, then raped them. Nolte ruined a good pair of trousers crawling around the stairway leading down into the basement, going over every tread and riser with magnifying glass and tweezers. In the end, Knudsen was happy. He had the kind of package he considered fit to ship.

Taken together with everything else, the FBI report that came back three weeks later had the look and feel of a twelve-foot fall from the gallows. Two Caucasian pubic hairs were found that were microscopically the same as pubic hairs in a sample taken from Kenneth Bianchi— one on the sheet in which Diane Wilder's body had been wrapped and the second in the sample from the stairwell. Three head hairs were found in the stairwell sample that matched those taken from Diane Wilder. Light-yellow nylon fibers identical to those in a sample from the carpets at the Bayside house were found on the two women's shoes and clothing, as well as on one shirt, a pair of pants, and a lint brush belonging to Kenneth Bianchi.

All in all, it was an impeccable piece of police work, and Varney and Salerno were left with little to do beyond showing their admiration for the men who put it together. The sophistication of these small-town detectives was impressive enough in itself, but what really made it striking was the cozy kind of lives they led. They didn't feel ostracized or traumatized or alienated—they felt right at home. They were hometown boys who were close to their parents and their children. Wight was big in Sea Scouts, Knudsen in school board and PTA. Nolte couldn't turn a corner without running into someone he'd known for twenty years. They didn't hang around together and they didn't hang around with other cops. Wight went scuba diving when he wasn't off running a charter. Knudsen took his camera up in the mountains and hills. Nolte plotted trips to see ghost towns and desert flowers. "This is God's country," Wight would say without blinking. Nolte would mention that he wasn't in police work for the spotlight or the glamour. Knudsen would toss in that, every time he went somewhere on vacation, he came back asking why the hell he'd left. Then he'd get around to saying that his place down on the Nooksack River was in sight of the house he'd lived in as a boy.

Mangan had the task force detectives out to his house for dinner. He lived on five wooded acres with a pond and a stream that had trout in it, and there were wild ducks out yakking on the lawn. Across the road was a cattle ranch, out back a dairy farm. One of the five horses grazing down by the pond had won a ribbon at the fair. The chief was nuts about his little tractor. Charlotte, his whirlwind wife, grew vegetables and flowers, groomed and fed the horse, bought beef by the side, put up all the ketchup, apple sauce, pickles, and jam the family used in a year. Terry was president of the parish council. Charlotte baked one hundred loaves of zucchini bread and sold them at the church bazaar. Megan was taking ballet. Sean was learning the piano. "Gee, it's great living in the country," Terry would say.

Race all that against Daryl Gates' scene, even though Gates, of course, had the spotlight and rated a place in the *Guinness Book of World Records* as the world's highest-paid police chief. Mangan's job brought other compensations. He got along great with the mayor and the district attorney. He was getting no complaints from the gay community, the black community, the Hispanic community—not even from the Lummis. He had no PR problems, no affirmative-action problems, no one demanding a citizen's review board, no Eulia Love. (In Bellingham's history, no officer has ever killed a citizen, nor has any been killed in the line of duty.) Mangan didn't have a headquarters staff so splintered into fiefdoms and emirates that to understand its subtleties required the wisdom of a Talleyrand. He didn't have troops who acted like the city's own Rhodesian constabulary or subalterns who lacked only plumed hats to express their vanity. What he had instead was a highly professional organization of unassuming men on a first-name basis with each other and lots of folks in town, and, just to make sure it stayed that way, he and the rest of his staff reported for duty periodically in patrolman's blue and spent a full shift out working the streets with the men.

You could write off the swift capture of Bianchi to good luck, simple procedures, and the basic decency of the town. Without runaways and drifters to prey on, Bianchi had to go after his victims in a way that resulted in his leaving a trail. The girls he went after weren't 'lude queens and floaters—they were girls who left notes for each other and remembered to feed the cat. The tips the police got weren't pranks or lies or freakish delusions—they were helpful tips from people who noticed things and cared. But once Nolte, Wight, and the others started building their case, they were unimpaired by the attitudes and postures that so often gummed up good police work in L.A. Bianchi didn't strike them as one of their own kind. They weren't impressed to be dealing with someone who was neither a dingbat nor a doper. They didn't glaze over at the sight of his police academy mustache and give the man a slide. They just went ahead and calmly did their job on him, and it made you wonder if the small-town approach to policing wasn't the solution after all. Could Varney himself imagine working in a place like Bellingham?

"Oh, yes. Yes. Very much so. Yes. You're damn right. Yes. I sure can. No problem being satisfied up there."

"Perhaps there is some part of Ken with whom I have not yet talked. If there is, let the right hand lift."

The right had slowly lifted.

As evidence mounted against him, Bianchi had continued to deny any recollection of the murders. He said he had no memory of any killing, and he said that even to Dean Brett, his own attorney, appointed by the court to defend him. Brett had practiced in Bellingham since leaving Stanford Law in 1972, and this was not his first homicide case. It was, however, his first case of any kind in which he found himself, at least initially, completely unable to get through to his client. Brett didn't doubt that the prosecution's case would be devastating, nor did he have any quarrel with the way the police had put it together. He saw Terry Mangan in church every Sunday and held him and his department in high regard. But he did believe that Bianchi's amnesia was quite genuine, and he saw hypnosis as the one available means to lift the veil. To accomplish this, he called on Dr. John G. Watkins, a psychology professor at the University of Montana, who was also an internationally recognized hypnotist and a widely published authority on dissociative reactions—the psychiatric term for the process of the mind that blocks off control over one's actions and accounts for both certain forms of amnesia and the existence of multiple personalities within one mind. Bianchi failed the arm-drop suggestibilty test and proved to be a difficult subject for hypnosis. But after forty-five minutes of trying, it looked to Watkins like he had him under. Working on intuition as much as experience, Watkins invited the right hand to lift, and the right hand lifted, and a whole new person was there.

"The changes in total personality were such that even the most seasoned actor could hardly have malingered them," Watkins wrote after the sesson. "Mildness changed to violence; reticence to talk about the crimes changed to bragging about them; soft voice changed to shouting; respectful words in talking about women changed to crude obscenities; posture and gestures were different; good use of English changed to short, ignorant verbalisms; solid cognitive reasoning now became concrete, childish exclamations. The personality changed in all modalities—perceptual, intellectual, emotional and motor."

In sessions with Watkins and two other psychiatrists, four personalities or shards of personalities wrestled their way to the surface. There was Billy, the liar, conniver, and thief, who postured and pimped and sent off for bogus credentials and sometimes caused Ken to sign "Ph.D." after his name. There was a second Ken, thoughtful, brooding, cautious, deeply perplexed by the circumstances of the Ken that everybody knew. There was "ISH" (the psychiatrist's acronym for "internal self-helper"), a powerless entity without deceit or guile, who introduced himself only as "Ken's friend." And then there was Steve, Steve Walker, the truly bad apple, the one who confessed to all the murders and said that Angelo Buono, a cousin of Ken's, had helped him out on many of the murders—in fact, had even led the way. Strangler, rapist, foul-mouth, snitch, Steve dealt strictly in the impermissible, and if he and Ken shared the same body, it was only proof that opposites attract.

Every time he emerged in the sessions, Steve made the same entry—"cussing, stormy, angry, complaining." He said that he and Angelo had just been "shootin' the shit" when they hit on the idea of picking up a girl and strangling her, just to see what it felt like. He called his victims "cunts" and said that killing them was "no fuckin' big deal." But mainly he raged against Ken and took cruel pleasure in the clever way he'd set Ken up to be caught. "I wanted him out of the way so fuckin' bad that I left myself a nice little trail," he boasted, "and I left him a nice little trail, and I thought I had the asshole cooked."

The doctors who discovered Steve, Billy, and the others were in accord as to their origins. Ken had created Steve as an imaginary playmate when, as a child of nine, he would hide under the bed to escape the whims of his mother. Four years later, when Ken's father died, Billy was invented to provide Ken with a charming new face to hide his heartbreak. Steve by this time had slipped into Ken's unconsciousness and become the pocket of rage that festered until it found release in the murder of Yolanda Washington; all the killings that followed were Steve's attempts to escape the dominion of Ken. Ken was amnesic of periods when Steve was in control and unaware of his existence. When Billy surfaced in Ken's actions, Ken would remember what he'd done but think it the result of his own compulsions. Ken loved Kelli and Ryan, their infant son, born six days after the last of the hillside murders; Billy liked Kelli too, even though he wasn't much of a husband; Steve, of course, hated both Kelli and the kid. Bianchi was not a person—he was a caucus, and every man wanted the floor. All except ISH, who stood helplessly by, rueing and remembering.

Curiously, some of the experts who studied the tests administered to each of the personalities without knowing where they came from or meeting Bianchi himself saw Ken and Steve as dead ringers psychologically. The tone was different, but the content was the same. Other experts disagreed, one saying that while Ken's Rorschach was that of a fairly normal and pleasant person, Steve's was the sickest thing she'd seen in forty years of practice. The tests were submitted to computer analysis and Bianchi came out a type 300.1 psychoneurotic—"hysteria, dissociation reaction"—the same diagnosis reached by two of the six analysts who saw him. Two others found him to be insane, but not for the same reasons, while the final two doubted that he was ever actually hypnotized and thought that Steve and Billy were invented right there in the Whatcom County Jail. After sixty hours of videotaped interviews, thirty-five more hours of sessions recorded but not filmed, every available test, and the accumulation of all of Bianchi's school and medical records, they sent the court almost four hundred pages of expert opinion showing them divided on even such questions as whether or not Bianchi's IQ of 116 made him smart enough to fool a psychiatrist. Had the case ever gone to trial, it had all the promise of being one of those learned wrangles that only succeed at convincing twelve more people that Freud must have really been nuts. But the interviews did provide the police with the name of Angelo Buono. And they also left the authorities keenly aware that, when all was said and done, the score was 4 to 2 that Bianchi was insane.

Knudsen was the man behind the videotape machine, and it made him gnash his teeth to see Bianchi winning so many rounds with the shrinks. To Knudsen's mind, nine out of ten psychiatrists were in the business of guiding killers away from the gallows—they'd say anything to convince you that the poor guy's mother made him do it. Looking through a one-way window, listening to the doctor cluck away as Ken recited all the horrendous things *his* mother had done, Knudsen would have to stifle an urge to burst in on them with a few well-chosen words about *his* mother: she'd done the same damn things, and he'd survived.

But of course she really hadn't. She hadn't dragged him around to every clinic she could find, then thrown a fit when the doctors told her that nothing was wrong with his wee-wee. She hadn't held his hand to the stove to discourage him from stealing. She hadn't forced him to go to his father's funeral wearing his father's shoes.

Knudsen, Wight, and Nolte would sit down together to watch the tapes: Kenny Bianchi starring in *As the World Turns*. Bianchi was fully aware of the camera (Brett being the one who insisted it be there), and the detectives had no doubt that he was using the doctors to play to them. Raging or polite, Ken or Steve, in a trance or not, he was full of helpful hints to get them hopping down blind alleys. Wight considered Bianchi about as good a con artist as he'd ever seen, but Nolte's view was different: To him, Bianchi was one of those people whom the deeper you looked into the shallower they got.

All were agreed that the man was an old-fashioned, foot-to-the-floorboards liar. He'd tell you anything to win your sympathy, and when one lie caught up with him he'd just tell another to wash it away. For example, he told Kelli he had cancer. Kelli had let him know that she'd checked up on one of his stories, and he hadn't been where he said. So Ken just reached back for a better curve ball and looked into the eyes of the woman who was the mother of his baby son and told her, Hey, I didn't want to say anything because I knew how much you'd worry, but the thing is I've got this cancer, and I was down in the hospital taking cobalt. And Kelli was so stunned by the news and so touched by his courage in not telling her before that all she could do was dissolve in tears and pray that the cancer would be cured. Only there was no cure for his kind of cancer.

One by one, they'd kicked away all his alibis. When he finally broke down and admitted that his story about driving around to get his head together on the night of the murders was a lie, he said that he'd really been out with another woman and hadn't mentioned it before because Kelli's feelings would be hurt; he was just toughing it out in jail to spare poor Kelli the pain. So Wight got on a plane and flew to Grand Forks, North Dakota, and there he found the girl Ken claimed to have been out with, and he came back with a statement saying none of it was true. And when Bianchi learned that he was fresh out of alibis again, he went to his last-ditch defense: he pretended to slip under the spell of the psychiatrists and came up with his old playmate, evil Steve.

At least that's how the detectives saw it. They had constructed a detailed profile of Bianchi as he was known in Bellingham, and no one among the dozens of friends and fellow workers they talked to had ever seen a sign of Billy or Steve. The person they knew was Ken—earnest, engaging, a little too eager to please. Besides, if Ken was supposed to be amnesic of periods when Steve was in control, where were all the blackouts? Bianchi had gone to a great deal of trouble setting the murders up, which meant that the strangler inside him was in control much of the time. But through it all, he was conscientious Ken, functioning well at a complicated job, giving no one an impression of mental slippage.

Still, when four out of six doctors agree, you'd better have your facts together if you're going to dispute them. Bianchi's insanity plea had made moot all the evidence they had that proved he killed the women; now the challenge was to prove that he knew what he was doing. Brett was serious and solid, the kind of lawyer who could get the most out of an insanity defense. He would make great use of Bianchi's school and hospital records—"mother needs help," one of them said. He would also underscore Bianchi's compliant behavior at the time of his arrest, espeically the way he freely gave the police permission to search his home, even though the basement was full of stolen goods. Telephones, chain saws, jackets, canned salmon and canned shrimp, tools that had never been used. Even a rural jury might readily believe that a thief who was crazy would welcome search of his cache, and that together with Bianchi's straight and likable manner might be enough to soften up some jurors for the shrinks. Nolte and

Wight had their work cut out for them. Together, they headed back east, and the Rochester police met them at the airport.

This was an agreeable time for the two detectives. They were thriving on their absorption in a fascinating case, and it was pleasant as well to match up with their colleagues in bigger cities and come away feeling like pros. Rochester was no different than L.A.—smooth and friendly, with the ritual shows of respect policemen accord each other. Men were assigned to drive them around the city. The department's files were open to them. Over dinner and drinks they swapped stories with New York detectives and were praised for the work they'd done.

Rochester was where Bianchi had spent most of his boyhood and where Billy and Steve were said to have been born. The transcripts of the psychiatric interviews were full of references to Bianchi's childhood friends, some of whom he said might know him better as Steve than Ken. Nolte and Wight scoured the transcripts for all the names they could find, and, although they knew that finding Steve might well mean losing Ken, they did go looking—"for blackouts, time lapses, and black lapses, fits of anger, violence, anything." No one was aware of the headaches Bianchi said he'd suffered as a child. No one was aware of Steve. Wight interviewed Bianchi's mother and came away with the impression that she'd done a hell of a job raising him "in the I-talian tradition." There were no blackouts, no seizures, no violence, just a long habit of lying. Ken's mother, Wight noted, was relieved to learn that he didn't really have cancer. As for the story of the father's shoes, Ken, the detectives reasoned, was probably embroidering on something his mother had said—"Now that your father has gone, you'll have to step into his shoes." But even if she had made him wear the goddamn shoes, what was so bad about that? Lots of kids would have been proud.

All along, many in Bellingham had felt that Bianchi was essentially a California phenomenon, and the prospect of a long and complex trial was not relished by those who looked ahead to its cost. So there was little outrage in Whatcom County when Bianchi made his deal with the authorities, agreeing to plead guilty to seven of his murders and to testify against cousin Angelo in exchange for being spared the threat of the gallows. Mangan and the prosecutor agreed that the plea bargain would remove a major millstone from their necks, make Buono's prosecution possible, and spare the victims' families the ordeal of reliving their losses through the long series of appeals that inevitably follow a death sentence—if a death sentence was returned, which no Whatcom County jury had ever done. Moreover, Washington State's death-penalty statute had never stood the test of Supreme Court review, and few thought much of its chances. No matter how they went about it, Bianchi was unlikely to suffer a penalty harsher than the one he was accepting: a minimum term of twenty-six years eight months in prison.

Nolte, Wight, and Knudsen could see the logic of it too, but that didn't make them feel any better. Their beautiful case would never see a courtroom, and all they could do about it was console themselves with manly metaphors. It was training for a fight that gets canceled. It was landing the king of all salmon, then losing it off the deck. But then Nolte and Wight flew down to Los Angeles and saw Angelo Buono in court, and that was enough to change their minds. Buono's was the coldest presence Wight had ever felt; just standing next to the man for a minute made it suddenly no problem to pack Bianchi up and ship him south. Nolte and Wight accompanied him on the plane ride. Ken, as always, was pleasant and polite. Mainly they talked about the weather.

"In the long string of murders he committed, [Bianchi] demonstrated that he had mastered the science of law enforcement and that he was a better policeman than any policeman on the force. . . . So, in the process of achieving his victory over the female authority figure by killing her surrogates, he also vanquished the male authority figure by eluding the police . . ."

Such was the opinion of Dr. Saul J. Faerstein of Beverly Hills, one of the six who examined Bianchi in Bellingham, and for a time it squared exactly with the opinion of the police. Faerstein thought Bianchi was faking hypnosis, had dreamed up his multiple personalities, and was actually a sociopath with "a sexual deviation disorder with features of sexual sadism and violence." But now that Bianchi has in effect become the lead man of the Hillside Strangler Task Force, the police are less inclined to present him to the public as a pathological liar. Unless his testimony is believed, there is little chance of convicting Buono. When they jury is shown the videotapes, they must accept the authenticity of Billy, Steve, and ISH.

This turnabout makes Wight and Nolte powerful witnesses for the Buono defense; if they are called, they will have to say that in ten months of searching the country they were rarely able to turn up evidence of Bianchi speaking a truthful word. They will have to report that the state's star witness is a man who would delude his own wife and mother into believing he was dying of cancer. They will have to say that Bianchi's friends and family never had the slightest intimation of Billy or Steve. The same testimony that might well have brought a death sentence for Bianchi in Washington could, in California, just as easily bring an acquittal for Buono.

Buono's jury may also be hard pressed to appreciate the moral necessity of granting Bianchi immunity in at least five of his murders in order to secure his dubious testimony against a cousin who on balance seems the lesser of two evils. Bianchi was the one who knew all about police work, who falsified his identity, and who demonstrated in Bellingham that he needed no help in his stranglings. Buono all the while worked in his auto-upholstery shop in Glendale, tucking and rolling, calling himself Angelo Buono, and after cousin Ken left town there were no more hillside murders. The concept of immunity is strained in such cases, and a jury might well be forgiven if it deemed it unfair to punish Buono worse than Bianchi.

The Buono prosecution was not helped when KNBC broadcast some of the Bellingham videotapes in December. Nice Ken and wicked Steve came off like caricatures of good and evil. Nor was it helped by two week-long series of reports by Jim Mitchell of KNXT, the first documenting the floundering of the famous task force and the second raising the possibility that Bianchi killed two Rochester girls before coming to Los Angeles. The trial, which probably won't begin much before the end of the year, promises to be a protracted affair. Buono's six lawyers hope to raise a million-dollar defense fund through the sale of FREE ANGELO buttons and other such enticements.

The detectives continue to thrive on the rich associations the case brought into their lives. Nolte plans to visit his task-force friends on a visit to Los Angeles this spring. Salerno is thinking about retiring in Bellingham. Everyone has the highest regard for each other.

It's a shame, of course, that he had to kill all those women—but why not look on the bright side? Would Timothy Cardinal Manning have otherwise paid him a Christmas visit? Would he be riding around in unmarked cars showing the detectives how the murders were done, showing them how to be good detectives? Would he suddenly be blessed with so many brand-new best friends—lawyers, psychiatrists, producers, agents—the kind of people he only pretended to know before it all began? It may be true that the gates will not open for Kenneth Bianchi before September 12, 2005. But that is not to say that many doors won't open well before.

Ken, as they say, has a whole lot going for him. Already he has turned down the first offers for the book, television, and motion picture rights to the story of his life; better offers are sure to come. With so many prison years ahead of him, he might be better off if he hadn't killed a black girl and two young Chicanas, but, then, isolation can work wonders. Likable, friendly, much favored by his lawyers, his doctors, his keepers at the jail, Ken stands a good chance of winding up a sort of Birdman of Alcatraz. He wants to become a lay Franciscan, and to purify his soul, he takes Holy Communion every morning.

1980

# pimps and

# poets

# The Case Against
# F. Lee Bailey

The day that Patty's lung collapsed, F. Lee Bailey flew down to Los Angeles in his twin-engine Turbo Commander to give a luncheon address at the Proud Bird Restaurant, arriving in good time to meet his hosts of the day, a management group from the Mattel toy company. Bailey looked formidable and fit in his inevitable three-piece suit, and considering that only the morning before he had stood in court to hear his wan young client sentenced to thirty-five years in prison, he was also in excellent humor. When a round of applause from the toy makers drew him front and center, he opened with a Dino-style booze joke, then coasted into a curious anecdote from the pages of his fabled casebook, a story about appearing for the first time before the Supreme Court and meeting Thurgood Marshall, who was then solicitor general.

*On September 18, 1975, nineteen months after she was kidnapped by the Symbionese Liberation Army, Patricia Hearst was arrested for bank robbery and illegal use of a gun. After a legal defense that she later called "disastrous," Patty was convicted and sent to federal prison. She served twenty-two months, her sentence commuted by President Jimmy Carter.*

". . . and Mr. Marshall, who was always a bit of a wit, came up and introduced himself, and he said, 'I understand you're the young hotshot lawyer.' I said, 'I want to thank you, Mr. Solicitor General.' And he said, 'Well, I'm the head nigger.' And I said, 'Well, we have a gentleman up in Massachusetts who's about to replace Senator Salton-stall and be a United States senator, which is higher than a mere solicitor general, and he says that he's the head nigger.' And then Marshall pointed to the bench and said, 'Next time there's a seat up there, I'm going to get it. And then I'm going to be *forever* the head nigger.'"

The story got a laugh. It got a couple of laughs, a couple of increasingly edgy laughs, it seemed to me. And because the story also seemed as improbable as it was tasteless, I made a note to call Justice Marshall to see if he recalled the meeting in the same terms Bailey did. Two days later, I reached him in his Supreme Court chambers, and at his invitation I read him Bailey's words, as transcribed from a tape I had made at the luncheon. There was a pause. Then Justice Marshall spoke.

"That's the most deliberate lie I ever heard," Marshall said. "Number one, can you imagine me at any time in the Supreme Court talking with anybody? Number two, I don't remember ever having talked to F. Lee Bailey. I might have met him and shook his hand, but I don't even remember that. I know I've never discussed Ed Brooke with him or anybody else. And I've never called myself a head nigger at any time."

"So the story is a total fabrication?"

"Total. Complete. Not one word of it is true."

It might be said that to go out on the banquet circuit and tell a Stepin Fetchit joke about Thurgood Marshall demonstrates a certain lack of judicial reserve in a lawyer—especially a lawyer so recently obliged to retreat to telling Patty Hearst's dad: Don't worry, Randy, I'll take this all the way to the Supreme Court. And if the story was not only a slur but also a canard, it seemed at least possible that the legend of F. Lee Bailey might be due for immediate review. Bailey's performance at the Hearst trial had disappointed even friendly observers who admired him still for his work in the Sheppard case, the Coppolino trials, and the court-martial of Captain Medina; but Bailey himself had made the verdict all the more a personal Waterloo by winning the case in the press before trying it in the courtroom, scoffing at the government's evidence on television, telling *Time* for its cover story, "The fact is, it's not a difficult case."

Before contemplating the many criticisms of his debacle in San Francisco, however, I thought it wise to let Bailey know what Justice Marshall had said about his funny story. After calling a dozen numbers in the East, I finally reached him at his home in Massachusetts. I told him the justice's reaction. There was a pause. Then Bailey spoke.

"You're kidding," he said.

"No."

"Oh, for Christ's sake. Well, I'm sorry he doesn't recollect it."

"He said he never sat with any private lawyers when he was solicitor general. He said the story's just an invention."

"Well, it's not an invention," Bailey said. His voice had the ring of complete assurance. "I'm sorry the Supreme Court justice feels that way. I was about to ask him to speak at an important matter. I was introduced to him and we did have the banter." Then Bailey said, "I think it would be distasteful if you published it."

"I don't know, Lee," I said. "It seems to me that it's a kind of significant little story."

"Well, maybe. Now that the man is sitting on the bench, I suppose it could be embarrassing even though it was banter. But I don't retreat from it. It's most unfortunate that he's taken umbrage at it. I recall it very well because I don't go to the Supreme Court all that often. That was one of two times, and the second time he was on the bench. I recall very specifically sitting with him. He introduced himself, and the story as I told it was just about the way it happened. I wouldn't be surprised, although God knows what, if Ralph Yarborough would recall the incident. We were sitting three abreast right next to the podium. Yarborough was on my right and Marshall was on my left, as I recall, although it could have been the reverse."

"Maybe I better ask Yarborough," I said.

"Perhaps you should. If he says it didn't happen you'll have to consider whether or not you want to publish it and get into a pissing contest."

Senator Yarborough was at work in his law office in Austin. It was Easter Sunday, but the former Texas Democrat had campaign debts left over from his defeat in 1972 and was intent on seeing them paid. "That explains your catching me in my office on Easter," he said, a little contritely. I was embarrassed to appear in need of third-person testimony to shore up Justice Marshall's word, but I told Senator Yarborough both sides of the story. He remembered meeting Bailey that day, he said. He remembered the long lines of tourists attracted by word that the Sheppard case was about to be argued. But he could not remember exchanging any words with Bailey, and he said that Marshall had been sitting on the other side of the podium. As for the story itself, he had no doubt.

"Never heard of it in my life and don't believe it," he said. "I do not believe it's true and the reason is—well, if Thurgood Marshall says it's a lie, I'd believe him. But another reason I don't believe it's true is that I've never heard such language from Thurgood Marshall. It's wholly out of character. It's not the way he talks. I don't believe the tale. Furthermore, I didn't hear of it, of course. I never heard the story before. Bailey played hell giving me as a reference because I never heard of the thing, and I just don't believe it."

Presumably, Bailey would be slow to propose a pissing contest unless he considered himself well equipped to win it. But one cannot avoid questioning the public conduct of a man who thrusts himself so relentlessly into the public eye. Having emerged from a nagging criminal fraud charge in Florida last summer—the case was dismissed for want of a speedy trial—Bailey entered the Hearst case like Ali coming out of retirement, and his immensely successful pretrial media blitz foretold a masterful approach to another Trial of the Century—the fourth or fifth in his sixteen-year career. His most generous appraisal of prosecutor James Browning's courtroom skills was "rusty"—hardly a match for the country's best-known lawyer, whose client, by the way, was said to have passed her polygraph exams, as the press learned on the eve of the trial. Experienced courtroom reporters concurred with Bailey's opinion that he was riding a certain winner.

But when defense attorney Leonard Weinglass won an illegal-search motion excluding more than a thousand pieces of evidence seized by the FBI for use against his clients, Bill and Emily Harris—an incriminating cache that included the carbine carried on the bank job—some doubts arose as to why Bailey had neglected to attempt to do the same in Patty's behalf. Then Patty took the stand and had to resort to taking the Fifth Amendment forty-two times to cover her activities in the year before her arrest. Then, during the final week of the defense case, Bailey also had an untimely commitment to conduct a criminal-law seminar in Las Vegas; frowns deepened when his solution was to fly back and forth every night for a week, strapping himself into the Turbo Commander around five every evening and getting back to San Francisco around midnight. Near the end, he appeared to go disastrously overboard in his cross-examination of the government's key psychiatrist witness, Dr. Joel Fort of San Francisco, the man who called Patty "the queen of the SLA." Bailey kept Fort on the stand for more than six hours, prying into why his family name had been changed from its Jewish original to Fort, denouncing Fort's credentials, even dancing grotesquely with the much-abused ghost of Lenny Bruce (whom Fort had seen as a patient). But in the end, Fort left the stand without suffering a wound, and the government's rebuttal case proceeded with gathering momentum until, at the end, only Bailey expressed shock at the outcome.

More than anything else, however, it was Bailey's final argument that made his services to Patty a terribly expensive going-away present from her folks. Browning's summation had been a 19,000-word marshaling of the facts in evidence—facts documented by movie films, tape recordings, pages from an anarchist's hand-written notebook, an Olmec monkey. Bailey came back with a 6,500-word free-style ramble marred by inexplicable references to the personal heroism of G. Gordon Liddy, an old best-seller, his love of flying, his preference for military courts—many things, in fact, except a portrait of Patty that could be believed.

The man the *Los Angeles Times* had called "Mr. Overwhelming" in the first month of the trial had simply lost to the man widely pictured as a stumbling, bumbling Ichabod Crane.

After the trial he said that the "hostility against Patty Hearst when I took the case a week after her capture was awful, just awful," adding that by the time she took the stand the balance was just beginning to tip the other way. This was the mirror image of the trial the jury saw; all the jurors who spoke to the press afterward said they wanted to believe in Patty's innocence; some wept and vomited as the guilty votes mounted; "We felt overwhelming sympathy for her," one said, "but then, at some point in everybody's mind, the sympathy was outweighed by the evidence"; at least one juror said he felt let down by Bailey—that the defense hadn't been there.

I was eager to hear what Bailey would have to say about these criticisms, but first I had to listen to the rest of his Proud Bird speech to the toy makers. Throughout it he displayed what seemed like a deep ambivalence toward his craft—praising court-martial law, British law, every kind of law but his own. But Bailey gives at least fifty speeches a year—according to his public-relations man he ranks up there with Ralph Nader and Dick Gregory on the lecture circuit—and he handled himself well in this one, providing a number of insights on the trial of his own volition when the well-mannered audience failed to ask. He was applauded warmly time and again, and the biggest laugh came when he related what he called "the lecture" that is given to "your ordinary, run-of-the-mill accused" when one such appears at his Boston law offices with retainer fee in hand:

"Sir, you have just retained what in our view is one of the most agile, professional, experienced criminal-law firms in the United States. Even at this moment, with your retainer in hand, I have dispatched to the field seasoned investigators who will ferret out each fact and circumstance that may be of aid to us in persuading the court of the righteousness of your cause, and at the same time eggheads from the Harvard Law School are proceeding apace to the world's best library, where, starting with Blackstone, they will research every statute and decision that might militate in your legal favor. And when the trial begins, the fancy footwork that you see in the courtroom will leave the air sparkling above the jury box at the close of each day. Meanwhile, continue with your plans to escape . . . "

I wondered if the story would get a smile from Patty, who was said to be resting comfortably after her forty-five-minute tension pneumothorax operation. Escape was, in fact, about all that remained to her. She had implicated seventeen people in her testimony, and now that she stood convicted she was ready to talk some more. She even named Wendy Yoshimura, a friend who had been kind, as an accomplice in a Sacramento bank robbery where a woman had been killed. Patty's word was without value, perhaps, but every prosecutor from San Diego to Philadelphia was ready to lend an ear. It was hard to imagine how she could have fared any worse with a Squeaky Fromme see-no-evil defense.

After the speech, Bailey hurried through the crowd to a waiting Fleetwood. I tagged along and soon found myself alone with him in the large backseat, headed for the Century Plaza Hotel. Bailey's aura of total self-assurance is an impressive personal accomplishment. Just looking at him, you know that here is a man whose house has both indoor and outdoor swimming pools. He scanned the franchised landscape along the San Diego freeway as I served up questions that seemed to turn into soft hanging curves as they crossed the small distance between us. We talked about his company, the Enstrom Helicopter Corporation of Menominee, Michigan, where Ernie Medina, the vindicated My Lai commanding officer, now serves as plant manager. Bailey said that he spent about one thousand hours a year in the air, all but three hundred or so at the controls of his own aircraft. That alone, I calculated, amounted to what most men would consider a half-time job—an average of twenty hours a week just flying. I remarked that in addition to his corporate duties, his lecturing, his writing (a third Bailey book, about flying, is scheduled to appear in June), and the odd jury trial, he must sometimes ask himself if he might not be spreading it a little thin.

"Certainly," he answered. "And the answer usually comes back yes."

When I asked why his closing argument had been so brief, so unresponsive to the evidence many jurors said had counted most, Bailey reacted as though I was the last of a trainload of morons who'd been pestering him for weeks with the same question.

"The problem with the final argument," he said with a heavy sigh, "is that it was done in a straitjacket. Browning was sitting there with the power to rebut, and a great many things I could have argued— that might have looked appealing on the surface—could have been devastated in rebuttal. I just had to stay away from it. The jury was either going to consider her a kidnap victim trying to survive, or they were going to consider her a very bad girl who had been doing bad things for a year and a half after her trauma. And we knew that was the choice. In fact, when the jury went out, the foreman said, 'I don't suppose we have much to deliberate. We're all here to acquit.' One of the women suggested they take an immediate vote, and they did, and it was seven-to-five for conviction, with mostly women voting guilty."

I reminded Bailey that his wife, Lynda, had been quoted as saying, "Oh, he left out so much!" Perhaps that suggested that he had forgotten some things he meant to say?

Bailey shook his head: negative. "She was troubled by that, because her idea was to get up and make all kinds of suggestions. She did not appreciate the nature of the rebuttal argument that I knew Browning had ready, and it would have been a corker. He's limited in his rebuttal to what I say, and as I found out time and again during the trial, when you open the door with an argument, you invite someone to talk through it with material that would otherwise be improper. Had I raised the fact that she kept the Olmec monkey for reasons other than having affection for Willie Wolfe, Browning certainly would have been quick to point out that there was no evidence to substantiate that. That's calling attention to her silence. Whether he would have gone far enough to point that out, I don't know, but I could easily have provoked him into calling attention to the fact that she did not retake the stand. And the reason she didn't is because I didn't want her taking the Fifth Amendment anymore."

Laughter spilled from the receiver when I called Browning's office in San Francisco the next day to inquire as to the nature of the unplayed corker. "That's just Bailey's track-covering," a prosecutor said. "We covered the waterfront in our summation. The judge advised us in open court that we were expected to give a full-fledged argument, that there wouldn't be any sandbagging. So there was nothing left. There was no door to be opened—it was all hanging out there."

A week after the trial, four senior members of the San Francisco bar appeared at a Press Club forum which began with the question "What was the weak point of the Hearst defense?" Vincent Hallinan, whose son Kayo had served briefly as Patty's attorney after her arrest, lost no time answering it:

"No amount of mischance, negligence, stupidity, or idiocy could have loused the case up worse than the way it was loused up. A case is won by meticulous and conscientious preparation. By finding everything that is to be found. By finding the Olmec monkey in Patty

Hearst's properties, by finding out what she had to say about the young man who was accused afterward of having raped her.

"What we have in this case is flamboyance. Showing off."

In obvious anger, Hallinan carried on for several minutes in the same spirit, winding up with a word of advice for the peripatetic Bailey:

"Unless the pickings in your own county are unduly sparse, refrain from foraging in foreign fields."

Bailey had followed his usual practice of requesting clearance for takeoff soon after the verdict came in, but Al Johnson, his boyhood hockey chum and law partner, was in the audience and he rose to stick up for the boss. "I consider those remarks intemperate, completely unprofessional, not worthy of any lawyer," he said, going on to accuse the senior Hallinan of several varieties of malice. It was Hallinan, however, who got in the last word.

"If you're going to give a client a story to tell," he said, "for Christ's sake give them one that can be believed."

In the press, the moral dismemberment of Patty continued while she lay in her hospital bed. She named more names. She confessed to a number of crimes for which she had not been charged. Al Johnson, who since the verdict had replaced Bailey as chief spokesman for the defense, said Patty hoped to study law or journalism; she had developed, it appeared, a masochistic fascination for the two estates that had served her the most cruelly. Bailey, meanwhile, had put a handsome distance between himself and San Francisco. He turned up in Bermuda, in Boston, in Washington, Los Angeles, Detroit. He appeared before a jammed breakfast gathering at the National Press Club and said the Justice Department, in its zeal to punish Patty, was risking innocent citizens' lives by impeding the FBI from arresting many people "only Patty can put away."

This appeared to be a clear attempt on Bailey's part to force up the market on Patty's damaged credibility. But it also seemed a bit reckless, alerting the underground to the urgency the defense was attaching to her desperate intentions to tell all. In the Fleetwood, I asked Bailey if he didn't think he was waving a red flag in the face of danger.

"What red flag?"

"Talking about people only Patty can put away."

"Certainly it's not a red flag. They know who they are. I'm not telling them anything." The sights along the freeway continued to hold his gaze.

"Yeah, but aren't you indicating she has future plans to testify against all kinds of people?"

"Um-hum. That's what they get for bombing her house. She's convinced they're not going to leave her alone. She really doesn't have an alternative."

As long as Patty remains in jail, Bailey said, the physical risk to her is not prohibitive. "The in-custody situation is really the better of several possibilities. You move her to another country secretly and you probably can't keep it secret very long. Or you can put her in a special section of the institution. The ability of this particular group to get an inmate to go in and sacrifice himself for the purpose of knocking off Patty is not very good. Not as good as organized crime might be able to come up with. But there's a continuing chance, no question about it. You can always slip something into her food."

It was a novel argument: as long as Patty stayed in prison, she was better off than she could ever have been had Bailey won her an acquittal.

When Patty was whisked in and out of Los Angeles to be arraigned on eleven state felony charges a week after the trial, Randolph Hearst was intercepted by reporters who wanted to know if he was content with Bailey's performance. Hearst said he'd just have to stick with Bailey's track record.

Bailey's criminal-law practice is without doubt the most dispersed in the country—he tries cases everywhere, and it is difficult to gain a clear impression of just how successful he is. Moreover, "winning" at his game is difficult to define, since in some cases any result short of death at the hands of a lynch mob must be looked upon as a victory of a kind. In *The Defense Never Rests,* Bailey's first best-seller, he estimates his acquittal rate at between sixty and seventy percent. While riding in the Fleetwood, I asked him if those figures still held, and he said by and large they still did.

Bailey was, of course, 0-and-1 in San Francisco. The last two clients before Patty had, by grim coincidence, both been sentenced in Fort Wayne, Indiana, on the same day, January 16 of this year. Bailey had pretrial motions to argue in San Francisco, so he flew into Fort Wayne on the Turbo Commander just long enough to stand for sentencings before heading back for the coast. The U.S. attorney there said he hadn't been able to resist kidding Bailey on his swift passage through the courthouse. He recalled telling him, "Two sentencings on the same day! You'll have to put that in your next book."

John Gaffney, a prosecutor in Suffolk County, Massachusetts, who is 5-and-0 facing Bailey in front of Boston juries, says that Bailey loses more often than not in the home courts.

"He's a PR man," Gaffney told me on the phone. "The guy has got all kinds of confidence. He exudes confidence. He's one of the greatest egotists who ever lived. Even losing, he doesn't feel that he lost.

"Bailey tries very few cases here in Massachusetts now because he gets beaten all the time. We don't even let him in the office here, because you can't trust him. If you talk to him off the record, he'll use it against you in court. Once he even bugged a conversation with a judge in the courthouse lobby. We had a couple of experiences with him, and we wouldn't let him in. Another reason why he doesn't practice here much anymore—there isn't any money here. Run-of-the-mill cases don't interest him. He's got to have a case that brings big money, or publicity, or both."

The night before the Hearst jury brought in its verdict, Bailey sat with a reporter in the lobby of the Stanford Court Hotel. As ever, Bailey was confident. "The line in Vegas is seven to two for acquittal," he said.

The reporter expressed some amazement—"Gee, Lee, even money I can see, but seven to two!"

No. Bailey said. That was the Vegas line.

I called Jimmy the Greek. In Vegas. "We had a thousand calls on that trial," Jimmy said. "Ladbrooke's in England. Women. People from all over. It was nuts. Because we never gamble on anything pertaining to people's lives. An election, a ball game, a fight. Not somebody's trial. It's an untrue statement that there ever was a line."

I called Harry Gordon at the Churchill Downs Sports Book in Vegas. "That's an out-and-out lie," he said. "That's just part of Bailey's act. We don't put out a line on tragedies."

I called the Little Waldorf and the Turf Club in Reno. Same deal.

I called Bailey at home in Massachusetts:

"You mentioned the night before the verdict that the Vegas line was seven to two, right?"

"Those were the odds we were told. I forget whether it was Vegas or Reno. The odds originally had been told to us, mostly by newsmen, as three to one after Patty testified. Then after she took the Fifth they went four to three."

"Because I know Jimmy the Greek a little . . . " I started to say.

"Jimmy the Greek was quoting even money when the jury went out."

"Jimmy was?"

"I don't know that that's true . . . "

"No, it isn't. Jimmy's position is that he doesn't book odds on tragedies."

"I know nothing about betting. I don't do it. Even when I go to Las Vegas, I don't go to a table. I'm just telling you that this was one of the ongoing jokes, you know, people sitting around waiting for the verdict, most of them reporters, and I would suggest that the reporters were probably making the odds up to get a reaction."

"Yeah, probably."

One final matter remained in dispute. The day before Patty was sentenced, transcripts of her interviews with two psychiatrists were leaked to the press, and stories in the *Los Angeles Times* and the *New York Times* both quoted the transcripts in support of the idea that Patty had doubts about her brainwashing defense from the beginning. "It just doesn't get rid of everything," she was said to have told Dr. Louis J. West, a UCLA psychiatrist who later testified at the trial. When I asked Bailey about this in the Fleetwood, he said that the press had taken the statement out of context and done "a dirty thing," making her appear to be saying the opposite of what she meant. "If you read further," he said, "you'll see what she is saying is that it isn't going to repair the damage done to her parents. She felt badly for them."

Since both newspapers had independently drawn the same inference, and since the transcript itself revealed no mention of Patty's parents, I called Bailey at home in Massachusetts. I told him my problem. He said:

"Have you tried the horse's mouth?"

"Patty?"

"No, no, obviously Patty's talking to no one. But you could call the people who conducted the interviews. Call West. See what he says."

It came out at the trial that Dr. West had written to the Hearsts before Patty's capture, outlining a defense not unlike the one that was decided upon once Patty was in hand. This damaged Dr. West's effectiveness before the jury, as did his inability to refer to documents and tapes that were judged inadmissible. "I wanted to have the jury hear those tapes, hear her tone of voice, hear what she was going through," he said. Like Dr. Fort, his opposite number in the witness box, Dr. West had found the trial a bitter experience, and his hopes were growing frail that the truth would ever out.

"What I was doing was prodding her," he said, describing the forty hours of interviews he conducted in her jail cell. "Up to then she was unable to tell anybody, not her lawyers, not her doctors, not anybody, everything that had happened to her—partly because she couldn't remember it all, partly because there were portions of it which, in terms of this defense, were the most favorable to her, in which she was the most victimized, that she couldn't bring herself to talk about because the memory was too painful. It would make her fall apart and she couldn't talk. So what I was doing was telling her that I had talked to her lawyers, saying that they seemed to be good people—hell, I didn't know them—and they seemed to have developed a reasonable defense, and what did she think about it. When she said, 'That doesn't get rid of everything,' she wasn't talking about evidence. She wasn't even able to formulate an idea like plea bargaining."

Dr. West backed Bailey up completely, in other words, but as I listened to him talk I became more and more aware that here at last was someone who expressed real compassion for Patty. Bailey's portrait of Patty in the closing argument was the product of an old-fashioned ex-Marine flyboy sense of life: he didn't seem to know that how-could-a-nice-girl-like-this-do-a-terrible-thing-like-that? is too naive a proposition to play in San Francisco. I told Dr. West that I was also having trouble squaring Bailey's picture of Patty as the damsel in distress with my reading of *Rolling Stone,* where she'd been quoted as telling Bill Harris, "Kiss my cunt, Adolf" when he called her "a bitch." As I listened to his reply, I realized I was hearing the final argument Bailey might have given, a plea for understanding that did not confuse or offend.

"*Brainwashing* was never a term Patty used," he said. "She never understood it and still doesn't understand what happened to her. I would explain it to her, and she always would say, 'I believe it because you're telling it to me, but it doesn't make me feel any better.'

"In the press, Patty was portrayed as though she were a normal person just like the other members of the SLA. The people in the SLA didn't realize what they had done to her. They didn't comprehend what had happened. They had kidnapped her, clubbed her down, imprisoned her, frightened her to death, and then they molded the resultant product to fit their wishes—Cinque deliberately, and the rest of them just going along with a process they didn't understand.

"And that product, that person living in a partly disassociated role, was still a real live person, still a human being, someone who had to get through every day. And she had likes and dislikes and had to eat and drink and go to the store and wasn't any longer the terrorized infant with a gun to her head. Wendy Yoshimura took pity on her. She found her in a pretty sad condition, and encouraged her to take a few tentative steps toward independence, to call her parents, to move away from the Harrises. Patty wanted to call her parents. She wanted to call Trish Tobin. But when it came right down to it, she couldn't make the calls. Not because she was afraid the FBI would find her. Because she had created a mental barrier she couldn't break through. And without knowing why.

"Patty's arrest wasn't a rescue. Not like a returned POW greeted back home by joyful parents, astonished to learn they don't blame him. Because the larger society obviously did blame her. She had no right still to be alive. That was what it was all about. And that's what it's still all about.

"The only way Patricia Hearst can redeem herself to the angry public is to die. Then maybe people will start to say, 'Gee, that poor kid.'

"Until then, they're saying what the Harrises said: 'That rich bitch, look what she's doing, snitching on her friends.' But what's happened to Patty is that she's been captured again, kidnapped in a sense, confined, cross-examined, interrogated, just like with Cinque, held by hostile persons obviously intent on destroying her life, who don't care about her as a person at all, who are just using her, smashing her, for their own purposes.

"Her defenses are shot. She no longer has any basis of saying, 'I don't want to talk.' Her lawyers say to her, 'We have determined that you should do this or that, you should tell whatever you can remember.' I wouldn't see her talking as ratting on anybody. I would just say she's somebody who's been pounded down by both sides to the point where all she can do in the world is tell what she remembers.

"She's one of the least understood people I've ever encountered. Everybody's talking about an imaginary person. They don't know her. She doesn't know herself. I see her as very fragile, very much in danger in every way. I think she is one of the saddest evidences of the ubiquity of human cruelty that I've ever run across. And if she teaches us anything, it's that the notion that it helps to be a child of the rich and powerful when you're facing the power of a group to be cruel, well, that's just one more fiction. The rest of us who aren't rich and powerful would like to think that it's true. But it isn't."

The Fleetwood pulled up in front of the Century Plaza. I asked Bailey if he had any doubts or regrets about his conduct of the defense.

"No, indeed," Bailey said. Then he went inside the hotel, looking formidable and fit.

1976

# George in the
# Afternoon

*G*eorge Segal was just being friendly when he agreed to be interviewed by the twenty-six students in my nonfiction writing class at the University of California at Santa Barbara. He got all dressed up and rented a Lincoln Continental to add a theatrical touch to the occasion, and we had such a good time on the drive up from Beverly Hills that our arrival in the classroom was a little chastening. An awkward moment passed before George declared himself ready to begin—a moment in which I thought he captured exactly the note of noblesse oblige that is part of every celebrity interview. The students asked questions for an hour and twenty minutes, and the following week all but one turned in a 1,000-word paper. Their disharmonious impressions of what George looked like, what he said, what he stood for, and what he was doing there in the first place struck me as highly amusing at first, leading me to take a sentence or two from each paper and arrange them into the composite interview that follows. But in defense of my students, and of the art of interviewing generally, I submit that our 25,000-word Segal dossier rivals in accuracy most government profiles, newsmagazine features, and other literary enterprises involving the work of many hands.

As George Segal entered the classroom, I prepared for my first exposure to a bona fide actor from Hollywood. I saw a blondish young-old man in a blue suit, an immaculately tailored blue suit, a wondrous unwrinkled work of expense. The suit and tie established a certain limit, a boundary beyond which those without an invitation could not go. He was a dolphin in powder blue under surveillance in front of us. George looked real sharp in his bright blue suit. Here was Mr. Conservative.

His hair had that enviable quality that suggests that it will never be any more or less tousled than it is. The green eyes looked almost too bright to be real. The chin was rock-hard mayonnaise. Hands in pockets, he panned the room with the smile of an impish boy. It was the smile of a man pleased with himself and with the position he has made for himself, the smile of a man who thinks he is in control. He directed a mocking stare toward everyone present. His blue-eyed gaze lingered peacefully on each student's face. I was struck by his candid but pleasant arrogance. He had no false pretenses or pompous mannerisms. The blond-haired actor was reverberating with the taut worry of a struck tuning fork. Could this calm, composed man be the same George Segal who pulled down his pants on the *Black Bird* set? Segal wasn't always this suave.

Segal rested languidly on a desktop. He perched atop a desk. He assured a commanding place on top of a table in front of the class. He clung to the table, knuckles curled tightly around its edge. His hands were resting motionless in his lap, but he seemed to be knitting all the flying, scattered vibrations into a low-keyed *om*. His posture suggested confident control as he sat upright on the table. He studied his questioners with an intent half-smile, folded his arms across his chest, crossed and recrossed his ankles. His brown socks and loafers matched the color of his hair. He epitomized grace, style, savoir faire. He was witty, smooth, confident, aggressive, unbearably urbane. While he was talking, Segal, who seems to be shorter in person than on the screen, used his arms frantically. "What I'm trying to do is be stoned about my life," the tall, ruggedly handsome actor said.

He was so patient and attentive to each question put forward, so direct and sincere in the ideas he gave back. It was clear from the beginning that this would be *his* interview, not ours. I was impressed with his wit, his verbal agility. I'm sure he'd said it all before on *The Tonight Show*. Segal's spirit was one of total openness to the flow of the discussion. Obviously, he was a man who was used to being in control. He was refreshingly candid about himself as a person, gracious enough to volunteer bits of information that I found very revealing. Whenever a query touched on his personal life he was quick to maintain a safe distance. "I'm naturally stoned in thinking about my life," the Hollywood actor said.

Always in complete control, Segal fielded ridiculous questions with professional ease. He stooped to answer familiar questions. He was patient about answering even the dumbest questions. Serious questions that touched on conflicts were treated as jokes or ignored. I was surprised at his willingness to answer whatever questions came his way. I was rankled by the interview. It was stilted and tight. His observations were colorful and lucid. Statements of double meaning were in abundance. The bass note was sincerity and cool. It was clear that he had learned the necessity of humility along the way. Who had more right to snobbism, sophistication, and conceit than one who had achieved so much since his meager existence in New York City? "What I'd like to do is live my life loaded," he said.

Many of his answers initially appeared to reflect a philosopher's logical system, but as time went on the inconsistencies came to the surface. Segal's self-confidence, his good humor, and his friendly, yet detached manner all indicated a man who had smoothed out the roughest edges in his life. A persistent whisper bade me wonder: is George Segal playing George Segal? After admitting to tantrums, exhibitionism, and a general lack of consideration during the shooting of his last film, Segal could look back on what happened and gain from it. "A little madness establishes respect," he said. "A little madness establishes sanity. By acting a little mad, you prove your sanity. You win fear and respect if you act a little mad. A little meanness establishes sanity. I'm a crackerjack actor. What I really want to do is be stoned about my life."

The actor George Segal and the man George Segal were both sitting on the table. George Segal, the person, did not exist for this interviewer. We only saw Segal acting. There certainly is a George in Mr. Segal. Thinking the way George Segal thinks often leads to personal isolationism. People who get where Segal is pay a very high price, both in psychological and real terms. His career has taught him that he has to be arrogant, I suppose. Obviously, success is something he has learned to handle with ease. I was amazed that after so much success he could still be so natural and real. "I'm trying to live stoned," he said.

Segal said he is his own worst critic. He prefers to rely on his own judgment of his work. He refuses to say which of his films he likes best. He said he thought *Where's Poppa?* and *Born to Win* were his best films because they dealt with real-life problems. Significantly, he garnered the most satisfaction from his role in *A Touch of Class*. He likes to make people happy, if only for a brief time. He thinks of himself as a teacher but would not say of what. "I'm just trying to be stoned about my life," he said. "I'm a top-notched cracker actor."

Segal always capped off every answer with a grin that overflowed into everyone around him. He kept that forced, fixed smile glued on. He genuinely wanted to make positive contact with everyone in the room, to make sure that each of us felt comfortable talking with him and felt a freedom to respond on an equal level. Unfortunately, now that he has it made, his concerns are centered on himself. The talk was primarily about the big me, número uno. Being a star, he has had to set up defenses. He was cynical, realistic, but interesting. Apparently he knows something about yoga. He sat there on the table and weaved a marvelous portrait of a content, successful person.

His nervousness seemed to lighten as the questions continued. I was struck by how calm and rational he was in viewing his own career. Sometimes he would drum his fingers on the table. He came across as perceptive and aware, making an effort to know the people who sat before him. His front was dropped to a minimum, and he tried to let the classroom set its own mellow tone. He was too convincing, too amusing. He was totally composed. As far as seeing George Segal goes, you remain the outsider. You see only the performance. "I'm a top-notch crackerjack actor," he said. I couldn't help but agree.

The interview ended before the shell that enclosed him could be entered. Much of the megafantasy had dropped away, and we were beginning to interview George Segal, man, rather than legend. Still smiling, now having about him an air of casual confidence that may not have been there when he entered, George Segal headed for the door.

1975

# The Guru Comes to Kansas

Allen Ginsberg is eating breakfast: sterile, plastic-coated Danish pushed crumbling into great Hasidic beard, sips of tea pale as tears, molecules mating in gastric Oneness, sleepy visionary poet munching morning food of Kansas students in afternoon of campus cafe. Excited elbows ring the table. Passing boobs' laughter is proof of holy isolation to students bent on truth pursuit. Imploring faces shine with want of Allen's talk. Allen has twenty years on the kids.

"Say, Allen," says an earnest sophomore. "Remember how I was talking about blowing up the railroad stations? And you said no, that it was better to sit in front of the draft board and everything? Last night? Well, anyway, don't you think it would also really be better if we got our hair cut and shaved and everything? I mean because then people wouldn't form an opinion. Allen?"

Allen looks up from his disappearing breakfast. Thirty minutes ago he was asleep in a borrowed bed, and he has not finished his tea. Yet Allen shows no trace of irritation with this familiar question. He suffers sophomores gladly, always has. "My hair's just there," he says, smiling didactically under the balding dome of forty years. "It's not a flag or anything. It's just there."

Not a flag, just there—a fine, disaffiliated head of hair. Ten years ago, when joke stores were selling Allen Ginsberg costumes to wear to smart parties, Allen himself looked rather soft and clerkish. Too many things were happening in his life for his face to register much beyond simple wonder and delight. But work, fame, baths in the Ganges—these things leave their marks. Now Allen has become the image of his poems, the angelheaded hipster sprung from the page. With beard and sunburst hair and comprehending eye he is like Whitman come back, or Moses. In the streets he is taken for a Skid Row evangelist. Onstage at a poetry reading, chanting Buddhist mantras and ringing his Tibetan finger cymbals, he could be a visiting Himalayan monk. And here, in this chromium cafeteria in the basement of the student union building at the University of Kansas, here in Lawrence (pop. 43,720), here he is a guru—no mistaking it.

Considering how Allen began his poetic career (Beatniks! The madhouse! Marijuana and worse!), it seemed wonder enough when the students of Prague elected him King of the May last year—one hundred thousand of them joining in the parade to carry him through the town. But even Allen is astonished by the breakthrough involved in finding himself a Guggenheim Fellow visiting the University of Kansas to read and talk with the students, to meet the faculty at parties and teas. The shocked hysteria that hounded him into middle age has suddenly slipped away. He can talk about drugs, homosexuality, world love congress, all his pleasures and beliefs: the students will listen and the *Kansas City Star* will carry a friendly story.

Allen's vast experience as a voluptuary and all-weather mental navigator has made him the obvious laureate of LSD and the sexual-freedom movement. But even home economics majors now seem able to hear all he has to say with wonderful, terrifying sophistication. His poems come in strong words—scatalogical insights, joyous whoops for any kind of love, cries from a mind stalked by a sense of decay and eventual doom. The language writhes with images in crisis and change as the threatened poet advances, taking soundings, scribbling back instructions for those who care to follow.

Sometimes the idiom falters, causing the poems to wheeze, Allen to miss his mark. His recent poems are even further departures from the polished standards he outraged with the three slender volumes he gleaned from his first years' work—*Howl, Kaddish,* and *Reality Sandwiches.* But literary responses to Allen's work have always sounded prim and inappropriate, for the beauty of these poems is in their humanity more than their line. Allen's humanity, his unqualified humanity, his almost Franciscan view of things, has won him a genuine influence he never quite achieved in his old Beat days, and Allen speaks today to the young of the world at large as the most famous and admired American poet. But even when he was just another mystical creep, his message was very much the same: be tender with all meat.

The kids around the table naturally want to hear Allen talk about reeducating the police, marijuana and LSD, all forms of soul research— how often does he get to Kansas, after all? But for the moment Allen has other matters on his mind. He is concerned because Peter Orlovsky—his friend and lover, "the strange tender ambulance driver" of his life—Peter cannot find a spot at the table for his breakfast tray. Hair to his waist, feet pink with chill in rubber shower slippers, Peter stands with his silent brother Julius at the edge of the tight little crowd. "Ladies! Gentlemen!" Allen says, and the students make way for the curious brothers. There is polite, uneasy silence while Allen helps Julius get started with his meal, pointing out the little sacks of sugar and the stick for stirring, unwrapping the crackers from their tight cellophane case.

Allen, Peter, and Julius have been traveling together—six months cross-country to New York in a used Volkswagen Camper. Allen bought the Camper last fall when the Guggenheim grant gave him

$6,000, more money than he had ever had before in his life. The trip is broken with stops for readings and visitations: Berkeley for the Vietnam Day demonstrations, singing mantras in the streets to calm both Hell's Angels and police; Big Sur for an LSD trip; readings in Los Angeles, Wichita, Lawrence, Topeka, Lincoln, Buffalo; a pilgrimage to the Kinsey Foundation in Bloomington, Indiana. As they roll, Allen sings and composes poems on a tape recorder. Peter drives. Julius listens, watches the scenery slip by; fourteen years in the back wards of state hospitals have transformed an agitated child into a wordless, fuming judge of no age at all—Julius is thirty-four, but he could be sixty, or ten. Allen and Peter look out for him, and they take him along wherever they go. "Julie," they call him, and sometimes "Buster Keaton."

Allen's eccentricities slide out of focus when Peter and Julius are around, even when Allen remains his eccentric best. Both Peter and Allen, for example, are occasionally given to taking off their clothes at parties and meetings and the like. When Allen does this, it is generally understood as a charmingly explicit statement of his belief in total cosmic nakedness. But when Peter unexpectedly undresses, not everyone is pleased. Allen sticks up for Peter doggedly and well. "Now, in perspective," he will say, "Peter took his pants off in front of the group of psychiatrists. And they were upset. But was it Peter who upset them or they who upset Peter? Or did they both upset each other?"

The talk with the students at breakfast leaves Allen excited and agitated, primed for the reading that is held that afternoon in the big student union ballroom. "Those kids!" he says. "They have a sexual awareness, an openness and tolerance and compassion that is absolutely ravishing. It's going to save the world. Ask any psychiatrist. He'll say it's fine. The kids are finally coming out from under the anxiety barrier." He leaves the cafeteria grinning exuberantly and, with a nervous hour to kill before the reading, starts off to visit the campus library, trailing an entourage.

Students have filled the ballroom to overflowing by the time Allen and his band arrive. Peter sits lotus-fashion on the stage by the lectern to fuss with the tape recorder and play the harmonium while Allen sings his mantras. Each mantra is a Buddhist prayer or sermon, but Allen values them mainly as a means to express simple emotion, and he sings them at his readings as an antidote to anxiety. His voice is just right for carrying the thin modal chant and, with cymbals ringing and poet clearly transported by song, the mantras cast a hypnotic lure over even an edgy, grudging audience: *Shiki fu I ku ku fu shiki shiki soku ze ku ku soku ze shiki* (Form is not different from emptiness, emptiness not different from form. Form is the emptiness, emptiness the form.)

Then the poems—and they strike with terrific impact, a great rushing cascade plunging down to primitive levels of love and dread, an avalanche of language and confession so frank that it stares from the poems like torches along a trail. Soon all forbidden words have been spoken, shouted, all forbidden pictures brought to mind. The thousand coeds present are in shock or gladly past it. No one stirs except to applaud.

Allen reads his work with fervor—timidity with these words would make schoolboy graffiti out of every crucial crunch. He prefaces the most direct of them with explanations that serve for one and all like deep breaths before a high-board dive: "The crisis we're all facing—like overpopulation, leaving the planet, the possibility of mass death, the hanging of the bomb over the world—it's made a situation where personal feeling has finally got to come out to the surface and become public. People have got to start telling the truth. So here goes, a purely personal poem."

And so onward, inward, downward into realms of feeling few poets have publicly explored.

Allen reads for two hours, the poems coming in scrupulous chronology of place and time. Berkeley, 1955; Paris, 1958; Lima, 1960; London, 1965—Allen growing older. When he is finished, there is nothing more to tell. The whispers of his secret mind are the possession of everyone present. The reading, like the poems, is a catharsis for Allen; he is subdued and touchingly open to the high-pitched flattery that swirls around him as he leaves. The students are deeply excited—less so, it seems, by the buckets of sexual revelation than by the larger spectacle of a man so completely able to tell the whole truth about himself, however difficult it is to bear.

Allen comes from what he calls a "Jewish left-wing atheist Russian background in Paterson, New Jersey"—his father a poet and teacher, his mother lost early to schizophrenia, Allen at eleven brooding vainly over the Spanish Civil War. He arrived at Columbia University in 1943 both burdened and enchanted with a vision of himself as a servant of the suffering masses, "a Poet-prophet," as he has written, "on the side of love and the Wild Good." But he was acutely aware that in fact he was only a trembling seventeen-year-old aesthete and he set about broadening his spectacled horizon with work as a dishwasher, stevedore, spot welder, night porter—anything open to an intellectual boy whose principal concern was with the doom of his desires.

Then two things changed him. He enthusiastically encountered the wild postwar hipster society of Times Square in 1945—"the whole apocalyptic vibration"—and, three years later, he had a vision.

"I was in an intermediate period at Columbia when I wasn't attending any classes, just writing some papers, living alone in Harlem up on the sixth floor of a tenement, separated from the people I knew as companions for several years already, like William Burroughs and Jack Kerouac. I was eating mostly vegetables and reading a lot of St. John of the Cross and Plato and Blake and Plotinus. And one day, while lying by an open window on a couch, reading Blake, my eye fell on the printed page, and suddenly I heard a voice pronouncing the words on the page—Blake's 'Sun-flower.'

"Well, this was a deep, earthen voice, like a fatherly voice, very tender and real, grave, deep, grave in the sentence, deep, like saying, 'Ah, Sun-flower! weary of time, / Who countest the steps of the Sun; /

Seeking after that sweet golden clime, / Where the traveler's journey is done; / Where the Youth pined away with desire, / And the pale Virgin shrouded in snow, / Arise from their graves, and aspire / Where my Sun-flower wishes to go.'

"It was talking about desire, I guess. Answering desire. And simultaneously I was having an illumination, very similar to some aspects of the illuminations you get with the psychedelic drugs—except deeper, more ample, more real, and more blissful than anything I've experienced since. Everything around me seemed completely alive, like a concretized intelligence, so that looking out of the window, all the cornices, the Victorian cornices of 1910 apartment houses of Spanish Harlem slums, they all became the handiwork of a creator—every brick and on up into the sky, the sun, the very blue substance of space."

Allen was so stunned at meeting Blake on his own mystic turf that he mindlessly let the year or so that followed slide into a shambles around him. Herbert Huncke, a Times Square thief and drug addict whose intrepidly accurate personal journals have recently elevated him from the underworld to the Underground—Huncke was staying in Allen's apartment with "a whole *Beggars' Opera* cast of thieves." Soon the place began filling up with silverware and fine oaken furniture stolen from apartment house lobbies. Huncke was far too sympathetic a creature for Allen to throw out, so Allen decided to move himself.

"There was too much anxiety and I didn't quite approve of the thieving," Allen says. "So I piled all my manuscripts in a car with a friend who was one of the robbers, and I was going to take them to my brother's house, seal things up, quit my job, and leave town. So out in Queens we turned the wrong way down a one-way street, at the end of which was a police car. The driver panicked and so did the cop and we swerved trying to get away until, all of a sudden there we were, riding down Utopia Boulevard at ninety miles an hour being chased by a cop.

"We swerved to take a side road, skidded, smashed into a telephone pole, turned the car over. Papers flying, my eyeglasses lost, all these stolen suits and silverware and suitcases all upside down. Chaos! I crawled out and just sort of wandered away from the scene.

"I'd had a funny visionary thing. Just before we turned into that street I was singing Hebraic mantras—'Lord God of Israel, Isaac, and Abe-ruh-ham!' So when I walked out of the crash it was like Jehovah coming in judgment, intolerant of thieving and messing around. Wow. Anyway—a great chain of causes leading to my being in the ridiculous spot of being in a crash, with all my manuscripts, all the letters from Burroughs, everything floating inside the wrecked hot car.

"Five minutes after I got home, about six big cops walked in and asked for Allen Ginsberg, and from then on it was a drag. A real bring-down for my teachers at Columbia—Trilling and Van Doren. Like I was billed in the *News* as 'COLUMBIA COLLEGE CRIMINAL GENIUS,' held captive by this gang of low-life people because of craving for dope.

"What a mess! Like was my father ever upset—it really brought him back. He—a nice middle-class teacher, a poet, there in Paterson— the idea of *anybody* going to jail was horrifying to him."

The police let Allen go with instructions to see someone about his head, so he wound up in a mental hospital for the next eight months. It was there that he met Carl Solomon, the mad friend introduced in the famous first line of *Howl*—"I saw the best minds of my generation destroyed by madness, starving hysterical naked . . ." Their meeting was a madhouse classic: "Carl was coming up from shock and he asked me, 'Who are you?' and I said, 'I'm Myshkin,' and he said, 'I'm Kirilov,' and so we sat around for the rest of that year discussing the doctors' sense of reality and whether or not it was right for us. Carl was having problems because he was getting shock. But I didn't have any of that. No medicine, no shock. For me it was like a hotel, like a very convenient monastery for me."

Back on the street, Allen began to drift perilously toward respectability and steady employment—book reviewer, market research consultant. He traveled some, wrote poems, relished his friends. But it was no good; he was getting nothing from his life beyond the wan pleasure of discovering that the necktie world no longer intimidated him. So, in 1955 he began a year of psychotherapy in San Francisco that flung open all forbidding doors.

"The doctor kept asking me, 'What do you want to do?'" Allen recalls. "Finally I told him—quit. Quit the job, my tie and suit, the apartment on Nob Hill. Quit it, and go off and do what I wanted, which was to get a room with Peter and devote myself to writing and contemplation, to Blake and smoking pot, and doing whatever I wanted.

"So he said, 'Go ahead and do it then.' So I said, 'What'll happen to me if I grow up with dirty underwear in some furnished room and nobody will love me and I'll be white-haired and won't have any money and there'll be bread crumbs falling on the floor?'

"And he said, 'Ooooh, don't worry about that. You're charming and people will always love you.'

"Such a relief to hear that! His own liking of me! So I realized— well, sure! Why not? And I went at it with a vengeance. I started really enjoying myself. I could get up in the middle of the night and write down a dream without worrying about getting up in the morning."

With such liberating winds in his sails, Allen sat down to write *Howl*. He wrote the entire first section in one afternoon. Looking at it later he was pleased to discover "a huge sad comedy of wild phrasing, meaningless images . . . poetry of mind running along making awkward combinations, like Charlie Chaplin's walk." In the act of writing *Howl*, Allen discovered the one guiding principle of all he has written since:

"I started it with the idea of writing what I really felt, summing up my life for the soul's own ear, tapping the sources of what was really inside me and expressing these things directly—outside literature, of course, outside the possibilities of social communication. Funny wrinkles of my own awareness, as Kerouac says—little secret aware- nesses. 'Fool,' said the Muse, 'look in thy heart and write!'"

"I didn't expect to publish it, but *Howl* was like really looking in the heart and writing. I wasn't wise enough at the time to realize that that alone would make it close to right. Kerouac put me on to the discovery that we're stepping forth into a time of irrevocable statement: speak now or forever hold thy peace. And then I realized that the exact area which is classic art and which everybody is interested in is just that—our secret personal doodlings. Art is something discovered from your own real nature."

Understandably, Allen was worried about his father's reaction to *Howl*; the poem is a catalog of the very words and feelings a son would try hard to conceal. But the paternal response was mild, and it included praise for screwball courage. Allen then perceived that all the niceties and conventions that had restrained him, man and poet, were nothing more than the "retrograde hangover of early Paterson provincial fear."

Allen floated enviably free of all ballast through the period that followed, swooping around the country raving, talking Zen, following the unpredictable shape of his mind. With Peter and with Gregory Corso, a fellow Beat poet and the author of *Gasoline* and *Bomb*, Allen lived like someone running a poetic medicine show. Culture snobs were grateful to have him show up superbly underdressed for their parties, and Allen would oblige by lecturing the ladies roughly about love and The Void. Whenever his vanity got the best of him, nudging the poet out of control, Kerouac, his friend and advisor, would warn him of the danger and denounce him as "a hairy loss." So, in 1961 he resolved to disappear into the Orient—for a while, at least.

Hardly a poet since Lord Byron has made so much of travel— Peru to take the magic drug *ayahuasca* with witch doctors, the Arctic as mystic yeoman in the merchant marines, the Péten rain forest in Guatemala to harvest cacao and dwell in a grass hut, Tangier "to vomit from the rooftops"—Paris, Havana, Prague. The most celebrated of these voyages, however, was his pilgrimage to India, where with Peter and Zen poet Gary Snyder he introduced American transcendentalist poetry to at least one of its spiritual homes.

His letters to friends were passed around and published, and splendid letters they were: "Spent all Tues. nite sleeping with ganjabum holymen in burning ghats—lost my shoes & wandered around high barefoot from one corpse burning to another with dishevelled hair & feeling crazy. Great nite."

Such radical departures from customary tourism naturally came to the attention of India's rather touchy police, and the poets were asked to leave. Allen appealed, claiming spiritual visas beyond the reach of law. "Well, if you're here on an *intellectual* level . . ." said the man from the Home Affairs Minister's office, and Allen and Peter were allowed to stay long enough to kindle a nettlesome literary revolt in Calcutta that the police are still trying to suppress.

But Allen's first mission was finding a guru, and he embarked devoutly on the guru-seeking exercise of wandering around for days muttering *"gurugurugurugurugurugurugurguru."* A lady guru thus discovered told him the obvious—Worship Blake! But the next, upon hearing Allen's story, said, "Oh, how wounded! How wounded!" and the searing truth of that plunged into Allen's heart and soul. He walked barefoot in the Himalayas, visited Tibetan monks in holy aeries, practiced yoga and breathing exercises, meditated high on ganja (India's legal marijuana), sang mantras, traveled to Japan to sit in Zen monasteries, said the holy sound *om* to himself until it became the very buzz of his body and brain.

Then, in the spring of 1963, while riding along on the Kyoto-Tokyo Express the day before sailing for home, Allen had another illumination:

"It came to me, everything at once, in a moment of great euphoric weeping. I saw the end to the moral necessity to enlarge my being, that I could just be myself as I am, *now,* me, to live in this form as a human being now. The whole visionary game was lost to me. I was alive in a body that was going to die. Then I began looking around the train and seeing all the other mortal faces—faces of weakness and woe, as Blake has it, and I saw how exquisitely dear they all were. Unique and frail, each a thing bound to die.

"So I pulled out my notebook while the illumination was still glowing in my body and while my breath was still fitted to weeping, and scribbled everything that came into my thought stream—all the immediate perceptions at the moment in the order in which I could record them fastest. Later on, that becomes known as a poem. Anyway, this was a poem called *The Change*, where I say, 'In my trainseat I renounce my power, so that I do live, I will die.'"

Allen returned from the Orient "bankrupt and softened," stilled by the realization that the period in his life that began with the vision of Blake had ended with the ride on the train—the past fifteen years were suddenly over. He would have to renounce all yearning for the visionary state, renounce Blake himself. It was clear that whatever the proper concern of poets was, it was here in this universe now; reaching it would require "direct vision, sense perception contact with the now of life." He could turn full-face to the increasingly bizarre event of his own life, and to a world getting more bizarre all the time, too. He was free to abandon all metaphysical groping in his poetry—good news to Allen and his readers alike.

The old New Jersey atheist quietly took command, but even now— three years after the train ride—Allen is easy to mistake for a person who grew up somewhere near the Japan-Benares border. He quotes tellingly from Lord Shiva, Vishnu, and the Zen masters, draws instructive analogies from the *Diamond Sutra*, cautions people that they have their karma, their destiny, to answer for.

Before the Oriental interlude of his life, Allen's social views had a way of sounding shrill and old-fashioned. Many in the avant-garde who greatly admired his poems found themselves, like Francophiles in France, constantly exasperated with their love. But now there is a note of knowing benevolence in even his most scattered thought, as in his appeal for the "tender comradeship" proposed by Whitman.

"Because of overpopulation and the highly centralized network of artificial communications," Allen says, "it has become necessary to have a breakthrough of more direct, satisfactory contact. It is necessary to the organism. This can be understood from the fact that if babies are not touched by human flesh, they can't develop. They just die. Tenderness is a food to the human organism, without which it perishes."

Surely no decent man would quarrel with this. But when Allen finishes reciting all that this proves or, at least, implies to him, he is left with scarcely an ally over thirty years of age—for no one trusts the potential goodness of man quite like Allen does. He is for total pansexual freedom; LSD for "the Faustian, Columbian, Ulyssean men who care to explore it"; the legalization of marijuana; pulling down flags; getting out of Vietnam—in fact, the whole gamut of unpopular ideas.

Flurries of indignation follow Allen, Peter, and Julius on their progress across the country. In Wichita the police arrive to break up a reading in a coffeehouse, then retreat sensibly after Allen instructs them in the full meaning of poetic license. The vice squad in Lincoln is ready and waiting when the Camper pulls into town bearing the poets, and an ecstatic reading to three thousand students at the University of Nebraska is followed by letters in the campus paper signed "Sickened" and "Disgusted"—plus others in Allen's defense, signed with names. A week later, readings at Indiana University produce demands for a legislative investigation: can academic freedom go too far?

But offending a legislator here and there scarcely describes the scale of moral combat Allen has grown accustomed to. His distinction, after all, lies in being equally distasteful to all worldly authorities, East and West. And he, in turn, regards all countries as police states, specifically including this one.

Whatever early hopes Allen might have cherished for people's regimes were dashed last year when he was expelled from both Cuba and Czechoslovakia in the space of the same springtime. In Cuba he was asked to leave "for violating the laws."

"I asked them which laws they meant, of course," Allen says, "and this Brown Shirt answered, 'You'll have to ask yourself.' A pure Kafka bureaucracy shot!"

Trouble in Prague began when the police found a meticulously accurate personal journal of all sorts of amusements and rejoicings that the King of the May had lost in the streets.

Allen raised no fuss about these ungentlemanly departures; the appalling irony of becoming a Cold War hero struck him mute. But there was no suppressing the scandal in London a few weeks later when Allen's part of a reading in Albert Hall turned into an obscene scream-duet with an audience of fully seven thousand. "A section of the audience began to barrack," a poetry critic later wrote. "Ginsberg, shaking his wild locks, responded with all the fire of an Old Testament prophet. 'Can we have some real poetry now, sir?' shouted an officer-class voice, and the incongruous 'sir' revealed an abyss of incomprehension."

Incomprehension is, of course, the very food of revolutionaries, and one wonders how well Allen would get along without it in large draughts. Unmistakably, he is a man who knows his karma when he sees it, and if he weren't the kind of poet he is, he would be a depressing case.

Whatever peril or error may lie in a career as an enthusiastic violator of world behavior norms, it seems to be good for Allen's work. His new poems are filled with extravagant attack on all that keeps men in their places, the shouted crowning of the senses—NAKED MAN THE HERO-CITIZEN AFTER ALL! And there are darker regions he has begun to explore: the question of dying childless; of life with Peter, the "long-haired saint." Even when he appears to be plunging headlong after the Wild Good, Allen keeps the best of himself for his writing. In the end he is, as he says, "always careful to keep myself together and pursue Poesy & have a forwarding address."

\*　　\*　　\*

The long cross-country trip ends with a day's rush of turnpikes—from Bloomington to New York—Julius asleep, the poets finally weary. They return to the clutter of the same small apartment on the Lower East Side that Allen has lived in for years; though *Howl* has sold through sixteen printings, Allen continues to live under an old vow of "relative penury"—$3,000 a year or so, and the rest for whoever needs it.

Allen begins a quiet week of writing, but his friends greet him like a circuit-riding judge. "The network," as he calls his circle, has spread out from Kerouac and Corso and Burroughs to include the likes of Bob Dylan, Lenny Bruce, Dr. Timothy Leary—and now everyone is plagued by trouble with the police. Soon Allen has launched two or three new committees in the name of total psychic freedom. He composes petitions, gives benefit readings, turns up on television, agitates, clips the papers, fires letters at the government.

He works at all his causes with Talmudic attention. He has assembled and all but memorized a vast library of studies which prove the beneficence of marijuana, for example, and his ceaseless campaigning for it has brought him out on the picket line (POT IS A REALITY KICK) and made him an inviting target for the police. A friend of his testifies in court that federal narcotics agents offered him soft treatment in his own case if he would set prudent Allen up for an arrest. Allen attends the trial, bathes judge and jury and government agents in the equivocal light of his great shaggy smile.

A young man trails Allen out of the courthouse and into a Chinese restaurant. There is an X cut in his cheek, fresh and still mottled with blood. Allen introduces him to his friends as a follow poet, and the poet gratefully takes his place at the table. The X looks like a one-letter suicide note. The poet tells Allen that he carved it with a piece of broken glass because he had slept through an appointment to meet a friend that morning.

"Yes, but why did you really do it?" Allen asks, and at first the poet cannot answer. "I'm nothing . . . and death is nothing, so I . . ."

Allen reaches across the table and lays a cradling hand on the poet's neck. "Now you just eat your soup," he says, and together they eat.

It has been a long time since Allen, like the young wounded poet, had only the tremor of his cornered intelligence with which to snare a crucial moment. Now his voice is clear in everything he does. Mantras are sung, cymbals set to ringing, poems preached over hushed rooms. Allen weeping says precisely what Allen screams with fury or what Allen, in his solitary work for the tenderness lobby, tells Washington:

"Dear Mr. McNamara. The first thing is, be calm. There is no essential threat to anybody's ultimate being. Not yours, you are also safe, as is the one supposed to be 'our' enemy. He is also safe."

1966

# Sinatra: One Hell
## of an Enemy

Frank can be one hell of a friend. The man will give you a $250 lighter, a $1,000 watch, a color TV, a Cadillac, a grand piano. When the IRS nailed Spiro Agnew for the two hundred grand in taxes he'd evaded, Frank was there to bail him out with a personal loan. Hey—what are friends for? Here's a man who's not hurting no matter how generous he gets. He's got one hundred suits, fifty pairs of shoes, thirty grand in cufflinks, sixty hairpieces. If you're a friend of Frank's, your days of worrying about cufflinks and hairpieces are over.

But Frank can be one hell of an enemy, too. His pals will punch you out in the men's room. You'll be out of the Rat Pack for good. Take how he treated Sammy when Sammy got uppity. Look what he did to Peter when Peter couldn't talk JFK into staying at Frank's place on a presidential visit to Palm Springs. JFK wanted to stay at Bing's place. So Frank put a freeze on Peter that hasn't lifted in all the years that JFK's been gone. That's the kind of memory the man has. You mess with Frank and you'll notice a terminal cooling.

Last December Frank celebrated his fortieth year in showbiz. The

Hoboken fireman's son had outlived Elvis, outlived the Beatles, out-lived even disco and the Bee Gees. Now The Voice was sixty-four and one thousand of his closest friends were gathered at Caesars Palace in his honor. Spiro Agnew was there. So were Lucille Ball, Milton Berle, Lillian Carter, Sammy Davis, Cary Grant, Dean Martin, Robert Mitchum, Dinah Shore, Dionne Warwick, Andy Williams, and Jimmy Van Heusen. Menachem Begin, Anwar Sadat, and Jimmy Carter couldn't make it, but they all sent telegrams. "The sound of your voice long has been a part of my life," Carter's message said. "When we recall the great events of our times and the important moments of our individual lives, it is always to the accompaniment of a song—done your way."

You'd think that this fullness of praise would be enough for any artist—especially a faulted, aging artist like Sinatra. Picasso never had it so good. Neither did Beethoven. Nobody ever made more money or more important friends. Who else springs to mind who's in a posi-tion to introduce Carlo Gambino to Anwar Sadat? Who else has had more beautiful women, more ecstatic audiences, more encouragement to think of himself as a living legend? And who has been forgiven more sorry excesses than this pockmarked idol, a man whose doctor gave him up for dead when he came in as a thirteen-pound forcep-scarred only child minus one of his earlobes. Thank God Sinatra's grandmother was there and had the presence of mind to snatch him up and stick him under a cold-water faucet. Otherwise the future crooner would never have taken a breath.

Sinatra could use a bath like that right now, for as the man has grown bigger he has also shrunk incredibly small. When his name appears in print without the required swoon, he sends telegrams as vile as Western Union will allow, telling you what a scumbag you are, how nothing you say means crap. Then, as a "husband and parent" concerned for the future of the Republic, he sends out vast mailings to business leaders and politicians urging a crusade against the powers of the press. And when his efforts fail to achieve his dream of censorship and you make him unhappy with what you have to say, he calls up a pal and gets you fired.

To appreciate the damage done by Sinatra's latest outrage, you have to have lived for a time in the airways of WNEW in New York, where for thirteen years there was in residence a peculiarly literate disc jockey named Jonathan Schwartz. Schwartz was an island of civility and intelligence in a sea of moronic teen talk. Novelist, journalist, nightclub singer of no small ken, Schwartz was further blessed with an anachronistic taste in music, perhaps the legacy of his father, Arthur Schwartz, whose songs include such classics as "Dancing in the Dark" and "I Guess I'll Have to Change My Plans." On his two weekend shows, Schwartz would weave a tapestry drawn from the works of Harold Arlen, George Gershwin, Richard Rodgers, Lorenz Hart, Jerome Kern, and Jimmy Van Heusen. Against the tides of pop, rock, and schlock, Schwartz was a reminder of what was and what will always be.

So when, the other weekend, Schwartz reviewed Sinatra's just-released album—*Trilogy,* a three-record set—he felt compelled to remark that it contained some severe disappointments. "Record one and record two are outstanding in every way," he said. "I'm sure they will enrich your lives as they surely and clearly enriched mine." But record three—a biographical suite composed for Sinatra by Gordon Jenkins—was something else. "As I heard it, and this is only my opinion, it is a shocking embarrassment," Schwartz said. "It is self-important beyond all knowing. One must avert one's eyes when one hears it, so deep is the embarrassment. It is impoverished . . . subservient."

Schwartz had been Sinatra's most constant and cultivated enthusiast through Frank's lean years in the sixties and seventies, but that wasn't enough to give him the right to say what he thought. Frank called his old pal, John Kluge, chief executive of Metromedia, the communications conglomerate that owns WNEW. Get him off the air, Frank said. Kluge called Jack Thayer, WNEW's general manager. Get him off the air, Kluge said. Thayer called Schwartz, the flagship voice of his station. You're off the air, Thayer said.

Everybody is denying everything, but that's what happened. Friendship outpointed freedom. The hitmen did their job. Now Frank and his pal Kluge can meet at Jilly's and talk about the scumbags and the gassers. Schwartz can go sing in a nightclub or write another book. But you won't hear that good old music on a Sunday in New York. All you'll hear is the gangster music that is made when Frank gets a real mad on.

1980

# Gee, Gordon

Here was the man who held his hand to the flame, holding out his hand, ready to shake with me. We shook. Very glad to meet you, we said. I couldn't tell from shaking if the hand was scarred.

Here was the silent one, the crazy one, the one who cooked his hand. County prosecutor, FBI man, White House "plumber," special counsel to CREEP—his career was an ascent into the sinister. He would rob, he would kidnap, he would kill for his president. As a child, he had eaten a rat to overcome his fear of rats. Now, as a man, he had held his hand to a candle to prove the power of the will. And when his dinner companions recoiled at the stench of burning flesh, this most unflinching of patriots looked them in the eye and told them that if the day ever came when the President wished it done, he would be proud to add his own name to his hit list.

Why not? Jack Anderson and Howard Hunt were already on the list, so what was one more life? Anderson's columns threatened national security. Hunt's hysterics put the stonewall stance in peril. There were times when you had to resort to executive action. You had to terminate with extreme prejudice. You had to kill to preserve the things that you held dear. If the day should come, he told Magruder and Mitchell, just tell me where to be and I'll be there. I'll stand on the corner while you sight me in.

Now he was standing in the kitchen of an apartment in Venice, the Latin Quarter of L.A., surrounded by reporters and writers. Renata Adler was there. She was following him around the country to do a profile for the *New Yorker.* The newspapers were there. TV was there, but without any cameras. This was a social evening. This was an evening that gave you a chance to press the flesh and see if the hand was scarred.

"Gee, Gordon," I said (a little joke I had invented in the car), "I hear your book is doing great."

It was in its second printing, he told me, grave as the FBI. The first printing was one hundred thousand. So was the second. The second was ordered eight hours after the publication of the first. Next Sunday, it will be number five on the *New York Times* best-seller list. Number four in *Publisher's Weekly.* Number one at Brentano's. *Time* had run a six-page excerpt. He'd made the *Today* show, *Good Morning, America,* and tomorrow he'd be on *Dinah!* At $13.95, his autobiography was a publishing event, a literary blue chip. It was a big book, an absorbing book, a book called *Will.*

"Why did you call it *Will,*" I asked, "when *Won't* would have been so much more on the money?"

This was another joke invented in the car, but Gordon did not get it. Instead, he explained that the message he was trying to get across had to do with the power of the will. That if you steeled yourself, you could accomplish anything. That the force of will was greater than the force of body or mind.

A number of guests were fellow graduates of the writers' workshop at the Terminal Island Federal Penitentiary, the last of the nine prisons which Gordon had served his fifty-two and one-half months. Of all the Watergate conspirators, no one served more time. Twenty-five went to prison, but some for only a few easy months. Gordon did four and a half years, including one hundred six days in solitary. He did hard time because he lived by his code. He would not snitch. He would not betray his standards. He would eat a rat. He would hold his hand to the candle.

I couldn't resist kidding him about his hit list. He'd made a big splash in *Time* and on the *Today* show admitting that he'd meant to kill Anderson and Hunt. But, gee, Gordon, Anderson and Hunt are both alive and walking around and taking their chances. What does it mean to be on your hit list?

Gordon fixed me with a look that only men who hold their hands to candles can achieve.

"I don't think I should be blamed for striking out when I never came to bat," he said.

I had heard Gordon say these same words on the radio and on television. I think they're even in the book. They are formula words, the kind of words an author speaks when he's in his second printing and he's on a national tour. And never mind that the baseball analogy describes a failed wish to murder.

Someone asked him about the Nazi stuff. Did he really show Nazi propaganda films in the White House basement? Was he really a Hitler buff? Gordon was prepared for this. It wasn't the White House basement, he said. It was the National Archives. And it wasn't Nazi propaganda films, it was Leni Reifenstahl, who was Hitler's mistress for a time, and her film is a classic document in the annals of propaganda, a juggernaut tour of Germany, with the banners snapping, the heels clicking, Hitler waving, the crowds waving back. The White House staffers loved it, Gordon said. "What an advance job," one of them had exclaimed.

As for the rest of the false reporting about him, that was what you had to expect when you kept your silence, when you were willing to stand at the corner and get hit. You had to go to prison and spend four and a half years doing your pushups and drawing up writs for other prisoners and writing the prison menu. You had to change "peas" to "Fresh June Peas" so the inmates wouldn't riot. You had to change "potatoes" to "Fluffy Mashed Potatoes." That's how Gordon spent his time while all the others were getting early releases and going on TV and writing books and selling them. But now Gordon himself had received a commutation from the President, and he was out of jail, and on a tour, and his book was in its second printing.

The only discouraging note was that this antihero of silence had finally decided to talk, or worse still, to write; silence had not been golden. But the rest was unchanged by all the long months in prison. Nixon was still a great man. Magruder was still pathetic. The ghosts had refused to go away.

Someone asked if he was bitter over the time he served in prison. Gordon said that John Sirica had taken four and a half years away and given them back at the end of his life. He was younger now than when he entered. He could do one hundred pushups every morning. He could run, he could fight, he could hold his hand to the candle. Someone flicked a Bic by way of invitation. Gordon fixed him with a look and held out his left hand, palm up. The palm was deeply scarred by fire.

Where did his strength of will come from, someone asked. Gordon was a man with a date with *Dinah!* and he was ready with an answer that captured the triumph of his fall.

"I was a miserable, unhappy child," he said, "as miserable a child as you can imagine. But I changed that. I became what I was."

1980

# An Indigestible Dinner
# with Professor M.

The visiting professor from Oxford regaled our little group with his joke about the shop near the campus where stupid white students could get made up in blackface. That way their teachers wouldn't dare let them fail. Everyone laughed mischievously, the salad was passed, and the visiting wit skipped on to the new courses being offered in Swahili: "Imagine, pretending that the patois of illiterate Arab slave traders is the precious 'cultural heritage' of these American blacks. What rubbish! What absolute rot!" The other diners, all members of the faculty at a university whose name is almost a synonym for troublesome new ideas, beamed with satisfaction: this Englishman certainly had a flair for putting their thoughts into words. I looked over at my old teacher, M., expecting him to be indignant at hearing this kind of talk bring so much pleasure to his table. But not at all. M. looked tickled pink.

I had seen M. only once in fifteen years, but I still drew so heavily on my memory of him that accepting his invitation to dinner meant running an important sentimental risk. M. had been the best and wisest of my professors, and in a sense I had never released him from standing watch over my ideas. He taught philosophy and I took every one of his courses simply because he taught them, a student lured into the study of the Great Ideas by the miracle of their life in his teacher's mind. It put me in a state of permanent awe to consider how much the man really cared every day about Spinoza.

So it caused a painful quake to see him encouraging this ersatz Evelyn Waugh, who was now leering around the table, looking, I thought, for a fight. "Spiro Agnew couldn't have put it better," I said (*argumentum ad hominem*), and that was all it took to set M. and the sharp-tongued don upon me.

Didn't I realize that the blacks were wrecking the university? That there wouldn't *be* any university unless this nonsense stopped? Did I know how impossible it was to teach these people? The Black Studies program was an absurdity, a disgrace, "an insult," M. said, "to any Negro with the pride and intelligence to want a decent education." The M. I remembered was a Kantian idealist, a philosophical position dependent on the kind of moral earnestness that ignores pragmatic effects. How could he be talking this way? In my dismay, I said something querulous about equality. "Equality!" M. shouted. "This love of equality means that *nobody* gets to learn how to do differential equations." This seemed a pretty desperate defense of the system and I said so. "Oh, yes, sure, I know, you're thinking I'm a racist," M. said. "Well, let me tell you who the real racists are. They're good white kids whose educations are being ruined by swarms of unmotivated and ill-educated blacks. And they're racists in the pure and simple sense of 'hating niggers.'"

It wrenched against the form of our relationship for me to be shouting back. It seemed futile and absurd to be arguing what seemed to me to be a basic question of freedom and justice in a room full of philosophers. Yet if the ideas learned from M. were to retain their validity, there wasn't any choice. I searched my mind for some remembered aphorism, for one of those long, telling drives from the back-courts of Western thought. But in the irony of the moment, I recognized that M. was still chancellor over all those ideas, and that left me with nothing better than the old sophist's dodge of Denying the Terms of the Argument. The university doesn't have a right to exist unless it serves all the people, I said, causing M. to flush crimson with disgust and the don to murmur, "Hmmmm, Mar*cuse*. Or is it Mar*cuss?* I can never remember if it's supposed to rhyme with *self-abuse* or *muss*."

Every day since that dinner, I think of another awful irony, another old idea that now I must evict. I've looked over my old philosophy texts and reread my term papers, all of which are richly strewn with M.'s always trenchant marginalia: "Your definition of Love?" "A case of Either/Or?" Nowhere is there any indication that the subject of racism ever once intruded on our study of all those spacious ideas, those filigreed moral systems. If we touched upon the notorious Nietzsche (" . . . nothing can be more terrible than a barbaric slave class that has learned to view its existence as an injustice . . ."), it was only to dismiss him as the visionary of the Nazis. I can't remember that any of us in that northern school ever considered racism as a moral problem for Americans. And why should we have? In all of M.'s classes I remember just one black, a smiling girl named Tommie who did her lessons well. Such is the relevance of a fifties education.

But has M. really turned into a racist? I can't believe that an intellect as strong as his could have been so afflicted by events. More likely, he hasn't changed at all. There is plenty of refuge for racism in the history of philosophy, even with the beloved Spinoza. And I was mistaken in thinking that the feelings I had at stake in our argument derived in some natural way from the Great Ideas. There is no connection. The past is broken off.

That leaves only the problem of passing judgment on a friend. M. is a custodian of civilization, the books, the archives, the great tradition. For him, everything depends on the survival of that privileged quiet where ideas may be fondled and exchanged. Now it is imperiled and he springs to its defense; only the conclusions of passion can be counted on, as Kierkegaard observed.

But the incapacity to cope with change is something philosophy is supposed to cure, and so I am short on sympathy. The times require a commitment to ideas that goes beyond "fairness" and friendship. Whether we know how we got there or not, M. and I both understand that we are on opposite sides in a war of more than words. There are no more consolations. This time, absolutely, it's a case of Either/Or.

1970

# The Rules of the Game

We will not send our swimmers, our divers, our water-polo team. We will not send our sprinters, our hurdlers, our jumpers and vaulters, our lifters, our wrestlers, our boxers. We will refuse to play basketball or ride horses or row sculls or sail, and we won't send tennis shoes or stopwatches or sweat shirts or Gatorade or anything else that might give aid and comfort to the enemy. We are staying home from the Moscow Olympics. And let the people of Afghanistan take courage from our resolve.

Our resolve is all we have to offer. It's a moral example to tide the freedom fighters through their hour of need. It gets cold at night on the Khyber Pass, especially when every bonfire draws a mortar shell. With their country overrun by Russian troops and armor, imagine the warmth that floods the hearts of the Afghan rebels to know that Randy Gardner won't be in Moscow this summer.

Gardner won't be there and neither will the one hundred fifty other American athletes whose lives since childhood have been focused on this summer, this moment, these games. In the brief life of an Olympic athlete, four years make all the difference. Most members of the current U.S. team were too young to reach their peak at Montreal four years ago and will be too old, if not too bitter, to try it again in Los Angeles in 1984. While politics is an enterprise endlessly forgiving of error, blunder, compromise, and confusion, Olympic sports are not. And to make this generation of our best athletes hostage to an empty, awkward gesture is to my mind a grave political crime.

If Carter's decision to boycott the Olympics were part of a coherent U.S. diplomatic offensive, one would expect the athletes to accept their sacrifice as readily as a surprising number have done despite the clear injustice of making them alone pay for a weak president's foolish ultimatum. But apart from a partial grain embargo and the restricted export to Russia of certain technological gear, the boycott is the sole U.S. expression of displeasure with the Soviets. It is a toothless growl that in point of fact serves Russia's interest by obscuring the real issue at hand: instead of directing world attention to events in Afghanistan, the boycott is a distraction.

While the heavy tanks roll over the Afghan highlands, while poison gases are deployed, parliaments and presidents around the world are pressured by us to concern themselves only with the unrelated issue of the games.

Having already won gold medals in mixed singles and international waffling, Carter has decided to take an inflexible stand here. Citing the "iron realities" of world politics, he has refused to consider any compromise, including the athletes' sound proposal that they compete in the games while refusing to take part in the ceremonies or to present themselves for medals on the winners' stand. Instead, the President warns that any American athlete who attempts to compete in Moscow independently poses a serious threat to U.S. security. Corporations that have pledged financial support to the U.S. Olympic Committee are intimidated by the threat of White House reprisals. The president's spokesmen dismiss as "noises" expressions of agony from athletes whose discipline and dedication put the rest of us to shame.

It now appears that when the flame is lit in Moscow on July 19, the United States may well be the only major power absent from the games. As few as six of the one hundred forty-three nations recognized by the International Olympic Committee are firmly committed to joining the boycott, and while two are puppet states—Honduras and the Philippines—four are at best accidental allies whose presence will not be greatly missed: Saudi Arabia, Malaysia, Egypt, and Djibouti. Apart from the Americans, the only athletes likely to take medals who probably won't attend are the Kenyans, victims of Muhammed Ali's ludicrous African tour last winter. The Olympics will go on. The Russians will remain in Afghanistan.

The White House grouses darkly about the dubious loyalties of allies such as Britain, France, and Canada, whose Olympic committees have voted to defy their governments and attend the games. But if the moral authority of Carter's stand is largely lost on the world, it is perhaps because the sanctity of a lesser nation's borders has not been a conspicuous American concern in other Olympic years. Through the sixties and into the seventies, we were invited to the games despite the uninvited presence of our troops in Vietnam, Cambodia, Laos, and the Dominican Republic; border crossing, indeed, was a sport in which we stood unsurpassed.

In 1968, when the Russians threatened a boycott of the Mexico City games, we cried foul over the unseemly mixture of sports and politics, and nothing was said to protest the fact that, just two weeks before those games began, more than one hundred students were gunned down by Mexican police in the Plaza of Three Cultures in what amounted to a brief but brutal civil war. Yet we held high the Olympic ideal and went there to compete. And when Tommie Smith and John Carlos went to the winner's stand and raised black-gloved fists during the playing of the "Star-Spangled Banner," they were denounced and even blackballed by the sports establishment for disgracing the pure idea of the games.

If you're up on your Kipling, you probably know that the instinct of the Afghan rebel would be to go to Moscow and knock the Russians out of their jocks. That feeling, perhaps too fiercely, is shared by many Americans. In this long, miserable season of ineffectual American conduct in world affairs, our proudest moment—shame to say—was the victory of the U.S. hockey team over the Russians at Lake Placid. We took a pleasure from that game that was jingoistic and probably misplaced but in any case was certainly preferable to skating primly away and refusing to play. Carter invited the hockey players to the White House and grinned and clapped them on the back and said great things about what an inspiration they were. Then he sunk back into the rigidity of his foolish ultimatum.

The first law of international politics is that you don't deliver ultimatums unless you're prepared to enforce them with vigor. And when Carter's February 20 deadline passed and the Russians remained in Afghanistan, Carter was stuck. One must think back to a time before Wilson to recall a president less gifted at dealing with the world at large. Bani-Sadr and the Ayatollah play him like a flute. The world money market ignores his imperatives. The Japanese decline to consider his demands. His one firm stand is the boycott, a classic example of the young being made to pay for the blunders of the old. It will accomplish nothing beyond preserving the credibility of a failed leader. The boycott merits defiance, and I hope our athletes can contrive some means of showing up in Moscow and living up to their dreams.

1980

# Billy in the Garden

illy Graham came alive for me last Inauguration Day, when I started thinking of him as an American Rasputin. Before, he had seemed an innocuous presence, even while earning more than $10 million a year for his various evangelical enterprises—and perhaps especially while golfing or praying with every president since Roosevelt. But on Inauguration Day I had to grant that Billy must have some really eerie gift for politics, or politicians. For here was a man who had stayed with the Johnsons through every trying hour of their final weekend in the White House—and had then outstayed his departing hosts to be ready at the door with blessings and benedictions for the Nixons.

Not that Nixon hadn't had Billy's blessing all along. The two had been intimate friends for more than twenty years, and both have said, in public and in earnest, that the other would make a good president. During the campaign Billy thought it best to affect a churchly distance, but there were some rather major lapses, as when he introduced his old friend to a crusade audience in Pittsburgh as a man more realistic than Jesus. If any doubts remained after the election, they were dispelled forever when the new president revealed that Billy had talked him into running.

One was left to ponder what else Billy might be able to talk him into, and for me the question was unsettling enough to recall Rasputin's haunting name. The idea of a revivalist once again holding spiritual sway over a sovereign, *our* sovereign, was far too intriguing to be dismissed because of obvious contrasts between Billy and Rasputin—one a barely literate peasant, the other a doctor of humanities from Bob Jones University; one a wicked Russian madman, the other foursquare on the side of American good. Leave it to Nixon, I told myself, to come up with a safe and sane Rasputin.

My own acquaintance with Billy was limited to attending two of his crusades—Seattle in 1951, in the tow of my aunt, and New York six years later, when Billy was at the height of his powers, packing Madison Square Garden nightly for sixteen weeks. I wandered in on impulse one night and, after climbing up into the final godless reaches of that sinister place, I was amazed to look down from the distance of a city block or so and recognize Billy away from the pulpit by the clear pale blue of his eyes. Now, with Billy back in New York for the ten-day crusade just ended, it seemed a cautionary move at the very least to see how the years had touched him.

It was a new and different Garden, a vaulting, pillarless arena of color-coded plastic seats, twenty blocks downtown from the old site; elevators and escalators took me to the Crusade Press Lounge, where I was issued a small brass badge saying MEDIA and a handsome press kit containing glossy photos and glossy biographies of Billy and the whole evangelic team: Cliff Barrows, George Beverly Shea, Grady Wilson and his brother T. W., Crusade Director Bill F. Brown (" . . . and what a giant for God that man is!" Billy said later on). A copy of *Decision*, Billy's monthly magazine, was opened to an article called "God in the Garden," that told how crusade advance men had spent two years organizing twelve hundred churches in the metropolitan area into "an uptight force determined to drive a wedge into the secular glob." The 2,000-voice choir was singing "Trust and Obey" as I entered.

Billy was sitting well back from the hydraulic pulpit on a portable stage crowded with dignitaries' chairs and banked on all sides with false shrubs and ferns. His face was tan with the sun of Key Biscayne, where he had spent the weekend with the president, resting up for the crusade. Four serious illnesses in recent years have made him watchful of his strength, but from the look of him it is easy to see why many of his followers believe him to be preserved by the purifying fire inside. He is fifty, but with just a touch of TV makeup, he still looks thirty-five.

His sermon, filmed for the twelve-city "television outreach" that brought the crusade "to millions upon millions of American homes," was another feat of preservation: the same glad voice, the same elucidating gestures, the same good-news Gospel. Some of his metaphors, though, were almost painfully contemporary (God is the infinite "heart donor"; our struggle is with "rejection"), and, like so many others these days, he seemed obsessed with the problems of sex and dope.

Night after night he returned to the attack on pornography, sensuality, lust, "trips of alcohol, sex, and dope." Times Square, he said, was "an open sewer" of depravity and vice, and he warned that "no city in history, no nation in history, has ever gone in for that kind of immorality and withstood the judgment of God." Student revolt was another obsession—revolt, he said, is a sign that the end is near. Can Nixon believe this, I wondered.

Billy was more encouraging about the future of the big cultural sins. Dismayingly so, in fact. "We don't have a race problem," he said. "We don't have a poverty problem. We don't have a war problem. The problem, ladies and gentlemen, is sin, S-I-N." When Christ comes to redeem us (and Billy says "it could be soon"), illusory problems such as these will vanish, being nothing more than symptoms of our estrangement.

My days as a Times Square thrillseeker ended when I was about nineteen, but hearing Billy talk about it in such vivid terms made me yearn to get up there the minute the service ended. A hot summer mist had polished the streets into broken black mirrors, and every doorway held a clammy nest of people waiting for the action to begin. As Billy had warned, there were a great many new pornographic bookshops, and all of them were crowded. "It's the rain," one dirty-book dealer told me. "These bums never buy nothin'." In the back room, a dozen men were plugging quarters into the peepshow machines. "Echhh, Jersey commuters, waiting for the bus," the dealer said.

It might have been Billy's doomsday preaching that made the famous street of shame seem so vacant and gloomy. But for all the facets of misery and breakdown, I couldn't find a trace of simple lust. I prowled around for a couple of hours, then headed for the subway home. On the way, I bought a sailor hat for my daughter in an all-night penny arcade; and while watching the lady sew "Anny" on the brim it struck me hard that this was the best thing I'd done all day.

1969

# How I Got To Be This Hip

I 'll never know what got into Youngblood the night he told me Iceberg Slim's fox-at-the-fistfight story, pretending the whole thing happened to him outside the Peppermint Lounge in Reno, Nevada, where we were passing the midnight hour at our usual table. We had such a good thing going—I the writer, he the pimp—that I hated to see it spoiled by this act of verbal plagiarism against one of my favorite authors. I suppose I was also a little insulted to discover that Youngblood had me figured for the kind of popcorn scholar who would be unacquainted with the sorrows and delights that fill the pages of *Pimp* (1967), *Mama Black Widow* (1969), *Trick Baby* (1967), *The Naked Soul of Iceberg Slim* (1971), and other, less substantial works comprising the oeuvre of America's foremost *maquereau-raconteur*.

There were ladies present, and they were Youngblood's ladies, so the players' code forbade my making it known that I was on to the brother's lame maneuver. The unlettered hags were hanging on to daddy's every word, unaware that in its original telling (see *Pimp* [Los Angeles: Holloway House, 1969], pp. 208–12) the fox-at-the-fistfight story is widely acknowledged to be one of the indispensable passages in all pimp writing.

Slim is drifting by in his LaSalle (for this is 1937) when he happens upon a street fight. Near the edge of the crowd he spots Christine, a silky-haired fox with a deerstalker walk and a moneymaking grin, all of which is presently being squandered on her insanely jealous husband, a scarfaced saxophone player named Leroy. It is no surprise to Slim that the lunatic Leroy is the cause of the commotion, the one who is beating a helpless old man to his knees with a little silver pistol. But when the master player observes that Christine is sobbing piteously, her tears inform him that Scarface is ready to take his fall. The sight of a prowl car swinging around the corner is Slim's signal to make his lightning move. Darting across the street, he arrives at Christine's side to touch a perfumed finger to her shoulder just as her knees are giving way. Chris is in the LaSalle before the rollers can get Leroy into handcuffs. Diamonds sparkle grandly as Slim waves a pleasant bye-bye and coasts off with his catch.

If Youngblood had bothered to tell the story better, I'm sure I would have overlooked the small crime of poaching in my readiness to applaud all philosophical statements uttered after midnight at the Peppermint Lounge. He might have noted, for example, how the story captured in distillate clarity the trick-or-treat sense of life that is the sine qua non of every winning street game. He could have called attention to the choreographed certainty of each person's moves, how victims and victimizers alike behave in strict obedience to immutable downtown street law. But no. All this slow-track hustler could see in Slim's story was an exhibition of the kind of pimping cool he aspired to so wantonly. In some displeasure I slipped inside my thoughts and let the fool talk himself into perdition.

Youngblood's stories usually came in the form of parables disproving the Golden Rule. I didn't mind their bitter content, nor the patronizing tone Youngblood would affect whenever a simple anecdote became a discourse in the street life. The premise of our relationship was that since I was neither pimp nor cop nor bartender, cab driver, crossroader, drug dealer, booster, card cheat, or ex-con, there were a great many things I wouldn't know about life. Youngblood was educating me. He was pulling my coat to those home truths you can hope to learn only by staying up late in places like Reno.

It took me a while to determine just what I was doing for Youngblood. At first I thought my role was more or less psychiatric, and it was true that Youngblood was looking much better now that I had taken custody of all his depressing secrets. But then I began to wonder if the prospect of fame, or its paperback equivalent, could have derailed the man's sense of *omerta* in the course of examining the local bookstalls, where the confessions of pimps, prostitutes, massage-parlor operators, and California call boys vied for space with the memoirs of muggers, rapists, fences, and hit men. Finally, after buying him several hundred dollars' worth of drinks, I arrived at the belief that the favor I was doing Youngblood was rather more refined. I was lending him that added dash of flash that comes from being seen with your biographer. Better than a pair of gold coke-spoon cufflinks, almost as good as a well-parked Continental, is a man with a notebook sitting next to you in a place like the Peppermint Lounge.

Youngblood would allude to his "street wisdom" as though he were dealing in revelation, in something as unlearnable as jazz or love. I would suffer these claims gladly for what I could glean in the way of professional secrets. How to park your car advantageously. How to guess who might be carrying worthwhile scratch. How to make a whip out of a coat hanger. How to behave when busted. It was a mean kind of wisdom, as pinched as a pawnbroker's stratagems or a beat cop's savvy. And yet, in hearing it, in copying it down in my notebook, I found myself acceding to an assumed naivete I never genuinely felt.

I had to stop and remind myself that even as a pale young boy in Seattle I knew the town better than the vice squad did. I was the rare child who knows where to go for whatever he wants long before he wants it. Call it a God-given talent, a gift of clairvoyance, but even today I can fall off a Greyhound bus in places I've never visited and five minutes later find myself talking to the only taxi driver in town who hustles on the side. Literary convention alone required that I accept the notion that Youngblood's superior criminality was evidence of his greater wisdom. This convention defined our roles and called upon me to apprentice myself to a false teacher whose sources were no different from my own. For if reading paperbacks gave one the authority to lecture on the street life, what did I have to learn from Youngblood?

As the dissembler rattled on with the tale of his bogus triumph, I brooded over my role as a cultural conduit through which the folkways of the demimonde were conveyed to the nonfiction-buying bourgeoisie. I had done my bit to advance the general awe of street people and their "wisdom," spending thousands of hours collecting the often trashy thoughts of those whose credentials consisted solely of having failed to escape the first traps life had set for them. Slim, I knew, would be the first to agree that the streets teach no more than mere survival. But whether it derived from an inversion of middle-class racism (the belief that blacks know what's happening) or from uncertainty over the meaning of the male role (pimps know how to treat women), something as misleading as a Noble Savage myth had grown up around even the most pathetic street people.

Discounting the many books about good and bad Mafiosi, and excluding as well all those that might be said to have a redeeming prurient appeal, the shelves were greatly burdened with the rantings and recollections of all manner of low-grade felons. Most of these works were paperback originals of the "as told to" school, and nearly every one had about it the let's-get-it-over-with ring of the blankest, purest hack work. Occasionally, one would discover a book of tremendous value and interest, such as Bruce Jackson's *In the Life* (1972), an archive of criminal attitudes and voices, or Elliot Liebow's *Tally's Corner* (1967), a study of street-corner society in the Washington ghetto. But often works that pretended to the highest levels of scholarship were afflicted with the greatest degree of credulity. A book like Christina and Richard Milner's *Black Players* (1973), which might have been good for a Ph.D. in anthropology at Berkeley or San Francisco State, was damp with a feeling of wonder that would have been excessive had their subjects been Sufi dervishes and not just San Francisco pimps.

Other books were the victims of their author's caution, for in venturing into mean streets it was tempting to take refuge in "composite characters" whose existence in life was doubtful. Sugarman, the star of Gail Sheehy's *Hustling* (1973), was a dead ringer for the almost-too-real Silky in Susan Hall and Bob Adelman's photojournalistic *Gentleman of Leisure* (1972). And though both were archetypal pimps much quoted and imitated by lesser players caught up in the Superfly craze, neither, to my mind, was fit to serve as Slim's valet. Something central had been lost in the act of imitation, and it did not matter if the copyist was the writer or the pimp. One was left with a sense of tardiness and loss akin to that experienced when shopping for primitive paintings at the airport in Port-au-Prince.

And yet here I was, feigning interest in the recycled reminiscences of the paperback-reading Youngblood. I was feeding both ends of a dim obsession, encountering the Heisenberg effect in spades. If the presence of an observer was driving pimps to cannibalize each other's confessions, the cycle of literature from the street would spin ever downward until it arrived at the image of the supercilious panderer seated across from me.

I was too slick to shortstop Youngblood's conversation while the foxes were in thrall. But when he capped his rap with a call for another Campari (Silky's drink, I think), fidelity to Iceberg finally compelled me to speak. My allegiance was not to Slim's philosophy—the sad fact is that his books are marred by an off-the-wall conversion to Christianity, something his disciples ignore in the same spirit that permits students of psychology to overlook the deranged footnotes with which the aging, post-orgone Reich vandalized his early works on personality.

What was sacred in Slim's writings was the truth of his moment of mastery, those too-short sugarplum years when his LaSalle was often mistaken for a metaphysical chariot. Silence would have been a disservice to the game.

"That fox's name didn't happen to be Christine, did it?" I queried slyly, slipping Youngblood a reference as clear in this context as Beatrice's name would be at a Dante seminar. Youngblood caught my eye and pretended not to hear. His laid-back ladies were still with us. "Anyway, your game is soulfully together, Jim," I told him, not forgetting that his name is Youngblood. "I can see that you are one pimping genius, white-on-white, outtasight! I never heard anything like that happening to anybody except maybe Iceberg Slim."

I'm pleased to say that Youngblood was man enough, as well as pimp enough, to come along peaceably. "Yeah, Slim sure had some times, Jack," he said, not forgetting my name is Barry. "You read his books, huh? I didn't know you was that hip."

1974

232

# how i got to be this hip

## Barry Farrell

### ABOUT THIS GUIDE

The suggested questions are intended to help your reading group find new and interesting angles and topics for discussion for Barry Farrell's *How I Got to Be This Hip*. We hope that these ideas will enrich your discussion and increase your enjoyment of the book.

Many fine books from Washington Square Press include Reading Group Guides. For a complete listing, or to read the Guides on-line, visit

http://www.simonsays.com/reading/guides

## DISCUSSION QUESTIONS

1. In the essay "On a Sailboat of Sinking Water," what does Farrell suggest happens to the imagination as we grow up? Is this a tragic loss, or a necessary function of maturing?

2. What did the author think of the use of drugs at Woodstock? What did he mean by "crossing a cultural Rubicon"?

3. How did the threat of the Weathermen affect other anti-government activists? Farrell asserts that repression can be a "state of mind." Do you agree with that statement?

4. Why did the author usually ride coach class in airplanes? Why did he feel guilty in first class?

5. What did the kite competitions illustrate about fatefulness? What was the omen that appeared?

6. In the essay, "In a Let-Burn Situation," why didn't the LAPD try to put out the fire? Why didn't the members of the SLA surrender rather than burn to death?

7. How did the fact that Patty Hearst's father owned several newspapers affect the coverage of her "kidnapping"? Did the SLA ultimately benefit from it? What role did language play in the media portrayal of the politics surrounding the treatment of the SLA?

8. Gary Gilmore insisted on the right to die and chose death by firing squad. Was there dignity in his choice of death? Why did it cause such excitement in the media?

9. In the essay "Stalking the Hillside Strangler," did you think that Kenneth Bianchi was insane, or just a good liar and actor? The author ends the essay on a sardonic note. Why?

10. What are the arguments the author makes against F. Lee Bailey?

11. In the essay "Gee, Gordon," what was Gordon's burned hand testimony to?

12. In the essay "How I Got To Be This Hip," what does the author feel that the role of the journalist is in street life? Does he himself subscribe to this? Why?

13. These essays were written over three decades. How has media coverage of events changed over this time period?

14. How did the events of the sixties change this country? How would Patty Hearst or the Weathermen be dealt with today?

15. What are some of the dominant themes that run throughout these essays?